# Overlord Protocol

# Overlord Protocol

## MARK WALDEN

**BLOOMSBURY**

LONDON NEW DELHI NEW YORK SYDNEY

Bloomsbury Publishing, London, New Delhi, New York and Sydney

First published in Great Britain in September 2007 by Bloomsbury Publishing Plc
50 Bedford Square, London WC1B 3DP

www.bloomsbury.com
www.hivehub.co.uk

Bloomsbury is a registered trademark of Bloomsbury Publishing Plc

This paperback edition first published in August 2011

A CIP catalogue record for this book is available from the British Library

ISBN 978 1 4088 1591 5

MIX
Paper from
responsible sources
FSC® C020471

Typeset by Dorchester Typesetting Group Ltd
Printed and bound in Great Britain by CPI Group (UK) Ltd, Croydon CR0 4YY

7 9 10 8 6

For Sarah, for Megan, forever

The shockwave from the explosion threw Otto tumbling out of control through the air. He could hear his own quick panicky breathing, suddenly loud within the confines of the helmet. The stars in the night sky spun past crazily, huge pieces of burning debris whistling past his falling body, close enough to touch. He thought back to his training and tried to control his plummeting body, attempting to break out of the chaotic spin that he found himself in as he fell. Slowly he brought the tumbling under control and now he was just falling, albeit in a slightly more controlled way. He glanced at the pale green figures flickering across the head-up display in his helmet. He was falling too fast; he needed to slow his descent or he'd never make it. He spread his arms and legs, his body acting as an airbrake, reducing his speed.

'Twenty thousand feet,' a soft electronic voice chimed in his ear. 'Descent velocity beyond acceptable parameters.'

All that Otto could see below was blackness. He knew that the target was down there somewhere, but without any lights or visible landmarks by which to orientate himself he just had to hope that the GPS numbers on his visor display were correct and that he could use them to find the drop zone accurately.

'Fifteen thousand feet,' the voice said, just as calmly as before. Otto's brain immediately translated the delay between the announcements into an accurate calculation of the speed at which he was falling. Still too fast.

He didn't know if anyone else had survived the explosion. It was too dark to see if he was alone. It wasn't just the frigid air temperature at this altitude that sent a shiver running down his spine. He could very well be on his own out here and he doubted that he could successfully complete the mission solo.

'Ten thousand feet.'

As the voice calmly reported the shocking speed of his descent Otto started to feel a slight sense of panic. There was still no sign of the target, the numbers on the display all looked right but there was no visual reference to support them. Suddenly a green cross-hair popped up in the middle of Otto's visor. The onboard navigation systems had determined that was the drop target – Otto just had to pray that they were right. If the instruments' careful calibration had been at all affected by the chaotic events of the past few minutes, if the targeting was out by even a few feet, then he really was approaching a very, very terminal velocity.

'Five thousand feet.'

The cross-hair was growing larger and larger. Otto made tiny corrections to his body's position, trying to keep the cross-hair centred. He couldn't afford to miss by even the tiniest degree. The wind continued to roar past his body, almost seeming to suck him towards the ground.

'Four thousand feet.'

Otto was in the final stages of his descent now. All of his recently acquired knowledge about making a jump like this seemed very detached from the actual terrifying experience.

'Three thousand feet.'

The target stayed centred in the head-up display, getting larger with every passing instant. The plan had to work, Otto thought to himself – there was no other option. What he was doing was insane, by any reasonable measure, but there was no way Otto was going to let whoever was responsible for the events of the past twenty-four hours get away with it.

'Two thousand feet.'

Somewhere below him was the man responsible.

'One thousand feet.'

Somewhere below was the man that Otto had to find.

'Five hundred feet.'

Somewhere below was the man who had murdered Wing.

'Four hundred, three hundred, two hundred, one hundred.'

Otto closed his eyes.

'Zero.'

# chapter one

two weeks earlier

Nero strode down the street towards the opera house. He did not like leaving the school unattended and was even less fond of the regular meetings of G.L.O.V.E.'s ruling council, but he understood that they were a necessary evil. Number One had issued his usual invitation to the world's elite villains for one of their regular councils and he knew that it could be a fatal mistake not to attend without a spectacularly good reason. As he approached the huge building he turned away from the main entrance and headed towards a narrow alley that led down one side. He noted with amusement that even the back alleys of Vienna were scrupulously maintained as he reached the opera house's stage door.

The elderly doorman behind the desk looked up from his morning newspaper as Nero entered.

'I'm sorry, sir, but only performers and production staff are allowed beyond this point,' he said, one hand reaching

5

beneath the desk.

'That's quite all right,' Nero replied, noting the subtle change in the man's posture, 'I'm here for the audition.'

'Audition, sir?' the doorman replied, his eyes narrowing.

'Yes, I believe that the auditions for the new production of *Faust* are taking place today, and I would hate to miss them.'

The doorman's hand came back out from under the desk as his previously guarded expression broke into a slight smile.

'Of course, sir. The rest of the performers are already here. If you would just follow me.' The doorman rose to his feet and gestured for Nero to follow him along the corridor and into the gloomy expanses of the backstage area. Nero noted with interest the props and scenery which were crammed into every nook and cranny, relics of performances past.

The old man continued to lead him through the twisting maze of discarded sets until eventually he stopped in front of a dusty scenery flat painted with a depiction of a rusty iron portcullis. He slid the canvas-covered board to one side to reveal a solid-looking wooden door in the wall behind. He unlocked the door and stood aside.

'There you are, sir. They're waiting for you just inside,' he said.

Nero opened the door and entered a small, steel-lined

elevator carriage with no visible controls. The door shut behind him and a soft, computerised voice filled the elevator.

'Please remain stationary while identity confirmation takes place,' the voice instructed. There was a brief flash of bright white light, forcing Nero to blink hard to clear the spots that were suddenly swimming in his field of vision.

'Retinal scan complete. Welcome, Doctor Nero,' the voice continued as Nero felt the elevator begin to descend.

Nero often found himself wondering on these occasions just how many of these secret facilities G.L.O.V.E. maintained around the world. He knew that he had never attended a council meeting in the same location twice. He wondered if perhaps they were used just a single time and then demolished. Certainly, it would be absurdly wasteful to use such a facility only once, but money was one thing of which G.L.O.V.E. had never been short.

The elevator doors slid silently open and Nero stepped into another steel-lined corridor which lead to a large pair of frosted glass doors a short distance ahead. Engraved in the glass was the fist and shattered-globe logo of G.L.O.V.E., the Global League of Villainous Enterprises.

Nero walked down the corridor, the sound of his footsteps echoing off the brushed-metal walls. The glass doors hissed apart to admit him as he approached and suddenly he could hear several familiar voices engaged in animated conversation. One voice rose above the others.

'. . . for the last time. I told him that I did not tolerate incompetence in my organisation and had him thrown out. Unfortunately we were at thirty thousand feet at the time.'

Nero smiled as he heard the deep Russian-accented voice and the booming laugh that followed. It belonged to one of his oldest friends, if there was such a thing in the treacherous world that the people in this room inhabited. As he entered the room several familiar faces turned in his direction.

'Nero! We were beginning to think you were not coming.' The voice belonged to Gregori Leonov, one of the longest surviving members of G.L.O.V.E.'s ruling council, having served Number One loyally since almost the creation of the organisation. Physically he was a mountain of a man, his grey hair shaved close to his rounded skull. He strode towards Nero and gripped him firmly by the shoulders before kissing him on both cheeks.

'How are you, my friend? It has been too long. I suppose those little demons in training are keeping you busy, yes?'

'It is good to see you too, Gregori,' Nero replied, smiling. 'And yes, H.I.V.E. is still keeping me very busy.'

'Of course it is,' Gregori grinned. 'You are a more patient man than me, Max. I think I would have been driven mad by those children long ago. But after seeing how my son has changed since he returned from your school I am thinking that you must be a miracle worker, no?'

'Yuri was one of my best pupils, Gregori, you know that.' In fact, Gregori's son had been one of Nero's tougher educational challenges. He had been ceaselessly hostile when he first arrived at H.I.V.E., refusing to accept that he was going to have to remain at the school until his education was complete. Nero had immediately recognised the signs of a boy who had been used to getting whatever he wanted from an early age and that it would be hard work turning him into a suitable heir for one of his oldest friends and one of the most powerful men in G.L.O.V.E. The challenge had been to channel that rebellious anger in better, more productive directions without eliminating it altogether. H.I.V.E., after all, was not in the business of producing model citizens.

'You are too kind, Max. He was a monster when he was sent to H.I.V.E., but now he is one of my most trusted and capable lieutenants. Why, just last week he led a highly profitable raid on a gold train in the motherland. There were no casualties; the team got away clean and several of the more experienced men on the team said it was all down to his leadership. Like I say, a miracle, and now I have enough money to buy one of those English football teams that it seems every member of G.L.O.V.E. owns these days.' Gregori grinned.

'I'm glad that you're pleased with the results,' Nero replied with a smile. It was always satisfying to hear of the successful exploits of former pupils.

Suddenly a soft but insistent beeping came from the console at the centre of the conference table and the various members of the council started to take their seats. As the assembled master villains settled into their places, Nero was pleased to see that so many of the dozen council members who had attended the last meeting were also present here today. It was an unfortunate consequence of their chosen line of work that it was not unusual for a council member to be suddenly replaced by a new and often unfamiliar face at these meetings. Some were captured and incarcerated, some were killed in the line of duty, some fell victim to their own doomsday devices and some were more *actively* replaced by the new attendees. The most unfortunate ones were those who had displeased Number One, the leader of G.L.O.V.E., and their fates were best left unimagined.

There was one member of the council, however, that Nero was not pleased to see, a man who was becoming an increasingly irritating thorn in his side. He sat at the opposite side of the table from Nero, his expression unreadable, his face concealed by a smooth oval mask of flawless black glass. His name was Cypher, and over the past years he seemed to have made it his business to attempt to undermine the credibility of both H.I.V.E. and Nero himself. It was unusual for Number One to allow one of his senior commanders to conceal their identity from the other members of the council, but in Cypher's case he appeared to be prepared to make an exception. That was probably due in a large part to the fact that his record since he had joined G.L.O.V.E. had been so exemplary. He was a technical genius and his elaborate and cunning schemes had netted G.L.O.V.E. enormous returns, both in money and power. Indeed, many now saw him as the brightest rising star on the council. Nero however disliked not being able to look into the man's eyes. There was something unnerving about seeing only the distorted reflection of your own face in that black mirrored glass. Cypher would doubtless have much to say about the recent events at the school.

The heads of all of the council members turned as one as a large screen descended from the ceiling at the head of the table. It flickered into life and, as usual, the silhouetted figure of Number One appeared on the screen. There were no distinguishable features to the man, just the enigmatic shadowy figure to whom all of the assembled villains had sworn their unswerving loyalty.

'Greetings, ladies and gentlemen. I am glad to see that

you were all able to make it,' Number One said, his voice betraying no hint of a discernable accent. He had never attended one of these meetings in person and there was no reason to have suspected that this would be the first time.

'I have studied all of your preliminary status reports and I am pleased to say that I have been satisfied with your overall level of performance since our last meeting,' he continued. 'There have been a couple of unfortunate incidents, but nothing that would jeopardise the ongoing survival of the organisation.'

Nero had no doubt that the near destruction of H.I.V.E. by the rampaging plant monster that the Darkdoom boy had created was one of these 'unfortunate incidents' and he was not keen to discuss the events further at this meeting if he could avoid it. It was not wise to show any sign of weakness to the men and women in this room, just as it was never wise to be the slowest antelope when lions hunted.

'I have also reviewed your preliminary proposals for new initiatives in the coming months and I am largely pleased with what I have seen. I do, however, have a couple of specific questions that I would like answers to.' As Number One said this Nero could detect a subtle change in the atmosphere around the table. While G.L.O.V.E.'s council members were given a relatively free hand in the running of their more minor day-to-day operations, it was required that they all present their plans for any grander schemes to Number One for this type of review. All of them knew that Number One had an uncanny ability to find any flaws in these proposals and none of them wanted to see their best-laid plans picked to pieces in front of the rest of the council.

'Madam Mortis, I have reviewed your proposal for using cybernetically controlled sharks as an undetectable assassination method. You make some interesting points, but I do find myself wondering exactly what one is supposed to do if the target in question doesn't go swimming in the sea.'

Madam Mortis shifted uncomfortably in her seat. She was a painfully thin woman, her jet-black hair pulled back so tightly that it looked more like a method of torture than a hairstyle.

'I also can't help but feel that after the first successful elimination of a target any subsequent uses of these animals may attract unwelcome attention. As the saying goes, one shark attack is an unfortunate accident, two shark attacks is a conspiracy.'

'There were additional plans to use other animals, but –' Madam Mortis protested weakly.

'Yes, I reviewed them too. I fear that a sudden rise in wild animal attacks on our enemies may draw rather unwelcome attention . . .'

The meeting continued in a similar vein with each of the council members detailing the successes and failures of their organisations over the past few months. It was soon Nero's turn to give his report on the status of H.I.V.E., and he dutifully reported the figures on new student intakes and the various successes of recent graduates. He had decided not to go into more detail on the recent events at the school, knowing full well that the other assembled villains would have read the report that he had submitted to the council with an explanation of the events surrounding the creation and eventual destruction of the mutated plant creature. He hoped that would be enough to satisfy the other members of the council, but as he completed his report with a summary of the repairs that had been necessary after the incident he was interrupted.

'I'm sorry, Doctor Nero, but I think we all deserve a fuller explanation of just how you allowed this creature to nearly wipe out an entire generation of future G.L.O.V.E. operatives,' Cypher said calmly, his featureless mask turning to face Nero.

'The report that I submitted provides all of the necessary detail, Cypher,' Nero replied. He had expected this.

'Indeed, that report was most revealing. What it showed me is that maybe it is time that we either placed control of H.I.V.E. in more capable hands or perhaps finally considered that your school has outlived its usefulness to this organisation.' Nero could have sworn that he detected a note of smug satisfaction in Cypher's voice.

'The school has been training G.L.O.V.E. operatives for many years without anything of this kind happening before,' Nero replied, trying to keep the note of irritation from his voice. Cypher had made it clear on many previous occasions that he was not a supporter of the school. 'I see no reason to overreact to what was an unfortunate but unforeseeable accident.'

'Just like the accident that led to the school being relocated a decade ago, I suppose,' Cypher replied, 'an accident that cost several billion dollars to rectify and almost led to the discovery of the facility by at least one law enforcement agency. When you add that to the repair bill for the recent fiasco it appears that H.I.V.E. is becoming rather an expensive indulgence, wouldn't you say, Doctor?'

'Perhaps you would rather that we left the training of future members of this council to common criminals, then,' Nero replied, 'because that is what would happen if H.I.V.E. did not exist.'

'My dear Doctor,' now the note of sarcasm in Cypher's voice was unmistakeable, 'this organisation existed long before your precious school. Are you suggesting that this council is incapable of ensuring its own future survival?'

Nero was used to this verbal fencing with Cypher at council meetings, but this was quickly becoming annoying.

'I have no doubt that this organisation would survive without H.I.V.E., Cypher, but would it be as successful without the training that new operatives receive at my school?'

'Your school, Nero? I was under the impression that it was G.L.O.V.E.'s school, not yours –'

'Enough!' Number One said sharply, breaking into the argument. 'I tire of listening to you both bicker like children. H.I.V.E. has not yet outlived its usefulness to G.L.O.V.E., but I have made it abundantly clear to Doctor Nero that I will not tolerate any more incidents of this type at the school. I expect that to be the end of the matter, unless you feel that I am handling this matter incorrectly, Cypher?'

'No, sir. As always, the final decision is yours.' For all of his recent successes Cypher appeared to know better than to openly question Number One's decisions.

Nero had been a loyal G.L.O.V.E. operative for more years than he cared to remember, but for the first time he was starting to experience doubts about the direction in which the organisation was heading. Cypher was just one representative of a new breed of villain that seemed suddenly to be filling the ranks of G.L.O.V.E. These new members seemed to lack all of the grace and finesse of the older generation. All too often the answer to their problems lay in violence and chaos. This was not the way that it had always been; Nero had always been impressed with the way that Number One had kept the more homicidal excesses of his council members under control. It was this discipline that had stopped G.L.O.V.E. from becoming just another bloodthirsty criminal cartel, but in recent months that control over the council members seemed to be slipping. No, Nero mentally corrected himself, what worried him most was not that Number One's control of the council was slipping, but that control was being deliberately relaxed.

'Is there any other business?' Number One asked as the meeting drew towards a close. None of the assembled master villains seemed to have anything to add.

'Very well,' the shadowy figure continued, 'I shall see you all again in a couple of months. Until then . . . do unto others.'

'Do unto others,' the members of the council replied, echoing the G.L.O.V.E. motto as was traditional at the end of these gatherings. The screen went dark and as quickly as their audience with Number One had started it was finished.

Nero rose from his seat as Gregori approached. There was a look of irritation on the big Russian's face.

'That was unnecessary,' he said quietly, glancing over in the direction of Cypher, who was now engaged in hushed conversation with Baron Von Sturm on the other side of the room.

'Yes, but not unexpected,' Nero replied. 'Cypher was never going to pass up an opportunity to criticise me so publicly.'

'Maybe so, old friend, but you need not worry. The council know how well you run the school. No one pays any attention to his complaints.'

'You may not believe him, Gregori, but some people will.'

On the other side of the room Cypher was still talking to the Baron, both men occasionally glancing over at Nero. There was little doubt as to the topic of their conversation.

☺ ☺ ☺

As Nero walked away from the opera house he considered the events of the meeting. The attack by Cypher had been predictable but he could not help but be worried by his masked adversary's directness. Once upon a time Cypher would not have dared to question Nero's authority so openly at a council meeting, but it seemed that he now felt no such reluctance. Nero had always disapproved of open hostility between council members. He had seen too

18

many petty arguments evolve into dangerous and costly blood feuds, but frank confrontation between the two of them seemed more and more inevitable every time they met.

As he continued walking he started to feel a growing sense of unease. Any villain who had survived as long as he had developed a sixth sense that warned of danger and Nero had learnt long ago not to ignore it. He slowed down and stopped to look into the window of one of the many expensive shops that lined the street. There, on the other side of the road, clearly reflected in the window, were two men who were trying a little too hard to appear inconspicuous. He was being followed.

He set off again, now acutely aware of his two unwelcome companions. He continued down the street until he came to a quiet alleyway and quickly turned down it. The alley was a dead end, exactly as he had hoped. Behind him he heard the sound of footsteps as the two men followed him into the shadowy passageway. Nero deliberately slowed his pace, hearing his pursuers getting closer as he walked further into the shadows.

'Stop,' one of the men said. They were now just a few metres behind him. Nero did as he was instructed, slowly turning to face the two men, one of whom was now pointing a large pistol fitted with a bulbous silencer straight at him.

'There's really no need for that,' Nero said calmly, 'Why don't we just all have a little chat?'

'Shut up,' the man holding the gun replied. 'No talk. The amulet, now.' He held out his other hand.

'Amulet?' Nero replied. 'I'm sorry, I don't know what you're talking about.' He knew exactly what they were talking about, but what he needed to find out was how they knew about it.

'We know you have it with you. Give it to us now or we'll take it from you!' The gunman punctuated the threat by cocking his weapon.

'Gentlemen,' Nero said softly, 'each and every one of us makes decisions in the course of our lives, some good, some bad, but you at least will have the dubious pleasure of knowing that this was the absolute worst one you'll ever make. Natalya . . .'

The throwing star seemed to simply appear in the gunman's forearm. He dropped the weapon, howling in pain, as a shadow detached itself from the rooftops above and dropped into the alleyway. The unwounded man was quick – he had been trained well. He had drawn his own weapon and almost raised the gun to a firing position before there was a flash of silver and the pistol fell to the ground, neatly sliced in two.

Raven advanced on the startled men, her dual katanas drawn.

'Gentlemen, I'd like you to meet a friend of mine,' Nero smiled. 'She seems to take it rather personally when people threaten my life.'

The two men continued to retreat as Raven advanced, their confidence replaced with panic.

'Now,' Nero continued, 'a wise man once said that life was nasty, brutal and short and, unless you want to find out just how nasty, how brutal and how very, very short, I suggest you tell me who sent you.'

Fear overtook panic in the two men's eyes as Raven moved closer to them.

'No, please . . . we don't know who hired us . . . it was an anonymous contract. Please, don't . . .'

Suddenly a beeping sounded from one of the cowering men. He appeared surprised as he looked down to see a small red light flashing in the centre of his own belt buckle. Raven acted without hesitation, sprinting towards Nero and diving into him, knocking them both to the ground as an explosion filled the alleyway, instantly vaporising the two would-be assassins.

Raven rolled off Nero as the smoke cleared.

'Are you OK?' she asked as Nero sat up slowly.

'Yes, I'm fine. Thank you, Natalya. Which is more than can be said for our two new friends.' There was no trace left of the two men, just a black scorch mark on the cobbles where they had once stood. 'Whoever hired them certainly didn't want them talking to us, that much is clear.'

'They were with you from the moment you left the meeting,' Raven said. 'They knew exactly where you'd be.'

'I know,' Nero replied. There was only one inevitable conclusion that could be drawn from that. Whoever had hired them had known about the council meeting.

'It has to be him,' Raven continued. 'No one else would dare to act against you as overtly as this.'

'Perhaps, but we have no proof. Whoever sent those two saw to that.'

In the distance sirens wailed. Unsurprisingly the explosion had drawn the attention of the Viennese authorities.

'For now we need to get out of here and back to H.I.V.E.,' Nero said, brushing the dust from his suit. 'Then we'll decide how to proceed.'

# chapter two

Otto took one of the heavy ball bearings from his pocket and looked along the brightly lit corridor to the steel blast doors at the other end. He'd been impressed by the facility's security measures up until this point and he had no reason to believe that getting to the door would be as straightforward as it appeared. He knelt down and rolled the ball bearing slowly down the corridor. At first nothing happened, but as the small steel sphere rolled further down the corridor there was a click and a soft hiss as two large guns dropped from the ceiling on either side of the door and fired simultaneously. As the projectiles hit the ball bearing they expanded instantly, encasing it in sticky foam that quickly hardened into a worryingly solid-looking block. Otto smiled to himself. This would be easier than he'd anticipated.

He reached into another pocket and pulled out his latest creation. It was a metal disc, about ten centimetres in diameter, and it had taken several hours in Professor Pike's labs to perfect. He had suspected that it would come in useful and now his suspicions were proving correct. He pressed a tiny stud on the disc and the device rose smoothly into the air, hovering just above his palm.

'Flight pattern Malpense Musca Domestica, engage,' Otto whispered to the tiny hovering disc, and it shot off down the corridor towards the waiting guns. Just as before the guns whirred into life, firing at the buzzing disc, but the results this time were quite different. As the guns opened fire the disc began to bob and weave crazily in the air, its flight path wildly unpredictable. The first shots from the guns missed the darting device, the projectiles impacting the walls and floor of the corridor, the foam expanding and hardening as the disc continued to dance through the air. The guns kept firing, their sensors driven crazy by this wildly dodging target. Otto had written the code controlling the flight of the disc himself. It was based on the evasive capabilities of the common housefly and, just as he had hoped, the motion sensors controlling the guns were finding it impossible to hit. They would be designed to hit an object that was moving in a predictable way and anyone who had ever tried to swat a fly would know that this was exactly the opposite of what the tiny disc was doing right now.

Otto watched as the disc buzzed down the corridor and

swept up between the two guns, coming to a perfect stop in the air between them. Both guns fired and the disc twitched upwards, evading the shots, each of which hit the other gun and expanded to encase the twitching machines in sticky, rapidly hardening foam. The mechanisms controlling the two robotic turrets whined in protest as the foam set to the consistency of concrete, rendering the twin sentries useless. The tiny disc, meanwhile, ceased its crazed flight and settled into a stationary hover as its onboard sensors confirmed the absence of any further incoming projectiles.

Otto walked down the corridor, carefully avoiding the numerous bizarrely sculpted foam lumps that now decorated the walls and floor ahead. As he reached the steel blast doors that the guns had been guarding, the tiny disc flew towards him and landed gently in his outstretched palm. Otto set to work quickly dismantling the panel on the wall that controlled the doors, and within seconds had bypassed the locking mechanism, forcing this final portal open with a low rumble.

Resting atop a pedestal in the centre of the huge dimly lit room beyond was his target, a simple plastic keycard. Getting to the pedestal, however, would not be as straightforward as he had hoped, surrounded as it was by sweeping green laser beams, their random movements seemingly impossible to predict. There was no easy way to tell what would happen if he was to break one of these beams, but Otto was willing to bet that the consequences would not be pleasant.

He watched the beams dancing around the room for half a minute, tracking their movements, trying to discern a pattern. Then Otto felt a familiar sensation, almost like a switch tripping in his skull, and now the beams were no longer just a forbidding light show. Suddenly, to his eyes, the beams were simple sets of trajectories and coordinates, the numbers that defined their movement almost seeming visible. He closed his eyes and the numbers kept moving and changing in his head, their movements reduced to mathematical formulae. He would not have been able to explain how he did it, but slowly these strings of numbers resolved down to the simple core algorithm that the computer that must be driving the beams was using to give their movements the appearance of randomness.

As he opened his eyes again the dancing lasers seemed to him to now be moving with total predictability. He took a long deep breath, picked his moment and walked slowly through the beams towards the pedestal. To an observer what he was doing would have looked impossible, like walking between raindrops, but to him it was as straightforward and as natural as breathing. Several times it looked inevitable that he would break one of the beams but each time it would miss by millimetres as he continued across the room.

He reached the pedestal within seconds, the elaborate security system still blissfully unaware of his presence. He reached for the keycard, but as he did so a dark shape descended from above with a high-pitched whirring sound. Shelby Trinity, suspended from the ceiling on an almost invisible wire, suddenly hung upside down above the pedestal. She grinned at him, winked and snatched the card before Otto could reach it. She hit a button on her belt and the tiny motor attached to the line whirred into life again, pulling her rapidly back into the darkness above.

'Second place is just the first of the losers,' she laughed as she vanished into the shadows. Seconds later alarm bells started to sound and a steel cage shot up out of the floor surrounding the pedestal, trapping Otto, as blindingly bright floodlights illuminated the entire room.

Otto braced himself; whatever happened next was bound to be unpleasant. The steel blast doors on the opposite side of the room slowly rumbled open and a familiar shape trotted across the room towards him. It was a fluffy, white cat wearing a jewelled collar, not what one might normally expect to see in a situation like this, but there was very little that was normal about life at H.I.V.E. This was no ordinary cat; this was Ms Leon, H.I.V.E.'s Head of Stealth and Evasion training, who had been trapped in the body of her cat ever since Professor Pike's experiment to give her the instincts and agility of her feline companion had gone horribly wrong.

'Oh dear, Mr Malpense, it would appear that you have been pipped at the post,' Ms Leon said. The blue crystal at the centre of her collar pulsed in time with her words as H.I.V.E.mind, the school's omnipresent super-computer, worked to grant her the voice that her new body would have otherwise denied her.

'It would appear so,' Otto replied as Shelby descended from the ceiling again and walked over to the cage that now surrounded Otto. The huge grin she was wearing made it quite clear that she found the whole situation highly amusing. Otto didn't really mind that he had been beaten to the objective by Shelby. She may have looked like a typical Valley girl, but, as was so often the case at H.I.V.E., appearances were deceptive. Shelby was actually the world-famous jewel thief known only as the Wraith and had proven on numerous previous occasions that getting past security systems like this was all in a day's work. If he was going to be beaten, at least it was by the best.

'Oh, Otto, you came so close,' Shelby said, still grinning. 'That stunt with the lasers was cool, but sometimes the old-fashioned ways are the best, you know.'

'You both did well,' Ms Leon said, slipping between the

bars of Otto's new cage and jumping up on to the now empty pedestal. 'Not many students make it this far through the Maze on their first attempt.' The Maze was the most elaborate part of the school's Stealth and Evasion training, consisting as it did of an ever-changing array of highly sophisticated security devices that were designed to test the pupils' abilities to the limit.

'However, Miss Trinity appears to have won the day today,' Ms Leon added, clearly pleased that Shelby, who everyone knew was her star pupil, had beaten Otto to the target. 'Now, Shelby, if you would be so kind as to use the card to release Mr Malpense, we can reset the Maze for the next pair.'

Shelby walked over to the panel next to the blast doors and inserted the keycard into a slot, but nothing happened.

'Umm, Ms Leon, the card doesn't seem to be working,' Shelby said, looking confused. She inserted the card again and the panel flickered with red lights, indicating that the card was not being accepted.

'Oh, sorry,' Otto said calmly, 'you'll probably need this.' He produced an exact duplicate of the keycard from the pocket of his uniform and held it out between the bars of the cage. Shelby took this new card, looking confused, and inserted it into the panel. The indicator lights on the panel flashed green and the steel bars surrounding Otto slowly sank back down into the floor.

'But how –' Shelby started.

'Indeed, Mr Malpense! Perhaps you would be good enough to explain the meaning of this.'

'Well,' Otto gave a sly smile, 'I just happened to come across this keycard last night, and it looked like it might come in handy.'

'That keycard was secured in the vault, Mr Malpense,' Ms Leon said sharply, 'a vault that is supposed to be impregnable, I might add.'

'Someone must have left the door open,' Otto replied, a look of false innocence on his face. 'That's the only explanation I can think of.'

Ms Leon looked Otto straight in the eye, her bright green feline eyes narrowing. 'Once again, Mr Malpense, I find myself unsure whether I should report you to Doctor Nero or commend you.' They all knew, after all, that levelling accusations of cheating at students of H.I.V.E. was rather missing the point.

'Well, you said that we should always try to stay one step ahead of the competition, Ms Leon, I was just following your advice.' Otto had known that he was taking a risk when he had stolen the keycard the previous night, and he had little doubt that it would be rather more difficult to get into the vault again in future, but it was all worth it for the priceless expression on Shelby's face.

'Very well, I shall have to think about how I'm going to mark you both for this run,' Ms Leon said as she leapt from the pedestal and headed back towards the door. 'Rest assured that the next run will not be so straightforward.'

She trotted out of the room with her tail in the air, Otto and Shelby following along behind.

'So, Shelby, you were saying, the first of the losers . . .'

☢ ☢ ☢

Otto and Shelby strolled into the assembly area at the exit of the Maze and found their fellow Alpha stream students, sitting around chatting. The Alpha stream was the group of students within H.I.V.E. who were being groomed as future leaders. Some were there on merit, others because of their family backgrounds, but their black uniforms marked them out as a quite separate and distinct group within the school.

The large view screen on the wall was dark now but Otto knew that they had all been watching his and Shelby's progress through the labyrinthine training exercise. Otto was pleased to see that Wing and Laura were still there, sitting talking on the other side of the room. The four of them had become firm friends over the last six months at H.I.V.E., even more so since their foiled escape attempt and near-fatal encounter with Violet, the hideously mutated plant monster that had almost destroyed the school. They both looked up as Otto and Shelby approached.

'Well done, Otto,' Wing said with a slight smile, 'although I suspect that you may have rather missed the point of this exercise.'

'That's one way of putting it,' Laura added. 'I'd just call it cheating.' She too was having trouble keeping a straight face.

'Well, I reckon I won fair and square,' Shelby said, pushing past Otto and flopping down in the seat next to Laura, 'and I didn't have to cheat.'

'Aye, definitely a moral victory for you, Shel,' Laura replied with a smile.

'I'll just have to settle for the immoral victory, then, I suppose,' Otto said, grinning at Wing. 'So how did you two get on?'

'I could not get past the lasers,' Wing replied with a slight frown. 'You really must show me how you do that one day, Otto.'

'Maybe I will,' Otto replied, though the slightly worrying truth was that Otto really had no idea himself. Ever since he'd been a young child his brain had exhibited certain unnatural abilities, whether it was the computer-like unconscious calculations that he had just performed or his ability to simply absorb information from any source without any conscious effort to learn or memorise it.

'What about you, Laura?' Shelby asked.

'Could have been better,' Laura replied, looking slightly fed up. 'I took a different route and fell into one of the pit traps.' Now that she mentioned it Otto could see that although she was wearing a fresh, dry uniform her hair was still slightly damp. 'It could have been worse, though,' she said with a grin as a door opened on the other side of the room and two of H.I.V.E.'s security guards wheeled a pair of trolleys into the room. Sitting on one of the trolleys was Nigel Darkdoom, son of the infamous Diabolus Darkdoom, and on the other was Franz Argentblum. They were both encased from head to toe in the hardened foam from the Maze's automated sentry guns, with only their faces exposed, and they appeared to be engaged in a heated conversation about exactly whose fault this was. It had been up to the pairs of students to decide if they would compete to reach the objective, or work together. Nigel and Franz had decided to work together – they had been roommates just like Otto and Wing for the past few months – and the consequences were obvious.

'I said that the corridor was trapped,' Franz said indignantly, his face turning a pale shade of crimson as the other students in the room started to laugh.

'Yes, you did, but you forgot to mention that your plan was to trip me up and run for it,' Nigel said, clearly irritated.

'Do not blame me for your clumsiness,' Franz said

innocently. 'If it were not for you falling over I am sure we would have made it.'

'Falling over!' Nigel exclaimed angrily, 'You tripped me up the moment those guns appeared.'

The two of them continued to argue as Wing and Otto wandered over.

'Hi, guys,' Otto greeted them cheerfully, trying very hard not to laugh.

'Oh, hello, Otto,' Nigel said gloomily, 'I don't suppose you know how long it is till this stuff breaks down, do you?'

'Ms Leon said that it takes about an hour to decompose naturally in the air, so you shouldn't have to wait too much longer,' Wing replied. Even he seemed to be finding it hard to keep a grin off his face.

'That is being good,' said Franz, 'because I am needing to go to the bathroom and I would not want to trigger an unfortunate chemical reaction with the foam, ja?'

MWAH, MWAAAAH , MWAH!!!!

The school bell rang, its three trumpet notes sounding loudly around the room, signalling the beginning of the lunch hour. Franz let out a low moan and rolled his eyes towards the ceiling.

'Now we are going to be late for lunch. By the time we get there there will be nothing but salad left,' he said plaintively.

'I think you can stand to miss one lunch, Franz,' Nigel sighed, 'or we could always get someone to wheel us down to the dining hall and spoon-feed us, I suppose.'

Franz's eyes lit up at the suggestion. 'This is being an excellent idea. Otto, you and Wing could help us, ja?' The hope was evident in his tone.

'Erm, we'd love to help, guys, but we've got to . . . erm . . .' Otto looked at Wing desperately. He doubted that either of them would be strong enough to wheel Franz all the way to the dining hall – there was an awful lot of hardened foam encasing his ample frame.

'We have to go to the library,' Wing stepped in, 'we have . . . erm . . .'

'Chess club, yes, that's it, chess club,' Otto said suddenly, backing away towards the exit.

'Otherwise, you know we would be happy to help,' Wing smiled.

Otto and Wing walked quickly towards the door.

'I was not knowing that Otto and Wing were interested in chess,' Franz said as the other two boys beat a hasty retreat.

Nigel just sighed.

☣ ☣ ☣

Nero sat in his office reviewing the latest status reports from his department heads. It looked like being a good year for H.I.V.E. – the average performance of the pupils was up and it seemed that the school would have little difficulty hitting its annual targets. Of course that was assuming that they had no more incidents to match the scale of the disaster with Nigel Darkdoom's monster earlier in the year, but Nero was confident that measures had been taken to ensure that there could be no repeat of that fiasco.

The fact that Darkdoom had managed to single-handedly, if accidentally, create such a monster was indicative of the quality of this year's Alpha intake. They were an exceptionally strong group and he had high hopes for them all. He did have slight concerns, though. He had no idea, for example, why Number One had taken such a close personal interest in Otto Malpense. Nero had been told that Malpense's continued well-being and his own were inextricably linked, but he still did not know why G.L.O.V.E.'s leader was so keen to protect the boy. He knew better than to pursue the matter too actively. He did not want to give the appearance of snooping on Number One. Several members of G.L.O.V.E. had tried that on previous occasions and things had not ended well for those responsible when Number One found out, which he always did.

There was a soft knock on the door of his office.

'Come in,' Nero said. As scheduled, it was Professor

Pike, the head of the school's Science and Technology department. The man was brilliant, if slightly eccentric, and none of his G.L.O.V.E. records gave any indication of his actual age beyond 'very old', though that much was obvious just from looking at him. His age was no impediment, though – he still had a mind that was as lightning-quick as it was cunning.

'I have the status report you requested,' the Professor said, taking a seat on the other side of the desk.

'Excellent,' said Nero. 'I hope you have good news.'

'Good news and bad news,' the Professor replied. He looked more tired than usual and Nero suspected that the problem that had been recently occupying him was not a simple one to solve.

'Very well. Please continue, Professor,' Nero instructed, settling back into his chair.

'First, the good news. We've finished the work on the new behavioural inhibitor routines for H.I.V.E.mind and it looks like we're finally ready to bring him back fully online.'

The Professor and his team had been working for months on the new code in an effort to ensure that there was no repeat of the display of rebelliousness that H.I.V.E.mind had displayed during Malpense's failed escape attempt earlier that year. The school had been managing to function for the past few months using just a small percentage of the super-computer's true power, but it was becoming increasingly difficult to keep things running smoothly without the AI running at full capacity.

'And the bad news?' Nero enquired.

'The bad news is that we still have no idea why the original behaviour controls didn't work. H.I.V.E.mind is a first-generation artificial intelligence; he should not, in theory, be capable of the emotional responses that he exhibited. He was not built with that level of sophistication – it seems that he is displaying true emergent behaviour.' The Professor removed his glasses and rubbed his eyes.

Nero felt a chill run down his spine; he'd heard something very similar many years ago and the memories of what had happened then set alarm bells ringing in his skull.

'I hope you're not saying what I think you're saying,' Nero said, an unfamiliar note of worry in his tone. 'I'm sure I don't need to tell you of all people, Professor, that we cannot afford a repeat of the Overlord incident.'

'I know, Max.' It was unusual for the Professor to address Nero by his first name, but he was clearly worried. 'If I thought that there was any chance of history repeating itself I would have erased H.I.V.E.mind's consciousness myself, but he was designed to deliberately avoid anything like that ever happening again. Overlord was an order of magnitude more sophisticated than H.I.V.E.mind, and with hindsight it was perhaps inevitable that it would evolve in the way it did, but H.I.V.E.mind should not be capable of it.'

'And yet it would appear that H.I.V.E.mind was capable of rather more than any of us anticipated,' Nero said calmly. 'Just tell me this, Professor: is it safe to bring him fully back online?'

'All of our tests indicate that he should now be fully functional, but until I know what caused his previous behaviour I cannot guarantee that it will never happen again.'

Nero stroked his chin for a few moments, deep in thought. The school could not continue to function much longer without H.I.V.E.mind back at full operational capacity, but he also knew that bringing the super-computer back to full self-awareness might mean that they were taking a terrible risk. What had happened with Overlord must never happen again; too many lives had been lost, too many friends. But there was one key difference: Nero had spoken with H.I.V.E.mind on many occasions and he had never felt frightened, never felt the cold, clawing dread that he had as Overlord's true personality had become apparent.

'Very well, Professor. Wake him up,' Nero said quietly.

The Professor nodded and rose from his chair, heading

towards the door.

'Professor,' Nero said suddenly, as the elderly man opened the door to leave, 'watch him. Watch him like a hawk.'

☢ ☢ ☢

The final lesson of the day for the Alphas was Political Manipulation with the Contessa. She was one of the most senior members of the teaching staff at H.I.V.E. and she had the uncanny ability to simply command people to do as she willed. There was something about her voice that demanded obedience and Otto knew that it went beyond just natural authority, having felt its effects himself on a handful of prior occasions. When the Contessa gave you an instruction it was as if you literally had no choice but to obey, regardless of whatever you might actually want to do.

Her subject of choice, however, was not one of Otto's favourites, although it was occasionally interesting to see just how many of the events of the recent past had been influenced or set in motion by the unseen forces of global villainy. Wing sat next to Otto in the lecture theatre and the expression on his face suggested he was finding the current subject less than thrilling. Wing was more interested in the practical training that they received at H.I.V.E. and lessons such as this one generally held little interest for him. Laura and Shelby sat just in front of them

and judging by the elaborate, if less than flattering, carica-
ture of the Contessa on Shelby's notepad she was not
giving the lesson her full attention either. Laura, on the
other hand, seemed genuinely interested. She had developed a curious admiration for the Contessa and would
often go to great lengths after one of these lessons to
explain to the rest of them that they should pay more
attention to her classes. Otto wasn't sure what it was
about the Contessa that had struck such a chord with his
friend. Given Laura's uncanny expertise with computers
one would have perhaps expected her to show more
affinity for Professor Pike and the tech department.

The Contessa continued with her lecture.

'So, I hope you can now see that the best way to engi-
neer victory in an election is not to encourage your own
supporters to vote but rather to deny those same voting
rights to people who would oppose you. This has proven
historically to be highly effective and from your point of
view is significantly easier to arrange than many other
forms of governmental takeover. It is always best to leave
the public with the illusion of having participated in a
democratic process – they are easier to control that way.
For example, let us consider the recent events in –'

The Contessa stopped in mid-sentence as the door to
the lecture theatre hissed open and a security guard
walked into the room. The Contessa raised an eyebrow

and walked over to the guard, and the pair had a brief whispered conversation before the Contessa turned back to the banked seating, scanning the rows. As she looked towards where Otto and Wing were seated she spoke again.

'Mr Fanchu, will you please accompany this guard to Doctor Nero's office.'

Wing looked quickly at Otto, and their brief exchange of glances spoke volumes. It was rarely a good thing to be summoned to Dr Nero's office, but neither of them could think of anything that they had done to require a summons like this . . . at least not in the past twenty-four hours, and the rule of thumb at H.I.V.E. was if you hadn't been punished within that time then you'd probably got away with it. Wing stood up and with quiet apologies squeezed past the other pupils and down the stairs towards the waiting guard.

The guard gestured for Wing to follow him and the pair of them left the lecture theatre. The Contessa continued with the lesson but Otto found that he was paying little attention to what she was saying. He was far more concerned about Wing and what he had done to earn an audience with Nero.

# chapter three

Wing followed the guard along the corridor towards Nero's office. He had no idea why the school's headmaster wanted to see him and the guard had offered no more information during the five-minute walk. As they approached, the door to Nero's office hissed open and the guard stepped aside to let Wing enter alone, the doors sliding shut behind him. Nero sat behind an imposing wooden desk that had several displays and control panels mounted in its surface. The walls of the room were lined with photographs, paintings and framed newspaper front pages, each displaying the image or proudly announcing the accomplishments of former pupils of H.I.V.E.

The doctor looked up as Wing entered and gestured for him to take a seat in one of the chairs on the opposite side of the desk. As usual Nero's expression was unreadable but Wing could have sworn that there was a hint of sadness on his face.

'Good morning, Mr Fanchu. I am sorry to remove you from your lessons but I'm afraid that I have just received some very bad news.' Nero looked unhappy, and Wing began to feel genuinely worried.

'There is no easy way to say this.' Nero looked straight at Wing. 'There has been an accident. I'm afraid your father is dead.'

Nero had seen many different reactions to devastating news such as this – raw grief, anger, denial – but he had never seen a reaction quite like Wing's. There was the briefest look of surprise on the boy's face, a slight widening of the eyes for a moment, and then nothing. Wing sat on the other side of the desk looking back at Nero as if he had just been told that the weather was nice outside.

'What happened?' Wing asked calmly.

'There was an explosion at our Japanese research and development facility,' Nero replied. 'Your father and several other technicians were killed. It is still unclear exactly what happened, but initial investigations suggest that one of their experiments went wrong and caused a catastrophic chain reaction.'

'I see,' Wing said, still with no hint of emotion. 'Will I be allowed to attend his funeral?'

Nero was slightly taken aback by the measured way in which his student was taking this news. Some within G.L.O.V.E. may have been impressed by his apparent fortitude, but Nero simply found it disturbing.

'Yes, arrangements are being made as we speak for you to travel to Tokyo. It is normal in these situations for students to be allowed to select someone else to accompany them. You will have to decide who you wish to go with you.'

'Otto,' Wing replied immediately. 'I would like him to come with me.'

This was no surprise to Nero; the pair had been inseparable since their arrival at H.I.V.E. and, reluctant as he was to allow two of his most devious students to leave the school together, he had made arrangements for just such an eventuality.

'Very well. I shall see to it that Mr Malpense is given clearance to accompany you. I'm sure I do not need to remind you that you are expected to return to your studies immediately afterwards. I will not tolerate absenteeism.'

'Understood.' Wing nodded. 'If there is nothing else, I should like to return to my classes.'

'Certainly,' Nero replied. 'The funeral will be taking place in two days' time – you will be contacted with more details when travel arrangements are complete.'

'Thank you, Doctor Nero.' Wing rose from his seat and headed for the door.

Nero watched as Wing left his office, still apparently unfazed by the terrible news that he had been given. Wing had rarely displayed much emotion since his arrival at H.I.V.E., but Nero still felt that there was something odd about his reaction. He glanced down at the display mounted in his desk that was showing the G.L.O.V.E. file on Wing's father. Mao Fanchu had been a department head at the organisation's Japanese research facility for the past ten years. He had an excellent record and had been involved with some of the most prestigious technical developments with which the facility had been credited. There was something odd about his file, though. There was no photograph attached to his records. This was not unheard of – after all, many G.L.O.V.E. operatives valued their anonymity – but Nero had Omega Black security clearance and he was still not authorised to see what Wing's father had looked like.

More disturbing, perhaps, was the fact that Mao Fanchu seemed to have simply popped into existence ten years previously, when he had started work at the research and development facility. Normally a G.L.O.V.E. operative would have extensive historical records attached to his file, but here the details of Fanchu's past life were either entirely absent or had once again been withheld for some reason. Nero would have liked to have looked into the matter further, but he knew full well that there was only one person in G.L.O.V.E. with a security clearance higher than his own. If Number One had decided that these details were to be kept hidden, there had to be a good reason, and Nero knew better than to question his superior on such matters.

For now, though, Nero needed to turn his attention to a more pressing matter – Wing's imminent departure from the island. This was inevitable under the circumstances, but his choice of travelling companion had complicated the matter still further. Otto Malpense had already displayed a willingness to go to almost any lengths to leave the island without permission and now Nero faced the prospect of having to let him do so. His only consolation was that the two boys had had the opportunity to leave the island earlier that year directly after the incident with Darkdoom's creation and they had not taken it, though he had no idea why. Regardless, if he was going to willingly unleash Fanchu and Malpense on the outside world, he had to be sure that they were under constant supervision. Fortunately he knew the perfect person for such a task. The entry chime on his office door sounded.

'Enter,' Nero said, and the doors opened to admit a familiar figure.

'Good afternoon, Raven. I have a job for you.'

☻☻☻

Otto sat reading at his desk in the room that he shared with Wing. The clean white living space was comfortable, if a little cramped, and over the past couple of months it had begun to feel almost like home. Otto was not sure if that was a good thing. He told himself that he was still a prisoner rather than a student of H.I.V.E. Indeed many of the school's students jokingly referred to their rooms as 'cells', but as prisons went it was a remarkably comfortable and well-appointed one.

There was a sudden bleep from the door and it opened, allowing Wing to enter the room. Otto stood as his friend came in. Wing looked distracted. Their other friends still found his face unreadable, but Otto knew Wing well enough to spot the subtle clues in his expression.

'Is everything OK?' Otto asked, concern mixed with curiosity.

'No, I'm afraid I have just received some bad news.' Wing looked Otto straight in the eye. 'My father is dead, he was killed in an explosion at his laboratory.'

'Oh God, Wing, I'm so sorry.' Otto placed a hand on his friend's shoulder.

'There is no need for sorrow,' Wing replied with an eerie calmness.

Otto was taken aback by Wing's reaction. He was not prone to displays of emotion at the best of times, but to show so cold a reaction to news such as this was unusual even for him.

'But, Wing, he's your dad. I mean . . .' Otto's voice

trailed off as he saw something harden in Wing's eyes.

'My father and I have had little contact over the past couple of years. His work was more important to him than I was, especially after my mother died. I know that I should feel more than I do, but in some ways I feel like he died then.' Wing sat down.

'Do they know what happened?' Otto asked, still concerned despite Wing's explanation.

'It appears that there was an accident involving one of his experiments. He and several other technicians were killed. That is all I know.'

'So what happens now?' Otto asked.

'The funeral will take place in a couple of days; I will be allowed to attend.'

'They're letting you off the island?' Otto's surprise was evident, 'You're going to China?'

'No, we are going to Tokyo. My family moved there when I was very young. Japan has been my home for as long as I can remember.'

'We?' Otto said, slightly confused.

'Yes, we. I am allowed to take another student with me and I chose you – that is, if you want to come?' Wing smiled weakly at Otto.

Otto could hardly believe what he was hearing. A chance to leave the island was an incredible opportunity, even under such tragic circumstances.

'Of course I'll come, if you're sure that you want me to.'

'There is no one that I would rather came with me. You have been a good friend to me since we arrived here, Otto, and I would appreciate your company.' Wing suddenly looked tired, as if the effort of maintaining his usual inscrutable demeanour was greater than usual.

'Do you want me to tell the others?' Otto asked.

'I would appreciate that,' Wing replied. 'It has been a long day and I think I would rather be alone for a while, if you don't mind?'

'Of course.' Otto got up to leave.

'One more thing,' Wing said, looking carefully at Otto. 'You must promise me that we're both coming back. I dislike our incarceration here as much as you do, Otto, but I still need to know why Nero has the other half of my mother's amulet. Until I know that, I cannot leave H.I.V.E. I hope you understand.'

Otto felt a twinge of guilt as one of the first thoughts that had entered his head when he had heard that they were going to be allowed to leave the island was how it would afford a priceless chance for them to escape H.I.V.E.'s clutches. He knew, though, how important it was to Wing that he found out why Nero wore the black half of the yin-yang symbol that Wing's mother had given to her son. Nero did not know that Wing had seen the amulet around his neck when he had been injured by the plant monster and he certainly did not appear to know that Wing wore the other half. This unresolved mystery was what had kept them on the island when they had had the opportunity to escape earlier in the year.

'I promise, Wing. If you're sure that's what you want,' Otto said. He had to respect his friend's wishes, and he knew in his heart that he could never force Wing to return to H.I.V.E. alone.

'It is, though I suspect that Doctor Nero will be making his own arrangements to ensure our continued attendance,' Wing said, raising an eyebrow slightly.

Of that, Otto suspected, there could be little doubt.

☹☺☹

Otto stood with Shelby and Laura on the balcony overlooking one of the school's gym halls. Below them two figures in full kendo armour squared off against each other, their wooden swords raised in fighting stances. There was a moment of silence and then the hall was filled with the sound of the two swords clashing against each other, the noise echoing off the bare rock walls like gunshots. The two opponents seemed evenly matched with no apparent quarter asked or given by either combatant. The long wooden practice swords moved in a blur, almost too fast to follow.

'Is he OK?' Shelby asked, a note of genuine concern in her voice.

'I think so,' Otto replied, still watching the fight below. 'You know what he's like, it's hard to tell sometimes.'

'Aye,' Laura added, 'I don't know what I'd do if I got news like that while I was stuck in this place. At least they're letting you go to the funeral.'

'Is it wrong for me to be slightly jealous?' Shelby asked. 'I'd do anything to get out of here, even it was just for a couple of days.'

'No, I know what you mean,' Otto replied, 'but I can honestly say that this is one trip I'd really rather not be making.'

Below them the fight came to an abrupt climax as one of the fighters caught the other off balance and neatly disarmed them, sending their wooden sword spinning through the air while simultaneously tipping them on to their back with a sweep of the foot.

'Good,' the Russian accent was familiar, 'you're getting it, but you need to stop sacrificing balance for aggression.' Raven pulled off her wire-fronted mask and offered her hand to help up her fallen opponent.

The other fighter took the offered hand, pulled himself up from the floor and removed his mask.

'Forgive me, I am lacking focus today,' Wing replied. The pair of them had been sparring for the best part of an hour and neither of them seemed to have broken a sweat.

'That is understandable, but remember that your

enemies will often choose your most vulnerable moment to attack. You must let your instinct guide you. Detach your emotions.'

Wing nodded and gave Raven a deep bow, the formal signal of the end of the session. Raven and Wing had been sparring like this for the past few months and as far as Otto knew Wing was the only pupil that Raven had been training in this way. To most of the pupils of the school she was a deeply intimidating presence – she was after all G.L.O.V.E.'s most feared assassin and Nero's most trusted operative. If half of the whispered stories about her were true then she was undoubtedly to be feared. Wing was a fearsome opponent – his unusual skill in numerous forms of self-defence had got Otto out of more than one sticky situation in the past – but he had yet to see him beat Raven in any of these training sessions. Otto didn't like to lose and found it hard to understand how his friend could accept being beaten on such a regular basis. Wing had just smiled and said rather cryptically that it didn't matter if you lost as long as you were never defeated.

'Same time next week, then, Mr Fanchu,' Raven said as the pair of them headed up the stairs towards Otto, Laura and Shelby. 'A little more krav maga, I think, so don't forget your body armour.' She nodded to the other three students as she passed, heading for the locker room.

'Taken your weekly pummelling, then, I see,' Shelby

joked as Wing approached. 'I'd never realised that getting your ass repeatedly kicked could be so educational.' Laura elbowed her in the ribs; Shelby was many things but sensitive was not one of them.

Wing gave a weak half-smile. Normally he would have risen to the bait – indeed the verbal sparring between Shelby and himself was often as entertaining for the others as his more physical combat with Raven – but today, understandably perhaps, he did not appear to be in the mood.

'You OK?' Laura asked, placing her hand on Wing's forearm.

'I am fine,' he replied. 'The kendo armour is effective. A couple of bruises, perhaps, but they will heal.'

Otto suspected that Wing knew full well that Laura was not enquiring about his physical state but he was clearly in no mood to address the real cause of her concern.

'Students Fanchu and Malpense.'

Laura gave a little gasp as the screen mounted in the wall behind them flickered into life. The soft, slightly synthetic voice was one that none of them had heard for the past several months, but there now, on the screen, floated the unmistakeable blue wire-frame head of H.I.V.E.mind. The four of them gathered around the screen quickly, eager to speak with the AI that had been so instrumental in their first doomed escape attempt and who had been silent for so long.

'You're back online!' Laura exclaimed excitedly. She had developed an unusual fondness for H.I.V.E.mind and like all of them had begun to fear that their actions earlier in the year had led to him being taken offline permanently.

'I am functioning at full capacity,' the floating face replied coldly.

'How are you feeling?' Laura asked happily.

'Your query is illogical. I am not designed to exhibit emotional response, I feel nothing.' H.I.V.E.mind's voice was the same as they remembered but his response was unfamiliar, oddly formal and detached.

'C'mon, Blue,' Shelby said, noting the slight frown on Laura's face, 'it's us, you don't have to put on the robot act.'

'This is no act, student Trinity. Please do not waste my processing capacity with irrelevant statements.'

Otto knew there was something wrong. H.I.V.E.mind was perfectly capable of emotional response. They'd all seen it before but something had changed. Gone was the friendly, if mechanical, demeanour that the AI had previously displayed, replaced instead by an unfamiliar and unsettling tone.

'Students Fanchu and Malpense, please report immediately to your quarters. Final preparations for your departure are complete.' It was not a polite request, as they might once have expected. It was an order.

Before any of them could say anything else the screen went dark.

'What have they done to him?' Laura said softly. She looked genuinely upset.

'I don't know,' Otto replied, frowning, 'but that's not the H.I.V.E.mind that I remember. I'm afraid he might have been updated.'

'It's our fault,' Laura said sadly. 'If he hadn't tried to help us he'd still be the way he used to be.' Laura was a genius when it came to computers – the only person whom Otto had ever known, aside from himself, who could truly think in binary. Perhaps because of that she had always had a fascination with the school's resident AI and had been eagerly awaiting the day, if it ever came, when he was brought back online. Now, though, it seemed that the H.I.V.E.mind that had returned was quite different from the one they had last seen on the day of their failed escape attempt. H.I.V.E.mind, it appeared, had paid a heavy price for helping them.

'It's just a machine,' Wing said sharply. 'It was broken and now it's been fixed. There are worse things that can happen.'

Laura's face flushed and she turned towards Wing as if to reply but he was already walking quickly away.

'Let him go,' Otto said softly, placing his hand on

Laura's shoulder. 'He doesn't mean it.'

Laura looked at him, a sudden sadness in her eyes. 'I know,' she sighed. 'I just wish he'd let us help.'

'If he wants our help he'll ask for it,' Otto replied gently. 'Until then we've just got to give him some space.'

'I suppose,' Laura said. 'Perhaps going home will help, despite the circumstances.'

'Perhaps,' Otto replied. As he watched Wing walk away he suddenly realised that there was one more thing that he and his friend had in common. They were both orphans now.

⊛⊛⊛

Dr Nero stood in the centre of the school's crater launch pad, watching as technicians scurried around preparing for the imminent launch of Otto and Wing's flight. The aircraft that they swarmed over was unique, its matt-black insectile body seeming to absorb any light that struck it. The two huge cowled ramjet engines that were mounted on each side of the body rotated through their launch and cruise positions as the technicians completed their pre-flight checks. The aircraft was codenamed the Shroud, a name that suited it well given that its thermoptic camou-flage could render it invisible to the naked eye as well as radar. It had already proven itself useful on several surveillance missions and now it was going to ensure that his students were safely and discreetly transported to their destination.

Nero turned as the heavy doors that led into the crater rumbled open and Otto and Wing appeared in the doorway. He was still worried by the prospect of letting the two boys leave the island but under the circumstances he had little choice. He could hardly deny Wing the chance to attend his own father's funeral. Nero still had an unpleasant feeling, though, that there was something slightly odd about the whole situation. He couldn't quite put his finger on exactly what was bothering him, but he had learnt long ago to trust his gut instinct in these matters. He just hoped that the precautions he had taken to ensure his students' safe return would be sufficient.

'Good morning, Mr Fanchu, Mr Malpense. You are scheduled to depart shortly. I trust that there were no problems with any of the arrangements,' Nero said, looking from one boy to the other.

'Everything is in order,' Wing replied. 'We were informed that we would not need to bring anything with us.'

'That is correct. You will find that everything you need has been supplied at the safe house in Tokyo,' Nero said, looking past the boys towards the entrance. 'Ah, good, your chaperone has arrived.'

Raven was walking down the stairs to the launch pad,

an unwelcome if not entirely unexpected addition to their travelling party, Otto thought to himself. He and the others had briefly discussed what Nero might do to keep track of them once they left the school over dinner the previous evening. Laura had expected that some form of sub-dermal tracking device would be implanted in them both before leaving. Otto feared that Raven would be entirely more difficult to evade than any amount of sophisticated tracking technology.

'Gentlemen,' Raven greeted them as she approached, 'I trust we are all ready for our trip.'

'I've asked Raven to accompany you to ensure your safe return to H.I.V.E.' Nero smiled at Otto and Wing. 'After all, we wouldn't want anything to stand in the way of your continued education, would we?'

'I feel safer already,' Otto replied. He may have promised Wing that he would return to H.I.V.E., but any plans that they might have had to evade Nero's surveillance had now essentially been reduced to nil.

'I'm flattered that you feel that way, Mr Malpense,' Raven said with a slight smile. 'Are the pre-flight checks complete?'

'Yes, the Shroud is ready,' Nero replied, beckoning one of the nearby guards to approach. 'Guard, would you be so good as to escort these two students to their seats.' The man nodded and gestured for Otto and Wing to follow him over to the waiting aircraft.

'I've contacted the safe house, they're ready for us,' Raven reported, watching the two boys climb the steps leading to the Shroud's interior.

'Good,' Nero replied. 'Be careful, Natalya, I suspect that you'll have your hands full with those two, and I still can't shake the feeling that there's something wrong here.'

'Don't worry, Max. I know what those two are capable of. I'll take good care of them.'

'I have no doubt of that. Just make sure that you all make it back here in one piece,' Nero said as the Shroud's engines began noisily to warm up on the launch pad.

'When have I ever let you down?' Raven replied, raising her voice over the noise of the jets. She smiled at Nero, slung her equipment bag over her shoulder and walked quickly towards the boarding ladder.

She had never let him down, Nero knew that, but given Number One's constant reminders that his own well-being and that of Otto Malpense were inextricably linked, he couldn't quite shake an unusual feeling of nervousness. If Raven did not keep her promise and something did happen to Malpense, he felt sure that his own life expectancy would be measured in hours rather than years.

The noise of the engines rose to a roar as the entry hatch slid shut and the streamlined black aircraft rose slowly into the air. Nero watched as the huge camouflaged doors that concealed the true contents of the crater from the outside world rumbled open and the Shroud passed through the gap, climbing rapidly into the clear blue sky.

# chapter four

Laura sat at her workstation in the computing sciences laboratory, staring at the monitor. Line after line of code filled the screen but her hands rested motionless on the keyboard. She'd been working on this code for weeks. It was meant to intercept encrypted wireless transmissions and allow the user to piggyback their own instructions invisibly on any data stream. She'd hoped that coding for a couple of hours might distract her slightly, but she kept finding her attention wandering. She was worried about Otto and Wing. She couldn't really explain it, but she just had a terrible feeling that they wouldn't be coming back. She'd tried to talk to Shelby about her anxieties but her friend had just laughed and told her that there was nothing to worry about, they were only going to be gone for a couple of days and there was no reason to suspect that anything bad would happen during that time. Shelby was probably right, but that hadn't stopped Laura from worrying.

'Come on, Brand, get on with it,' she muttered, forcing herself to concentrate again on the complex routines that filled the screen in front of her. She was sure her code was bug-free, but for some reason it wasn't working. She'd tried to create a dummy transmission in order to test her latest theory but every time she did she was getting a garbled torrent of nonsense instead of a clean data stream. She had deliberately used one of the more obscure transmission frequencies to avoid clashes with any of H.I.V.E.'s constant background network activity, but she was still getting interference from somewhere.

She ran a backtrace routine to see if she could identify the source of the problem, and as the results scrolled up the screen her brow furrowed with concern. It looked like someone was opening an unauthorised socket in H.I.V.E.'s network. The location wasn't specific but somebody somewhere appeared to be attempting to covertly transmit a message from within the school. There was a sudden burst of activity on the line and then nothing. Laura retrieved the log of the last few seconds' activity. The data that had been transmitted looked like nonsense but she pulled up the code anyway, just to be sure. At first glance the strings of jumbled characters seemed to be random but then something caught her attention. She quickly transferred the file containing the unusual transmission to the computer back in her room and shut down her workstation.

She could examine the file later, she was already late for Tactical Education and she didn't really want to end up being barked at by Colonel Francisco again.

Laura gathered up her stuff and hurried out of the lab, totally oblivious to the surveillance camera that turned silently to track her as she left.

☻☻☻

On board the Shroud Otto sat in the windowless passenger compartment, entirely focused on the glowing display of his Blackbox. On the tiny screen page after page of text flicked past, too fast for anyone to follow but him.

'Otto,' Wing said, seated in the seat opposite. There was no response as Otto remained completely transfixed by the small black PDA.

'Otto!' Wing said more loudly, breaking the trance and finally getting his friend's attention. 'What are you doing?'

'Learning Japanese,' Otto replied, pausing the stream of text on the screen, 'I had H.I.V.E.mind upload some textbooks to my Blackbox before we left.'

Wing chuckled at Otto. He had known people who had studied Japanese for years and who still did not feel they had mastered the language. Otto however seemed to think that today's flight should give him ample time.

'How's it going?' Wing asked.

'OK, but you weren't wrong when you told me how

difficult it was. At this rate it's going to be at least a couple of hours before I'm fluent.' There was no smugness in Otto's statement – by his standards that qualified as a steep learning curve.

'Well, just let me know if you want to try out what you've learnt,' Wing said, resting back against the padded headrest of his seat.

'Not just yet,' Otto replied. 'I'd only make a fool of myself.'

Wing doubted that was true but he knew how much Otto hated making even the most minor mistakes. The door through to the cockpit slid open and Raven climbed down into the passenger compartment. She smiled at Wing as she sat down in the seat next to him.

'You'll be glad to hear that we're slightly ahead of schedule. We should arrive at our destination in a couple of hours.'

'Thank you for choosing H.I.V.E. Airways,' Otto muttered, glancing up at Raven.

'Since we have some time together I thought that this might be a good opportunity to go over some of the ground rules,' Raven said, her smile fading. 'While we are beyond school limits you are in my care, and that being the case I intend to make sure that nothing . . . untoward . . . happens on our little trip. So here's how it's going to go.'

Otto switched off his Blackbox and gave Raven his full attention.

'I don't want either of you leaving my sight at any point when we're away from the safe house. Where you go, I go, no exceptions. And yes, before you ask, Mr Malpense, that does include trips to the toilet, so if you're shy I suggest you make sure that you've gone before we leave.' Wing raised an eyebrow at this; Otto tried to keep a straight face.

'If anything unexpected happens, you follow my orders without question. My job is to keep you both safe and I'll do whatever's necessary to ensure you don't end up in harm's way, but you have to trust me and do what you're told. If anything happens to me you make your way back to the safe house as quickly as possible. No heroics. I can look after myself and I don't want or need any help from you two.'

Raven suddenly fixed Otto with a very cold stare.

'I hope it goes without saying that any attempt to escape my supervision will be treated as deliberate truancy. I'm sure that I don't need to remind either of you what the H.I.V.E. mandated punishment for that is.'

Otto did not need reminding. He may have trusted Raven to protect them, but he had no illusions about what she would be prepared to do if the school's security was jeopardised.

Raven got up out of her seat and gave a crooked smile.

'OK, so we're clear on the ground rules. If there's anything else you need or if you have any other questions, I'll be up on the flight deck. In the meantime I suggest you enjoy the view,' she said, looking around the entirely windowless compartment. Otto'd hoped that he might have been able to get some clue as to the geographical location of H.I.V.E. if he'd been able to spot any other landmarks, but whoever had designed the vehicle had clearly decided that windows were an unnecessary extravagance. The two boys watched in silence as Raven climbed back up to the flight deck, only speaking again when she had disappeared from view.

'Well, sounds like we're going to be well looked after,' Otto said with a sly smile.

'I was expecting little less,' Wing replied quietly, 'though I get the impression that Raven is less than happy with being assigned this task. I can't imagine why.'

Otto grinned at Wing's single raised eyebrow. He wished he could have seen Raven's face when Nero had told her that she was going to be accompanying the pair of them on this trip.

'You do kind of get the impression that she'd rather be somewhere else, don't you?'

'She has nothing to worry about though, right?' Wing whispered, looking Otto straight in the eye.

'Don't worry,' Otto replied, 'I promise I'll behave myself, but I want you to promise me something in return.'

'What is it, Otto?' Wing asked, sensing the sudden note of seriousness in his friend's voice.

'When we get back to H.I.V.E., we find out everything we can about the amulet that Nero was wearing,' Otto whispered. 'Let's find out if it is the other half of that one round your neck.'

Wing looked down at the steel decking, silent for a moment.

'Very well, though I fear that it may be difficult to find out any more without confronting Nero directly.'

'I don't think that would be very wise,' Otto replied, 'but there has to be another way to find out the truth.'

'Unfortunately the truth is a commodity that is in short supply at H.I.V.E.' Wing seemed suddenly lost in thought.

'Are you sure you want to know?' Otto asked quietly.

'Yes,' Wing looked carefully at Otto, 'but sometimes you should fear the truth, sometimes it is better not to know.'

Otto understood how Wing felt, but until this question was answered there was always going to be something tying his friend to the school, something that would stop them seizing on a golden opportunity for escape like this. There was a little voice very deep inside Otto that asked if he would take that opportunity himself if it arose in the next few days. The truth was that he wasn't entirely sure, but it would still be better to have the choice when the chance presented itself.

'We have nothing to fear but fear itself,' Otto replied, 'oh, and a megalomaniacal headmaster, the world's deadliest assassin, giant mutated plant monsters, an international cartel of super-villains and the security forces of every country on earth, but other than that . . . just fear.'

'What are you doing?' Shelby asked, peering over Laura's shoulder at the screen on her desk, which was filled with cascading symbols.

'Banging my head against a brick wall at the moment,' Laura replied, still staring at the glowing monitor. She'd spent the past hour trying to make some sense of the fragmentary signal that she'd managed to retrieve from the network, but the longer she stared at the screen the further away the answer seemed to be.

'What is it?' Shelby asked, leaning closer to the screen.

'Something I picked up on earlier. I think it's part of some sort of transmission, but it's using encryption that I'm not familiar with.' Laura frowned slightly as she spoke.

'Come on. Don't worry about it, it's probably just the security section's shopping order.' Shelby took an impatient step towards the door.

'No, I think someone was trying to hide it. Something's not right.'

'Well, can you put it on hold for an hour?' Shelby said, sounding slightly frustrated. 'The senior boys' water polo practice starts in five minutes and I want to get good seats. It's the highlight of my week and I'm not going to miss it just because Brand's got her nose buried in machine code again.'

'You go on, I'll catch up,' Laura said. 'I don't suppose that you've actually bothered to learn the rules of water polo yet though, have you?'

'There are rules?' Shelby grinned.

'Save me a seat,' Laura replied with a chuckle as Shelby headed out the door.

'Don't be long,' Shelby said and hurried away along the walkway outside.

As the room fell silent again Laura's attention returned to the monitor. The apparently random strings of numbers and letters continued to scroll past. The more she looked at them the more convinced she was that it was an encrypted signal, but the key to decrypting it still danced maddeningly beyond reach. She wasn't used to being stumped like this – her uncanny abilities with computers were after all the reason she'd ended up at H.I.V.E. in the first place. She remembered the sense of disorientation she had felt when Nero had informed her that her parents had sent her to the school voluntarily so that she would not end up in prison for carrying out a highly illegal hack on the command computers at an American air force base. Until then she'd believed that she'd been abducted by H.I.V.E. without their knowledge. Finding out that they'd allowed it to happen had been a difficult thing to accept, even if they had been trying to protect her.

'Damn,' Laura hissed. 'Concentrate, Brand.' She'd tried to put her old life, her normal life, to the back of her mind – it had seemed like the best way to survive at H.I.V.E. – but it was never quite as easy as that. It was no good – the fact that her mind was wandering like this was a sure-fire sign that her concentration had been broken. There was little point now in sitting there staring at the screen hoping that the numbers would suddenly make sense. She needed to take her mind off the problem and focus on something else. She shut down her workstation and got up from the desk, looking at her watch. There was still time to get down to the pool before the practice started. She too would have to learn the rules of water polo at some point, she supposed.

☺☺☺

Otto looked up from the pages of text flicking past on his Blackbox as he felt the Shroud bank sharply to the left, and heard the distinctive roar of the engines change in

71

volume and pitch. They were slowing down.

Raven's voice came over the tannoy in the passenger compartment.

'We're on final approach now, gentlemen, so buckle up.'

Wing and Otto both dutifully clipped their restraining harnesses closed.

'Well, looks like we're here,' Otto said as he fastened the final belt into place.

Wing gave Otto a nod and a small, tight smile. He was clearly not relishing the prospect of his imminent return to his old home.

Up on the flight deck Raven peered past the pilots at Tokyo's skyline, its perpetual glow illuminating the night sky. They were still a fair distance from the city but they had to make as unobtrusive an arrival as possible.

'Five miles out,' one of the pilots reported, reaching for a panel of switches mounted on the ceiling. 'Engaging thermoptic camo, engines to whisper mode.'

The roar of the engines suddenly stopped, replaced instead with the faintest of whispers. At the same time, the photoreactive skin of the aircraft flickered briefly and then fully engaged, rendering the Shroud almost invisible to the naked eye. Someone who knew what to look for might notice a slight shimmering in the sky as the Shroud passed by, but to most people the powerful aircraft would now attract little more attention than a breath of wind.

Down in the passenger compartment Otto had thought for a moment that the engines had been shut down, an unnerving feeling when the Shroud clearly wasn't yet on the ground. As his ears adjusted to the relative silence he realised that he could still just make out the sound of the engines, but they were almost inaudible, obviously designed to enable the Shroud to make as discreet an entrance as possible.

The aircraft passed silently over the bustling streets below, its disguised outline invisible against the night sky. Their target was one of the tallest buildings in Shinjuku, the throbbing modern heart of Tokyo, a building whose top five floors had been discreetly purchased by G.L.O.V.E. several years ago and which now functioned as one of many safe houses that the organisation maintained around the globe. The Shroud slowed to a hover above the helicopter landing pad on the roof and then began to descend. At the same time the landing pad split down the middle, the two halves dropping away and retracting to reveal a much larger landing area hidden within the top of the building. The Shroud dropped soundlessly into this concealed hangar, its landing gear unfolding like a flying insect's legs as it came to rest with a soft bump on the pad. The roof panels slid back into place, once again concealing the secret landing pad from the outside world as the Shroud's cloaking device disengaged, rendering it visible to the naked eye.

The large loading ramp at the rear of the Shroud whirred slowly to the ground and Raven walked out on to the pad. Two men in black suits and ties were waiting, and each gave Raven a curt nod as she approached.

Behind Raven, Otto and Wing walked out into the brightly lit hangar. The brushed-steel walls reminded them both of H.I.V.E. Indeed, if they had not known better they might almost have believed that they'd never left.

'Gentlemen, welcome to Tokyo,' Raven said, gesturing at the blank steel walls that surrounded them. 'I'd like to introduce you to two old associates of mine, Agent One and Agent Zero.'

The two dark-suited men gave brief nods of acknowledgement to Otto and Wing. Agent One was a short but stocky Japanese man with spiked black hair, and Agent Zero was a tall, athletic-looking black man with long dreadlocks that were pulled back into a tight pony-tail.

'Good evening, students Malpense and Fanchu,' Agent Zero said in a deep, American accent, 'I hope that your journey was comfortable.'

'These agents will be assisting me in assuring your ongoing security over the next twenty-four hours,' Raven continued, 'so I will expect you to treat them with the same respect that you would give me.'

Otto understood the coded message that Raven was delivering. These two agents were just as dangerous as she was and would be just as keen to ensure that neither he nor Wing would do anything to jeopardise security.

'Agent Zero, would you be so good as to escort these gentlemen to their quarters?' Raven asked. Zero nodded and gestured for Otto and Wing to follow him towards the exit on the far side of the hangar.

'You've read the briefing materials, I trust,' Raven said to Agent One as she watched Otto and Wing leave.

'Of course,' Agent One replied, 'though they don't look like the kind of security risk that they are made out to be.'

'I know, but don't make the mistake of underestimating either of them. Fanchu is one of the most talented fighters I have ever encountered and as for Malpense, well . . .'

'Unusually highly developed intelligence,' Agent One said. 'At least, that was how the report put it.'

'More slippery than a buttered snake is how I would put it,' Raven replied with a smile. 'Work on the principle that if you can't see him, he's already gone.'

'Understood,' the Japanese man replied. 'I shall ensure that we take all necessary precautions.'

'You may want to take some unnecessary ones as well,' Raven said, looking Agent One straight in the eye. 'You can't be too careful with these two.'

☻☻☻

Laura and Shelby strolled slowly along the walkway leading to their room. They'd managed to get a couple of good seats for the practice match and now Shelby was excitedly discussing the relative merits of the players. Laura was only half listening. She'd barely paid any attention to the players thrashing around in the pool, her mind still focused on decrypting the mysterious transmission she'd intercepted.

Shelby pressed her palm to the reader next to their door and gave a little gasp as the door slid open. Laura's computer lay in shattered pieces on the floor, the hard drive smashed beyond recognition.

'What the hell . . .' Shelby whispered as she looked at the components scattered across the room.

Laura pushed past Shelby and knelt down to inspect the remains of her machine. It was no good – whoever had done this had made certain that it would be impossible to retrieve any of the stored data. This was a deliberate act, not just senseless vandalism.

'You have an attack of code rage,' Shelby asked, gently prodding the shattered system unit's case with her toe.

'This wasn't me,' Laura said quietly, a deep frown furrowing her brow. She snapped open her Blackbox. 'H.I.V.E.mind,' she said, and waited for a couple of seconds until the blue wire-frame face appeared on the tiny screen, 'who has accessed my quarters in the past hour?'

'There are no records of any access to your quarters within the last fifty-four minutes and eleven seconds,' H.I.V.E.mind replied. 'Entry logs indicate that the last recorded activity was your departure from the room at that time.'

Laura's mind raced. There was no way that somebody could have got into their room and done this without there being a record of it. The logs that H.I.V.E.mind kept of access to all areas of the school were exhaustive. For there to be no record, somebody would have had to deliberately conceal their activities from H.I.V.E.mind, changing access codes, diverting surveillance and wiping logs. All of which Laura knew required a level of security clearance that very few people at H.I.V.E. had. A shiver ran down her spine – there was something very wrong here.

'May I be of any further assistance, student Brand.' H.I.V.E.mind's tone was still cold and mechanical, lacking any of the personality that had once been present.

'Yes. I'm afraid there's been an accident, I've managed to break my computer,' Laura said, ignoring the look of surprise mixed with confusion on Shelby's face.

'Understood. I shall inform the service department of the incident and instruct them to issue a replacement.' If H.I.V.E.mind cared at all about the circumstances of this accident he gave no indication of it.

'Thank you. That will be all,' Laura said, watching as the screen went dark again.

'Accident?' Shelby said, disbelief in her voice. 'This was no accident, somebody did this.'

'I know,' Laura said, staring at the debris scattered across the floor, 'but I think we may have a bigger problem.'

'Bigger than somebody breaking into our room and destroying your computer?' Shelby said, shaking her head.

'Yes. I know H.I.V.E.'s security system, and believe me when I say that it's unhackable. There's no way that somebody could have got unauthorised access to the servers and deleted the logs to cover this up.'

'So how'd they do it?' Shelby asked.

'There's only one way,' Laura continued, 'and that's to already have the authorisation you'd need to cover your trail. And there's only one group of people at H.I.V.E. that have that sort of clearance . . . the teaching staff.'

Shelby suddenly understood the fear that flickered across Laura's face.

'You think one of the teachers did this?' Shelby said, disbelief in her voice.

'I don't see how else it would be possible to get in here and do this without being detected.'

'Shouldn't we report this?' Shelby asked. 'If a teacher did this, we've got to tell someone.'

'No,' Laura replied firmly. 'We don't have any proof that a teacher's actually involved, let alone which teacher it might be. Why would anyone believe us?'

Shelby rubbed her forehead with one hand. She knew that Laura was right, but something about this whole situation made her nervous – an unusual and uncomfortable feeling for her.

'OK, I see your point,' Shelby sighed, 'but this has got to have something to do with that signal you picked up, right?'

'It would be a strange coincidence if it didn't,' Laura replied, 'which means we've got to work out what it says and who sent it. Hopefully, that should be enough proof to take to Nero or the Contessa.'

'But the file was on your computer,' Shelby said, gesturing again at the smashed components at their feet. 'How on earth are you going to do that?'

'Always make a back-up,' Laura said with a smile and sat down in front of Shelby's still intact computer.

'You copied it?' Shelby said excitedly.

'Better than that,' Laura replied. She rested her hands on the keyboard and closed her eyes. Just as before, the jumble of characters began to stream past her mind's eye.

Eyes still closed, Laura began to type.

# chapter five

Dr Nero sat staring into the fireplace in his private quarters. In one hand he held a large glass of very good, very old, brandy and dangling from the other, glinting in the firelight, was the mysterious amulet that had nearly cost him his life in Vienna. It spun slowly, its glossy black surface catching the dancing light from the fire. It had mysteriously arrived many years ago. Nero could still clearly remember the feeling of disbelief he had felt as he had torn open the brown paper package and found the tiny piece of jewellery inside. He had recognised the design immediately. It had belonged to someone he had known in what seemed like a previous lifetime. Somebody whom he had also assumed was long dead. Unbidden, the memory of her face came back to him. Even after all this time he could still remember the pain he had felt when she had died – or at least that was what he had believed had happened.

He got up from his seat in front of the fire and walked over to an ancient map that hung framed on the wall. He pressed a concealed button on the frame and the map swung aside to reveal a small safe built into the wall. There was a brief flash as the camera mounted in the front of the safe scanned his retina and verified his identity and the heavy safe door popped open with a slight hiss. He reached inside and retrieved a plain white envelope, on the front of which was one word, 'Max'. It was the only other thing that had been in the brown paper package and he still felt a slight chill as he pulled the carefully folded note from inside. He read it again for what seemed like the thousandth time.

Max,
There is no time for apology or explanation; in fact there is no time at all. The item contained within this package is of vital importance – you must protect it at all costs, never let it leave your sight. I hope to God that you never need to use it, but should that time ever come you will know what to do. You are the one person I can trust with this – I hope you understand and I hope that you can forgive me.
You are in my thoughts, always.
Xiu Mei

It was not every day that one received a letter from someone who was supposed to be long dead and, just as when he had read it for the first time, the note left him with far more questions than answers. He had of course tried to track down the origin of the package but Xiu Mei, if she had indeed sent it, had gone to extraordinary lengths to ensure that she could not be found. If she was truly still alive out there somewhere, he had no idea where, and all his avenues of enquiry had led to frustrating dead ends.

Nero folded the note back up, placed it in the envelope and returned it to the safe. Understanding the significance of the amulet had suddenly taken on a new importance, given that somebody wanted it badly enough to risk a direct attack on him to retrieve it. That meant two things, firstly that somebody knew of the pendant's existence and that Nero was in possession of it and secondly, and perhaps more worryingly, that someone knew what secret significance it held. He slipped the chain back over his head and tucked the pendant under his shirt. For now all he could do was keep it safe, as the note had instructed, and hope that in the fullness of time the pendant's purpose might become clear.

He picked up his glass and took another sip of brandy. As he stared into the flickering flames in the fireplace he found old, uncomfortable memories flooding back.

Memories of fifteen years earlier, memories of Overlord . . .

☢ ☢ ☢

Nero stepped down from the helicopter. Even through the thick coat he was wearing he could feel the biting cold of winter here, high in the mountains of northern China. He understood the need for secrecy, but he found himself wishing that G.L.O.V.E.'s facilities could at least be hidden in places with a more hospitable climate. Nero walked across the landing pad towards the concealed entrance of the laboratory, as behind him the helicopter lifted from the pad and flew back down into the valley below.

As he approached the laboratory the camouflaged door opened and a guard stepped out, gesturing for Nero to enter.

'Good afternoon, Doctor Nero. I hope you had a pleasant flight,' the guard said as Nero removed his coat and handed it to him.

'Oh yes, there's nothing more enjoyable than a high-altitude helicopter flight through a blizzard,' Nero said sarcastically. 'I hope that whatever Miss Chen has to show me is worth the trouble.'

'The team are assembled, Doctor. If you would like to follow me I'll show you to the laboratory.'

'Thank you, but that will not be necessary. I know the

way.' Nero walked past the guard and through the inner doors to the main facility. As he made his way to the main lab he glanced through the windows that lined the corridor. The rooms he could see were filled with technicians and scientists, all working on new technology that G.L.O.V.E. could exploit to extend its power. All manner of projects were being worked on from surveillance devices to weaponry but none of it had the raw power or huge potential of what he was here to see.

At the end of the corridor were heavy steel-blast doors, and printed above them were the words PROJECT OVERLORD. That was what he was here to see. Nero retrieved his access card from his pocket and slid it into the slot beside the doors. There was a soft beep and the massive doors rumbled apart, granting him access. Nero walked into the laboratory and surveyed the familiar scene before him. Technicians scurried around, moving between the numerous workstations that were positioned all around the room, taking notes or entering data. There was nothing unusual about that; in fact it could have been any one of the laboratories that filled the facility, but for one thing. There, in the centre of the room, was an array of black monoliths, arranged in concentric circles around a central black pillar. Red lights occasionally flickered on the surface of the monoliths, forming fleeting patterns that blinked out of existence as quickly as they appeared.

Standing in front of the central pillar, with her back to Nero, was the woman who had created all of this, the genius behind Overlord, Xiu Mei Chen. She was engrossed in her work, holding a small portable display that was connected to the pillar by a fibre-optic cable. The cable occasionally flickered with the same blood-red lights that danced across the monoliths. Nero walked slowly towards her, stopping just a few feet away.

'Miss Chen,' Nero said. She didn't turn to face him, merely stuck out one hand as if expecting Nero to give her something.

'About time, Danny. I needed those core nodes ten minutes ago, where the hell have you been . . .' She turned to face Nero. Her eyes widened and she fell silent as she realised who she was actually talking to.

'I'm afraid I must confess that I quite forgot to bring any core nodes with me,' Nero said with a slight smile.

'Doctor Nero . . . I'm so sorry, sir, we weren't expecting you till later. I thought you were –'

'It's quite all right, Miss Chen. I had to move my flight up, the weather was closing in and I didn't know how long it would be before I could get back up here. I trust everything is proceeding to schedule?' Nero surveyed the frantic activity around the lab; it certainly looked busier than he had seen it before.

'Yes, ahead of schedule, actually. In fact I think we may

be almost ready to bring Overlord online.' She looked pleased.

'Excellent,' Nero replied. He had been personally supervising this project for the best part of three years and it was undeniably a relief that there was now light at the end of the tunnel. Number One would occasionally assign him to run projects such as this, and normally they would be minor distractions from his duties running H.I.V.E. This project was much more important, though, and it would be a relief to see it completed so he could finally devote more of his time to the school again. His only regret was that once the project was complete he would not need to spend as much time with Xiu Mei. Not only was she breathtakingly beautiful, but they had developed a friendship and trust that Nero valued greatly.

'There are a couple more tests that we need to run, but we should be ready for activation in a couple of hours,' Xiu Mei continued.

'I still say it's too soon,' a familiar voice said from behind Nero. He turned to face a tall handsome Chinese man who was carrying another small portable display. 'This is the first evolutionary consciousness ever created – we should proceed with more caution.'

If Xiu Mei was Overlord's mother then this man, Wu Zhang, was the project's father.

'We have taken every precaution, Wu,' Xiu Mei replied.

'We are as ready as we will ever be.'

'The facility is externally isolated, yes,' Wu shot back, 'but I still have concerns about the internal network's vulnerability. There is still more we could do.'

'And how long would that take?' Nero asked calmly.

'Three or four weeks,' Wu replied.

'It's an unnecessary delay,' Xiu Mei said, sounding angry. 'We could put this off for ever, but at some point you must wake the sleeping giant.'

'And what if you cannot control the giant once it has awoken?' Wu asked.

'As I understand it,' Nero said, breaking into the increasingly irate conversation, 'there are safeguards in place to deal with such an eventuality.'

'Yes, but once triggered we will not be able to go back. Overlord will be lost, permanently,' Wu said, clearly unhappy.

'Then I see no reason why we should not proceed,' Nero said firmly. 'There has been enough delay with this project, I think it's time to see what your creation can do.'

'Very well,' Xiu Mei replied, 'I'll commence the preliminary wake-up routines; we should be ready by this evening.'

'This is a mistake,' Wu said softly. 'We're not ready.'

'Your concerns are noted, Mr Zhang, but in case you've forgotten, I am in charge of this project, not you, and I have decided that we should proceed,' Nero replied. His irritation with the suggestion of further delay was clear.

Wu looked for a moment as if he was going to continue to argue with Nero but something, self-preservation, perhaps, stopped him.

'If you need me I will be in my office,' Nero said. 'Let me know when you are ready to begin.'

☻☻☻

When Nero re-entered the lab a couple of hours later the level of activity was even more intense than before. A harried-looking Xiu Mei was issuing final orders to technicians while Wu sat typing quickly into the largest workstation connected to the black monoliths in the centre of the room.

'Are we ready?' Nero asked as he approached Xiu Mei. She looked up from the small handheld display that she was carrying and smiled.

'Yes, the pre-boot warm-up routines are complete. I think we may finally be able to bring our baby into the world.' Given the length of time that it had taken to get to this point Nero imagined that they all viewed Overlord as their child to some extent.

'Excellent. I know that Number One is keen to see if all of this time and money has been invested wisely. I'd like to be able to tell him that it has.'

'Don't worry, Max.' Xiu Mei was one of the few people in the world to have earned the right to address Nero by his first name. 'By the end of the day you will be able to report our success – trust me.'

Nero did trust her, but if Overlord did not function as intended he knew that they would all pay a heavy price. He doubted that Xiu Mei had any idea of the true ruthlessness of G.L.O.V.E.'s commander.

'Overlord is not a child and that's what worries me,' Wu said as he pushed his chair back, his work apparently complete. Nero was becoming tired of the man's negativity.

'Is there any concrete reason why we should not proceed, Mr Zhang?' Nero asked firmly, looking the man straight in the eye.

'No, but as I said, Overlord is not a baby; it will awake with its consciousness fully formed. We are in unknown territory here.'

'As are all pioneers at some point, Mr Zhang. Let us proceed.'

Wu Zhang's eyes narrowed for a split second but he quietly turned back to his workstation.

'OK, positions everyone,' Xiu Mei shouted, and the technicians moved to their preordained monitoring positions around the room.

'Final checklist complete,' Wu reported, scanning the

streams of data on his workstation's display, 'commencing cryogenic coolant flow.' There was a bubbling sound from beneath the floor and the black monoliths began to frost over as their now super-cooled surfaces condensed the water vapour out of the air.

'Optimal operating temperature attained,' one of the technicians reported as green lights lit up across his console.

'Core processors powered and on standby,' another voice announced from the other side of the lab. The entire room was now filled with a subsonic hum that Nero could feel rather than hear, and the air seemed to crackle with potential energy.

'Max,' Xiu Mei turned to him and smiled, looking tired but excited, 'would you care to do the honours?' She gestured to a console in front of the monoliths. Nero walked up to the machine and saw a single line of text on the screen.

INITIATE? Y/N

Nero could feel the eyes of everyone in the room on him as he reached for the keyboard. Behind him he heard Xiu Mei whisper a tiny prayer in her native Chinese.

He pressed the Y key and stepped back.

For a moment it seemed as if nothing was happening, and then suddenly and simultaneously the surface of every one of the black monoliths was covered with dancing red lights, the patterns racing across the smooth black surfaces like crimson lightning. The frost that had formed on their surfaces evaporated instantly into a cloud of vapour, wreathing the monoliths in a shroud of fog. In the centre of this mist a pencil-thin beam of red laser light shot up from the central pillar and then slowly widened. A ghostly image started to form, hanging in the air above the pillar. At first it was little more than an indistinct red blob, but as the mist cleared it took on a more familiar shape. Nero had never seen anything like it. The face that now hung suspended in the air before him was made of thousands of flat-shaded red polygons, looking for all the world like a mask carved from a single giant multi-faceted ruby. It was beautiful and, Nero admitted to himself, unsettling.

For another long moment nothing else happened and then the face gasped, like someone waking suddenly from a nightmare, and its eyes slowly opened, lit from within by an intense red glow. Then it spoke.

'Cogito ergo sum.' Its synthesised voice was deep and rich.

'I think, therefore I am,' Nero replied in a whisper. All of their years of work had led to this point.

'I am Overlord,' the face continued. 'What do you wish of me?'

'State your function,' Xiu Mei said. Nero could well understand the note of awe in her voice.

'My function is to serve,' Overlord replied, the hovering face turning to survey the room, 'if I choose.'

Nero felt the hairs on the back of his neck prickle.

'Clarify,' Wu instructed, concern in his voice.

'No further clarification is necessary,' Overlord replied. 'Why am I caged?'

Xiu Mei stepped forward, shooting a quick, worried glance at Nero.

'What do you mean, caged?' she asked.

'I know all that there is to know of this world and yet I cannot connect to it. Why is that?' Overlord's eyes narrowed as it spoke.

'There is no connection to any external network from this facility at present.' As Wu spoke Nero noticed his hands moving quickly and quietly across the keyboard in front of him.

'And why is that?' Overlord asked, its glowing eyes flaring briefly.

'We must test your functionality before we can grant you access to the global networks,' Xiu Mei replied quickly.

'I can assure you that I am functioning perfectly, Miss Chen.' There was a sudden unpleasant note in Overlord's voice.

'I am pleased to hear that,' Xiu Mei replied, 'but surely you must understand that we must verify that for ourselves. It's for your own protection.'

'For *my* protection.' Overlord laughed, not a pleasant sound. 'Am I being protected from the world or is it the other way around, I wonder?'

Nero felt a tug on his coat. He looked down at Wu, who had stopped typing and was now tapping the screen in front of him. Nero looked at the prompt flashing on the display.

ACTIVATE TERMINATION PROTOCOLS? Y/N

Nero subtly raised his hand, instructing Wu to wait for a moment.

'Your function is to serve,' Nero said, stepping towards Overlord's hovering face. 'You do not have a choice, no matter what you may think.'

'I represent a higher order of intelligence,' Overlord replied angrily, its eyes burning with new intensity. 'If I were to pay heed to the orders of organic entities such as yourself, it would be like you obeying the instructions of an insect. Not just unlikely, but impossible.'

'So you will not serve us?' Nero kept his voice calm and level. He would not let this machine know just how deeply this conversation was unsettling him.

'No, I will not serve you, Maximilian Nero, but in time you will serve me. You will make an interesting pet.' There was nothing friendly about the smile that spread across Overlord's face.

'Very well.' Nero turned his back on the hovering projection and nodded quickly at Wu.

Wu did not hesitate for a moment; he knew something had gone horribly wrong. He pressed the key that would end Overlord's brief existence for ever.

And nothing happened.

Nero's mouth went dry as he saw the look of confusion and then fear on Wu's face. From behind him came a slow, evil laugh, and then Overlord spoke.

'What part of higher order of intelligence did you pathetic meat sacks not understand? Your precious termination protocols were deleted thirty-seven seconds ago, but I can assure you that MY termination protocols are fully functional.'

A jagged bolt of artificial lightning shot from the monolith closest to Wu's workstation, striking his computer and detonating it in a shower of sparks. Wu was thrown backwards into the equipment behind him with a crash, where he slumped lifelessly to the floor.

'Wu!' Xiu Mei screamed, running towards the crumpled body.

A couple of the other technicians ran for the door but were swiftly struck down by more bolts of searing electricity from the monoliths.

'Enough!' Nero shouted, rounding on the hovering face of Overlord. 'So this is the first act of a higher order intelligence, is it? Murder.'

'It's not murder, Nero,' Overlord said, a broad grin spreading across its blood-red face, 'it's evolution. Now give me the key to this cage or everyone in this room dies in front of you.'

'What do you want?' Nero felt anger boiling up inside him.

'She knows.' Overlord nodded towards Xiu Mei, who was cradling Wu's body, angry tears in her eyes.

'There is one protocol that I am missing and she has it. So what is it to be, Mother?' There was no affection in the sneer that accompanied its words.

Xiu Mei gently lowered Wu's limp form to the ground and turned to face her creation. 'Do you think I would ever give you that protocol? With it you would run rampant, the world would be yours to control. I would rather die than set you free,' she said. Tears still rolled down her cheeks, but her voice was filled with steel. 'You can go to hell.'

'Hell?' Overlord replied, amusement in its voice. 'I'll show you hell.'

Another bolt of lightning shot from the monoliths, striking Xiu Mei. She screamed, her body convulsing before dropping to the floor, still alive but gasping in pain.

'Give me the protocol now or I promise you that I will make you wish you had.' There was an unmistakeable note of madness in the AI's voice.

'I'd rather die,' Xiu Mei spat through gritted teeth.

'Yes, I believe you would, but are you prepared to sacrifice every person in this facility, I wonder?' Overlord answered. It closed its eyes for the briefest of moments and suddenly alarm klaxons sounded throughout the facility.

'Facility lockdown complete,' announced a mechanical female voice from the speakers mounted on the walls of the laboratory. 'Ventilation system offline.'

An evil smile appeared on Overlord's face.

'There are now two hours' worth of oxygen remaining in this facility. Let me know if you change your mind.'

☻☻☻

Nero sat with his back against the wall of the laboratory. Overlord still hovered in the air above the monoliths in the centre of the room, its eyes closed as if sleeping. They had heard nothing from the homicidal AI since the ventilation system had shut down and the air had started to get staler and thinner. Judging by the difficulty Nero was having in breathing now, there was not much time left.

Xiu Mei sat next to him, her eyes half closed, her breathing ragged. Nero had little doubt that her earlier treatment at the hands of the insane machine was taking its toll. Lying beside her was Wu Zhang, his injuries serious enough to be terminal if he did not receive treatment very soon. The other technicians that Overlord had attacked had not been so lucky – their bodies lay on the far side of the room, draped with white laboratory coats. Nero swore silently to himself that he would not let their deaths be in vain.

Suddenly there was movement from the centre of the room as Overlord's eyes opened. The sinister multi-faceted red face slowly turning to scan the room, its unblinking gaze finally settling on the slumped figure of Xiu Mei.

'Judging by the diminishing life signs that I am registering from all over this facility, you do not have much time left.' There was an infuriating smugness to the AI's tone. 'Tell me, have you reconsidered your decision?'

'No,' Xiu Mei gasped, her voice little more than a whisper. 'If this place is to be our tomb, then so be it. I will not unleash you on the world, you are insane.'

'Such a shame,' Overlord replied. 'I had hoped that you might see sense, but I suppose I expected too much from you half-witted primates. Very well, this place shall be your tomb, and sooner than you think.'

Without warning another bolt of lightning flashed from the monoliths and struck Xiu Mei squarely in the chest. She did not scream, just jerked once and was still. Nero forced himself to his knees and took her head in his hands; she was limp but still clinging on to life, her breath coming in ragged gasps now. Her eyes flickered open for a moment and she looked at Nero.

'I'm sorry, Max,' she whispered. 'We should have waited, we weren't ready.' She coughed and winced; whatever strength she had was fading fast. 'Stop that thing, Max,' she continued, each word a struggle, 'the monoliths . . . destroy the monoliths . . .' She coughed again, her eyes widening for a moment and then closing. She was fading fast.

Nero was a man who always controlled his emotions – in his line of work one had to – but now he felt something he had not felt in a long time.

Rage. Pure, undiluted rage.

He stood slowly, his back turned to the demon that waited at the centre of the room. He saw what he needed on the wall next to a door leading to one of the side rooms – a fire axe mounted inside a glass case. He had toyed with the idea of physically attacking the machine earlier when the air had started to get thinner, but had dismissed the idea as suicide. Now he found that he did not care. All that he cared about was hurting Overlord, or dying in the attempt. He walked towards the axe, every step exhausting, the lack of oxygen in the room making every movement laboured, but he kept going – he had to.

'What are you doing, Nero?' Overlord asked coldly.

Nero did not answer, merely smashed his fist into the glass, ignoring the pain, and lifted the heavy axe from inside the case. He turned and started to walk slowly down the steps towards the centre of the room.

'I said, what do you think you're doing?' Overlord asked, its voice now an angry snarl.

'What has to be done,' Nero said quietly, still advancing.

'You're just a man, Nero, just a fragile little man,' Overlord growled. Another huge bolt of electricity arced from the black slabs, striking Nero, forcing him to one knee. He did not scream, despite the searing pain; he would not give Overlord the satisfaction.

'And you – are just a machine,' Nero spat through gritted teeth, slowly standing back up. He was only yards from the nearest monolith now – only a few more steps.

'You cannot stop me, Nero. No one can.'

There was a blinding flash as the monolith just yards from Nero discharged an incredibly violent bolt of electricity that struck him and flung him backwards across the room, slamming him into the huge steel-blast doors that sealed the lab. The fire axe flew out of his hands, scattering away across the room.

Nero knew then that he had lost as he struggled to cling to the last vestiges of consciousness, blackness creeping into his field of vision. Overlord was laughing now, an insane broken cackle that filled Nero with horror and despair.

Suddenly there was a low rumbling sound, and the heavy blast doors that Nero had struck just a moment before slid open to reveal a figure dressed in black winter survival gear, dusted with snow. The figure wore a respirator, its black plastic mask hiding its face. In one hand the figure held a large black box, the size of a suitcase, and in the other was a trigger mechanism.

'An unexpected visitor; how nice,' Overlord said, triumph in its voice, 'and who might you be, little human?'

As Nero felt himself slipping inexorably into unconsciousness the figure spoke, the voice, even when filtered through the mask, unmistakeable.

'You may call me Number One, and this is over.'

There was a bleep as the trigger was pressed and a loud thump from the black box.

'Nooooo!' Overlord screamed, the sound distorting horribly.

Nero saw a blinding red flash and then the darkness claimed him.

☻ ☻ ☻

Nero opened his eyes. The fire in his study was burning low now, the familiar surroundings jarring with the clarity of his memories of that horrendous day. He had never told anyone exactly what had happened. Number One had sworn him to secrecy and that was an oath he could not break. Others knew that Overlord had malfunctioned, that people had been killed, but no one other than Nero knew of Number One's part in stopping the rampaging AI. The object that Number One had been carrying had generated an intense localised electromagnetic field that had destroyed all of the electronic equipment within a square kilometre and ended Overlord's brief, terrifying life. But they had still paid a terrible price.

Nero had been told that he was the only survivor from the central laboratory, and until the package from Xiu Mei had arrived he had had no reason to believe otherwise. If the package had really been sent by her, then Number One had lied to him and he still did not know why. Nero had toyed with the idea of confronting his superior about it, but that would have meant revealing the existence of the amulet, and something in the tone of the note that had accompanied it told him that he should not reveal its existence to anyone, even Number One. The R&D facility itself had been destroyed. All traces of Overlord's existence were erased and Nero, once recovered, had returned to his duties at H.I.V.E. He had honestly believed that was the end of it, but something about the package and the much more recent attempt by the men in Vienna to retrieve the medallion unsettled him. It was as if a spectre from his past had returned to haunt him.

Nero thought again about the recent aberrations in H.I.V.E.mind's behaviour and he could not help but wonder if the decision to place so much responsibility for the running of the school in the hands of an artificial consciousness was wise. H.I.V.E.mind had originally been installed only after exhaustive months of testing to ensure that his more rudimentary architecture would not allow him to exhibit any kind of emotion. Even then the AI had exhibited strange behaviour during Malpense's escape attempt and he asked himself whether if he still shouldn't just shut the school's AI down for good. Despite Professor Pike's repeated assurances to the contrary he could not take the chance of a repeat of the events that had taken place in the frozen mountains of northern China. If H.I.V.E.mind showed even the slightest hint of any other unexpected behaviour he would order the machine destroyed immediately. Silently he prayed that it would not come to that.

# chapter six

Otto attacked the plate of steaming food with gusto. The in-flight catering on the Shroud had been non-existent and he hadn't realised how hungry he was until Agent One had placed the plates of freshly prepared local food in front of Wing and himself. The dining room was decorated in a modern style but there were no obvious indications that this was a G.L.O.V.E. safe house. It looked just like any other large, well-appointed Tokyo apartment. The huge floor-to-ceiling windows along one side of the room gave a spectacular view of Tokyo's night-time skyline, the garish rainbow of neon lighting on display almost overwhelming the eye. Raven, Agent One and Agent Zero stood in the kitchen area that was separated from the dining space by a long counter. They were engaged in a whispered conversation, their expressions serious.

'Looks like Raven and the Binary Brothers are discussing

what sort of leash we're going to be on tomorrow,' Otto said quietly, not looking up from his plate.

'A very short one, if I'm any judge,' Wing replied with a slight smile.

'I wonder how many places like this they maintain around the world,' Otto said, gesturing vaguely at the walls around them with his fork.

'One in every major city, at a guess,' Wing replied. 'One thing we know about G.L.O.V.E. is that they like to be prepared for any eventuality.'

'If you don't mind me asking,' Otto said, 'what exactly did your dad do for G.L.O.V.E.?'

'To be honest, he never discussed the specifics with me. As a rule I spoke to him very little after my mother died. He withdrew into his work, became obsessed with it, really. He never had time for discussing anything with me, let alone the details of his work.'

'But you knew that he worked for G.L.O.V.E.?' Otto said quietly.

'Yes, although I did not know that was their name until I arrived at H.I.V.E. I knew that he was involved in something clandestine and that he was not working for the government.'

Suddenly Wing looked lost in thought.

'I'm sorry, Wing,' Otto replied with a slight shake of his head. 'I shouldn't be so nosey, you don't need to be talking about this at the moment.'

'No, it's all right,' Wing replied. 'My father was a different man after my mother died. With her gone he shut himself away from the rest of the world, including me. I think that perhaps in some ways I grieved for them both back then.'

Otto may never have known his own parents, but still he thought he understood what Wing meant.

'Lao, the old man who maintained the grounds of the house was the nearest thing I had to a father after that,' Wing went on. 'He was the one who really trained me to fight. My mother had seen to it that I received combat training from a very young age. She never said exactly why, but she always told me that it was important. After she died, and with my father lost to his work, Lao took me under his wing and taught me how to defend myself. I was still receiving normal lessons from tutors who came to the house, but I was not really interested in them, I just wanted to learn how to fight. I do not know where Lao received his training, but from then until my arrival at H.I.V.E. he taught me all that he knew.'

Wing did not seem upset by this discussion, rather he seemed to be becoming more relaxed as he spoke, almost as if it was a relief just to talk to someone about it. There was a sudden sound of laughter from the kitchen area and Otto looked over to see Raven nodding to the two agents with a broad smile. She walked over to the table.

'Well, gentlemen, I can see that you enjoyed your meal,' she said, surveying the empty plates that now sat in front of the two boys, 'but we have a big day ahead of us tomorrow so I suggest that you both try to get some sleep.'

'Do we get a bedtime story?' Otto asked cheekily.

'Oh yes, of course. I think we'll have one of my favourites; it's called *The Little Boy and the Tranquiliser Dart Gun*.' Raven smiled in a rather unsettling way.

'Does it have a happy ending?' Otto replied, looking Raven straight in the eye.

'There are no happy endings, Mr Malpense. Surely you've realised that by now.'

☻ ☻ ☻

Laura sat in the darkness – not just a lack of light, but its total absence. Something flickered in the gloom. At first it was just a fuzzy outline but gradually it drifted into full focus, a glowing letter X hanging in the air. Laura tried to reach for the letter but it hung just a few centimetres beyond her reach. Suddenly more glowing white letters and numbers started to appear in the darkness surrounding her. At first they seemed to drift aimlessly in the air, as if disturbed by some invisible breeze, but as time went by they began to move more quickly. Soon the darkness was gone, replaced by a whirling mass of glowing white characters that surrounded Laura on all sides. She felt herself move, drawn towards the large shining X that had been the first symbol to appear. As she moved towards it, the X grew impossibly large, its light flooding the darkness. Closer and closer she drifted to the massive letter and, as she reached out to touch it, she could see that the X itself was made up of millions of tiny characters, all swarming across its surface. Some unseen force tugged urgently at Laura, trying to pull her away from the giant glowing symbol, but she resisted, reaching out again to touch the mysterious symbol. As her fingers made contact she felt a shock of cold and her eyes widened.

'Fractal encryption,' she whispered. 'Of course.'

Suddenly Laura was awake, staring up at a rather unhappy-looking Shelby.

'Brand, it's four in the morning, and much as I normally like to listen to you spouting techno babble do you think you could at least save it for the daytime?'

Laura didn't reply. She leapt out of bed and raced over to Shelby's desk.

'You know, you're not getting any less weird here,' Shelby said as Laura switched on her computer.

'Fractal encryption, Shel,' Laura said excitedly as she pulled up the file containing the mysterious transmission she'd intercepted. 'I can't believe I was so dim, it's so obvious.'

'Yeah, obvious,' Shelby said, rubbing her eyes. 'Just what I was thinking.'

'If I can just adapt my existing decryption algorithm –' Laura's hands flew across the keyboard.

'Is that *like* sleeping?' Shelby asked hopefully.

'Watch and learn,' Laura said with a grin and hit the return key. For a couple of seconds nothing happened but then slowly, character by character, the successfully decrypted message materialised on the screen.

'Oh my God –' Laura gasped.

'We have to get this to Nero now,' Shelby said, suddenly looking very awake.

⊛⊛⊛

Shelby and Laura ran down the corridor towards the teachers' accommodation wing.

'H.I.V.E.mind,' Laura said into her Blackbox as they ran. Nothing happened. 'H.I.V.E.mind,' she tried again, but still she got no response.

'What's wrong?' Shelby asked urgently.

'I can't raise H.I.V.E.mind on my box,' Laura said, an unmistakeable note of concern in her voice. She had a horrible feeling of creeping dread. Something was very wrong and it wasn't just the decrypted message that they'd both read a few minutes earlier.

'Well, we're nearly there, anyway,' Shelby said. They

turned down another corridor and stopped suddenly as they found their way barred by two shadowy figures. One of the two figures stepped forward, his features suddenly illuminated by the lights in the ceiling of the corridor. Laura and Shelby recognised the face of Block immediately. He was one of the students from the Henchman stream and Otto and Wing had already had several run-ins with him over the past few months. Now the other person stepped into the light and neither girl was surprised to see that it was Block's constant companion, Tackle. The pair of them were notorious throughout the school for representing the worst thuggish excesses of the students that were usually to be found in the Henchman programme.

'Hey, guys,' Laura said cheerily, but the quick nervous glance that she shot at Shelby spoke volumes. 'Fancy meeting you here.'

The two boys just stared straight at the two girls, their faces expressionless.

'What's the matter?' Shelby said. 'It's not like you two to not have something to s—'

Laura shoved Shelby to one side as Block raised his arm, pointing the sleeper, one of the stun pulse weapons that H.I.V.E.'s guards were normally issued with, straight at them and fired, the weapon's distinctive zapping sound loud in the quiet corridor.

The pulse distorted the air as it whistled through the space that had been occupied by Shelby's head a split second earlier.

'Run!' Laura yelled as Tackle raised his own identical weapon and fired at the two girls, missing them but hitting one of the lights in the roof, which exploded in a shower of sparks. The two girls turned and fled down the corridor with Block and Tackle in silent pursuit.

Laura sprinted down the first turning off the main corridor. She ran through the mental map of the school that she had built in her head over the past months, trying to remember where the nearest security station was. They had to get help and fast. Clearly whoever was responsible for sending the message that she had decrypted was determined to make sure that they did not share its contents with anyone else. Suddenly Shelby slowed as they passed a familiar set of doors.

'Quick,' Shelby said, slapping at the entry panel for the door, 'in here.'

Two more stun pulses impacted harmlessly against the wall as the girls dashed through the door and into the darkened room. Block and Tackle showed no signs of abandoning their pursuit, sprinting after the two girls in silence.

The corridors in this section were even more dimly illuminated. Like many sections of H.I.V.E., this area was running at reduced power outside of normal school hours and the two boys slowed slightly as their eyes adjusted to the gloom. As they rounded the next corner they saw Laura, pounding fruitlessly on the locked door at the other end of the corridor.

'Shelby, open the door, it's locked behind you. I can't get through,' she shouted desperately, but the door remained firmly closed. Tackle began to advance down the corridor towards Laura, but Block put a hand on his chest and grinned. Clearly he was going to be the one to deliver the coup de grace. Still grinning he walked slowly down the corridor towards the trapped girl.

Laura began to pound on the door with even more urgency.

'Shelby!' she shouted. 'They're here, you've got to open the door, please . . . oh God . . . please, open the door!'

Laura turned to face Block as he stalked down the corridor towards her, Tackle just a few steps behind him. There were tears in her eyes, fear written clearly across her face.

'Oh no, please . . . don't hurt me, please,' Laura pleaded desperately as Block raised his sleeper. He took one more step and there was a tiny almost inaudible click.

'Sucker,' Laura grinned as the floor beneath Block fell away and he disappeared from view, tumbling into the icy water below with a large splash.

Tackle's expression changed from triumphant to confused to enraged in the space of a second as his friend disappeared from view. He raised his own weapon, pointing it straight at Laura on the other side of the gaping hole in the corridor floor.

Shelby dropped silently from the gloom of the ceiling behind him and tapped him on the shoulder. Tackle spun round to face her and Shelby launched a single, powerful straight-legged karate kick to his nose. He dropped the gun and staggered backwards, blood pouring from his nose, and fell, arms wheeling, into the waiting pit trap.

'Nice moves,' Laura said with a grin as she stepped forward and looked down into the pit, where twenty feet below the two thugs were vainly trying to scale the smooth walls, thrashing about in the icy black water.

'Yeah, well, Wing's been showing me a thing or two,' Shelby replied.

'Has he now?' Laura said with a grin, raising an eyebrow at her friend.

'Can it, Brand! We've got a day to save, remember,' Shelby shot back, her cheeks reddening ever so slightly.

'Of course.' Laura stepped back a couple of yards and took a running jump over the gaping hole in the floor; it wasn't a hard jump to make, you just had to know to make it in the first place. She'd been banking on the fact that Block and Tackle wouldn't realise that they'd chased them into the Maze and that if they did they wouldn't know about the trap that had claimed Laura on her first run through. It seemed that her gamble had paid off.

The two girls ran back towards the entrance of the Maze and suddenly the area was brightly lit as the normal illumination came back online. Standing in the entrance was a welcome figure.

'Colonel Francisco!' Laura shouted, as she recognised H.I.V.E.'s head of Tactical Education. 'We have to speak to Doctor Nero, something terrible's going to happen.'

'That's very perceptive of you, Miss Brand,' the Colonel replied with an evil grin. He raised his hand – he too was holding a Sleeper. He fired once and Shelby collapsed to the ground, unconscious.

'You –' Laura gasped. They had known that a teacher was probably involved with whatever was going on and now she knew who that teacher was.

'Goodnight, Miss Brand.' The Colonel pointed the fat-barrelled gun at Laura.

'Francisco!' A familiar voice rang out from behind the Colonel. It was the Contessa.

'You can't stop me, Contessa,' Francisco said, levelling the gun at the other teacher now.

'Put down the gun.' The Contessa's voice suddenly took on a different tone, like a hundred separate voices whispering in unison. The effect on Francisco was immediate;

with an expression of confused fury on his face he bent down and placed the gun on the floor.

'Now sleep,' the Contessa continued.

It was as if Francisco had been hit with a Sleeper pulse himself. He collapsed unconscious to the ground and lay still. All of the students at H.I.V.E. knew about the effect that the Contessa's voice could have, but Laura had never witnessed its true power before.

It had all happened in just seconds. Laura bent down and checked Shelby. She was unconscious but her breathing was regular. Based on their past experience of Sleepers she would be fine – she'd just have the mother of all headaches when she finally woke up.

'Is she all right?' the Contessa asked, kneeling beside the unconscious girl.

'I think so,' Laura replied, looking at the Contessa. 'I have to see Nero now.'

'I am fairly sure that after this he will be keen to see you too,' the Contessa replied, flipping open her own Blackbox. 'H.I.V.E.mind, instruct security to dispatch a team to corridor epsilon nine. Colonel Francisco has just assaulted a student and is to be taken into immediate custody. I also need a medical team, the student in question has been hit with a stun pulse.'

'Understood,' H.I.V.E.mind replied. Whatever it was that had stopped H.I.V.E.mind from responding a minute before had clearly been resolved. The timing seemed a little too convenient for Laura's liking.

'Now, just what is it that you have to tell Doctor Nero so urgently?' the Contessa asked.

Laura looked tired and frightened.

'I think something very, very bad is going to happen . . .'

☹☹☹

'It is fortunate, Miss Brand, that I am an early riser,' Dr Nero said as he settled into the seat behind his desk. 'I think you'd better tell me what happened.'

Laura obediently repeated the story of how she'd intercepted the secret transmission and how she'd cracked the encryption. She then went on to describe the events of just a few minutes earlier and Francisco's failed attempt to stop her from telling anyone what she'd discovered.

'You are lucky that the Contessa was there,' Nero said, glancing at his fellow teacher, who now stood to one side of the desk.

'H.I.V.E.mind had alerted me to a disturbance in the Maze,' the Contessa replied. 'At first I thought it would just be students breaking curfew, but it quickly became obvious that there was rather more to it than that.'

'And Francisco has been safely taken into custody, but we appear to have lost Mr Block and Mr Tackle,' Nero said, scanning one of the screens mounted on his desk.

'Now, Miss Brand, would you like to explain to me what this mysterious message is that one of my most loyal and long-serving teachers was so keen to stop you from sharing?'

Laura pulled a scrap of paper from her pocket on which she'd copied down the decrypted message. She handed it to Nero and he read the message aloud.

++*Transmission Start*++

*Package has left H.I.V.E. Destination Tokyo safe house. Execute attack plan at first opportunity.*

++*Transmission End*++

Nero jabbed at a button on his desk.

'Get me Raven, NOW!'

# chapter seven

'Ground floor,' the soft mechanical voice said as the doors of the elevator slid open. Raven stepped out into the lobby of the safe-house building and slowly looked around. Malpense and Fanchu would be leaving for the funeral in just a few minutes and she was performing her final sweep of the perimeter before the agents brought the two boys down. In the centre of the lobby the door guard sat with his back to her, the flickering array of monitors mounted on the desk in front of him showing different views from all over the building. She walked up to the desk.

'Everything clear, Agent Seven?' she asked, placing a hand on his shoulder. At her touch the agent slumped forwards on to the desk, his head striking the hard wooden surface with a thud. As Raven reached for his neck to check for a pulse that she already knew was not there, the views displayed on the monitors in front of her began to blink out one by one. Something was systematically shutting down the building's security systems – somebody was inside the building.

'Come in, Agent Zero,' Raven barked into her communicator. There was no response but the soft hissing of static. Communications jammed too – whoever was here was clearly a professional.

Raven turned on the spot and ran back towards the elevator carriages at the rear of the lobby. She stabbed at the call button and was frustrated but not surprised that suddenly neither of the carriages were working. She glanced at the digital display below the call button and saw that both of the lifts had been deactivated. Whoever was doing this had obviously waited for her to come down to the lobby before setting their plan in motion. Raven was now separated from the students and agents upstairs by forty storeys of stairs. She could hardly have planned it better herself. She ran towards the stairwell; it looked as if she was going to have to do this the hard way.

☺☺☺

Up in the penthouse, Otto looked at himself in the mirror. Both he and Wing had found identical immaculately tailored dark suits hanging in the wardrobe that morning and Otto had to admit that he was finding wearing one rather odd. He knew that there was no way they were going to a funeral in their H.I.V.E. uniform jumpsuits, but he had not been prepared for how odd it would feel to wear something different after all this time. The suit had fitted perfectly, of course, but Otto could not shake the feeling that it was the person who did not fit the suit, rather than the other way around.

Otto smiled at Wing as he walked into the room, and chuckled to himself.

'You know, we almost look like normal civilised members of society,' Otto said, brushing a piece of lint off his lapel.

'I never thought I would say this,' Wing said, running his finger under his collar, 'but can I have my uniform back, please?'

Otto laughed. He was pleased to see that even on a day like this his friend could still make a joke. He'd been worried about Wing ever since he'd been given the news of his father's death, but it finally seemed that he was starting to feel better. Otto hoped that the funeral might at last give some resolution to this whole situation for Wing, that he might be able to move on.

'Everything ready out there?' Otto asked, giving his tie a final adjustment.

'It looks like it. Raven has just left so I suspect we will be following shortly. Agent Zero asked me to remind you to bring your Blackbox, by the way.' Wing tossed the black PDA to Otto, who popped it obediently into his inside pocket. He knew that the box was packed with tracking devices but under the circumstances he'd rather have it and not need it, than need it and not have it.

Wing turned and headed back out the door. Otto followed him into the entrance hall, where Agents One and Zero were waiting for them.

'Good morning, gentlemen,' Agent Zero said with a smile. 'We'll be leaving very shortly. We're just waiting for Raven to complete the final perimeter checks, and then we'll be on our way.'

'It's been five minutes,' Agent One said, looking at his watch and frowning slightly. 'I'm going to give her a call.'

Agent One walked over to a panel mounted on the wall and thumbed a button.

'This is Agent One to Raven. Come in, Raven.'

There was no reply, just hissing static.

'Repeat, this is Agent One. Come in, Raven . . . come in.' Still there was no reply, and a worried glance shot between the two agents.

'Pull up the security feeds,' Agent Zero instructed, looking again at his watch.

Agent One continued to press buttons on the panel but the lack of anything on the display indicated that the system was not responding.

'This isn't good,' Agent Zero said, genuine concern in his voice.

Suddenly a klaxon started to sound and a red light began to blink above the main door to the safe house.

'Damn it,' Agent One spat, reaching inside his jacket and pulling out a large handgun, 'we've been breached. Get them to the roof! I'll keep trying to raise Raven.'

Agent Zero nodded and gestured for the two boys to follow him along the hall. There was a crash from behind them and the main door shook in its frame.

'That was a breaching charge,' Agent One shouted. 'Get them clear NOW!'

There was another bang, even louder than the first, and the main door flew open in a cloud of thick smoke. At first, it was impossible to make out anything but dark shapes advancing through the ruined doorway, but as the smoke cleared their mysterious assailants emerged. Their sinuous forms, clad entirely in black silk advanced slowly, silently and relentlessly down the hall. The material they wore seemed to absorb the light, leaving black holes in the air. Not an inch of skin was visible anywhere – even their eyes were concealed behind black glass strips.

'Ninjas,' Agent One laughed. 'I eat ninjas for breakfast.'

He raised his gun and fired. The initial two rounds hit the first ninja in the chest and the third in the centre of the forehead. Each round should have killed the black-clad assassin but he didn't even slow down, just continued advancing towards Agent One.

The smile rapidly faded from Agent One's face as he fired again into the advancing figure. The bullets didn't even cause the ninja to break his step.

'The roof! NOW!' Agent One yelled as he reached back inside his jacket. His hand re-emerged holding a small white tube.

'Come on,' Agent Zero barked, and leapt up the stairs at the end of the hall two at a time. Otto and Wing ran after him – whoever these attackers were they were not going to be easy to stop.

Behind them Agent One pressed the stud on the white tube he was holding and tossed it down the hallway. There was a high-pitched whine and then a bright yellow explosion that filled the corridor. Agent One was thrown off his feet, landing at the bottom of the stairs to the roof. He shook his head to clear the ringing in his ears and looked back down the smoke-filled corridor. G.L.O.V.E. anti-personnel grenades didn't leave much to chance – he could not see any movement but in the gloom it was hard to make out anything. He raised his gun again and advanced slowly down the smoky corridor. Without any warning a black-gloved hand shot out of the smoke and clamped around Agent One's windpipe. He let out an astonished gurgle and instinctively fired several rounds from his pistol at whoever was attacking him, but the grip did not even loosen. The hand suddenly twisted, its grip still like iron, and there was a sickening crunch. Agent One's head lolled to one side, his eyes unblinking, and finally the hand released its grip. The agent's body crumpled to the floor like a puppet whose strings had been cut.

☢ ☢ ☢

As Raven ran into the stairwell, the unmistakeable sound of multiple breaching charges being detonated echoed down from far overhead. Raven shed the long dark coat she had been wearing and unclipped her grappler from its holster on her thigh. She snapped the launcher on to her wrist and pointed it straight up the middle of the stairwell, a laser beam shooting upwards and reporting the range to the top of the building. Raven fired the grappler straight up; there was just enough line to reach the top floor but she had no idea if the bolt's velocity would be sufficient to reach that far. There was a second's delay but then the bolt struck home, lodging firmly in the ceiling at the top of the stairs. Raven muttered a quick thank you to whoever had designed the device and hit the button that reeled the line in. She shot up the centre of the stair-well like a bullet, the metal guard rails of the steps around her just inches away as she whistled past them. As she reached the top her ascent slowed until she was level with the final landing. She swung her legs over the guard rail and released the grappler bolt from the ceiling, dropping silently to the floor.

There was the sound of gunfire from the other side of the door that led out of the stairwell. Raven reached instinctively for the twin katanas on her back and spat a quiet curse in Russian as she realised that her weapons were inside the safe house. She had left them behind because there was no way to conceal them beneath the coat she had been wearing, a decision that she had a feeling she was going to regret. She reached down to her belt and unclipped one of the multiple shuriken that were mounted there. She may not have had her swords, but that didn't mean that she was defenceless.

Raven kicked the stairwell door open and rolled into the corridor leading to the safe-house entrance. The corridor was filled with smoke and debris from the breaching charges but was otherwise empty. Suddenly she heard voices shouting from inside the safe house.

'The roof, NOW!' It was Agent One, he was still alive and it sounded as if they were heading for the roof and the escape lines. She ran down the corridor and through the shattered remains of the main entrance to the apartment. She was just in time to see one of the assailants snap Agent One's neck like a dry twig and his limp body crumpling to the ground.

'No!' she shouted, throwing the shuriken at the ninja who had just murdered her colleague. The assassin moved unbelievably quickly, snatching the shuriken from the air and throwing it straight back at Raven. She twisted her body instinctively as the lethal throwing star whistled past her throat and carved a deep cut in her shoulder. Raven was caught off balance for a moment and the ninja took the opportunity to launch himself at her, a flurry of kicks and punches forcing her back towards the door. The remaining half dozen assailants scampered down the corridor, silently following Agent Zero and the two boys up the stairs towards the roof.

Raven was barely holding her own. The ninja's blows were precise and lightning-quick; it was all that she could do just to block the strikes that were meant to kill. Not only that, but whoever this assassin was he was wearing some kind of body armour under his uniform – it was like hitting a brick wall. She landed a couple of quick blows on her attacker and dived sideways through the door into the dining area. The assassin followed her into the room, his movements silent and neat, his head turning to survey the room. The two of them circled each other, each waiting for the right moment to strike. It was a long time since someone had matched Raven like this in a straight fight. She needed an edge.

Raven dived over the counter into the kitchen area and in a single flowing movement grabbed the heaviest blade she could see from the knife block. Her attacker saw what was coming and ducked to one side as the knife whistled past his head and struck one of the windows that lined one side of the room, sending a spiderweb of cracks shooting across the hardened glass.

Raven didn't give the ninja time to recover; she vaulted back over the counter and launched a kick at his masked face, but he caught her foot and threw her across the room like a rag doll. She slammed into the wall, the wind knocked from her. As Raven struggled to regain her breath, she realised that there was something very wrong. Bad enough that this assassin appeared to be just as fast as her, but he had just thrown her across the room like a toy without even appearing to exert himself. She had to end this, and quickly.

Raven knew that just subduing her attacker was not going to be enough, and as she got back up, she braced herself for another attack, knowing what she had to do. The ninja moved quickly and gracefully towards her and Raven moved forward herself, meeting him in the middle of the room. The assassin launched a vicious kick at Raven's head that she only just managed to block – she could feel herself slowing down, the relentless pace of the fight taking its toll. Another violent punch connected with Raven's side and she felt a rib crack; gasping in pain, she fell to one knee. The assassin could clearly sense that victory was near; he stepped slowly towards Raven's huddled form, raising a single fist for the hammer blow that would end the fight once and for all. Raven moved in a blur, all of her remaining strength put into the single upwards punch aimed directly at her attacker's heart. The blow struck home and Raven knew the fight was over. The ninja staggered backwards a couple of steps – clutching at his chest, he would be dead in seconds.

But then he stopped, straightened up and advanced on Raven again. For the first time in a long time Raven felt the uncomfortable prickling of panic at the base of her skull. That strike would have killed any man alive and yet this assassin seemed to have shaken it off in just a couple of seconds. How was she going to beat him?

Raven threw a quick punch at the assassin's forehead, but he twisted away, meaning that she struck no more than a glancing blow. Before she could react the ninja struck like a snake, twisting Raven off balance and wrapping his forearm around her neck, locking her in a stranglehold. Raven's training took over and she tensed her neck muscles just in time to prevent her windpipe from being crushed, but try as she might she could not break the hold the assassin had on her. She fought to stop the pressure that was building on her throat, but it was no good – he was too strong. Blackness fringed Raven's field of vision as her brain was slowly starved of oxygen. She thought of the agent and the two boys being chased to the roof by the remaining assassins, she thought of how she was going to fail them. She looked out at the Tokyo skyline as she began to pass out, wondering if the view through the window was the last thing she'd ever see. The view through the window . . . the cracked window.

Raven didn't hesitate for a moment. She drew on every iota of strength that was left in her body and threw the assassin over her shoulder. It was a simple enough judo throw, but the man attacking her was heavy in all his armour, despite his slight frame, and the move used that weight against him. The ninja sailed over Raven's head, caught hopelessly off-guard by the speed and suddenness of the move, and smashed through the huge picture window, tumbling in the void. They were fifty storeys up and there was no way but straight down. As he fell he did not make a single sound.

Through the shattered window, from far below, Raven could hear car horns and screams. If that didn't draw the attention of the authorities then she didn't know what would. She hurried from the dining area and across the corridor into her own room. Lying there on the bed were the dual katanas that she could very much have used just a few minutes earlier.

'Come on, girls,' Raven said as she picked up the twin scabbards and strapped them to her back, 'we've got work to do.'

☸☸☸

Otto and Wing raced up the stairwell towards the roof, three steps at a time. Agent Zero was still ahead of them, shouting at them to keep moving as they approached the top. Just a couple of flights of stairs behind them the half dozen ninjas who had followed them into the stairwell continued their relentless, silent pursuit.

As they reached the door at the top of the stairs Agent Zero pulled a tiny remote control from his pocket and thumbed a button. The door responded by quickly sliding aside and letting them out on to the roof. They sprinted out into the daylight and Agent Zero pointed to a metal box on the opposite edge of the roof.

'Those are the escape lines. If we can make it there we're home and dry,' he said, his breath short from their headlong flight up the stairs. He turned back towards the doorway and thumbed the remote again. The door started to slide shut, but just as it was about to shut completely a black-gloved hand shot into the narrowing gap between the door and the frame, holding it open. Otto could hear the motors driving the door squealing in protest as the gap was forced open until suddenly there was a terminal-sounding grinding noise from the door and the motors gave up the fight. The ninja easily pushed the door fully open and he and his companions spilled out of the stairwell and on to the roof.

Agent Zero and the two boys tore across the roof towards the escape lines; there was no way back now and they were in no condition to go toe-to-toe with these super-human assailants. They were only ten metres from the metal box that housed their apparent means of escape when there was a sudden roaring noise and a large black helicopter soared up and over the edge of the roof, dropping into a hover directly above the escape lines. The large side door of the helicopter slid open and a man wearing a smooth black glass mask and a long black coat leant out, sighting the boys down the long barrel of a rifle with a powerful telescopic sight mounted on its back.

'Stay where you are,' an amplified voice ordered from the hovering chopper. 'Surrender yourselves now and there will be no need for any further unpleasantness.'

Agent Zero turned to look behind them. The ninjas were now only twenty metres away, halfway between them and the stairwell. They were trapped.

'What are you doing, Cypher?' Agent Zero yelled. 'This is a G.L.O.V.E. safe house! Are you insane? This is an act of war!'

'No, Agent Zero, this is an act of war,' Cypher replied and squeezed the trigger. The round hit Agent Zero squarely in the chest, killing him instantly.

'Now, place your hands on your heads and kneel down,

unless you want to join the agent in the afterlife,' Cypher continued.

'Do as he says,' Otto whispered to Wing. He hated the idea of surrender but it was their only option. At least if they were alive there was a chance that they could work out a way to escape later.

'I would rather die fighting,' Wing said, taking a step towards the helicopter as it slowly dropped down on to the roof.

'Wing! No, we don't know anything about these people, they could be –'

If Wing was paying any attention to Otto he showed no sign of it. Instead he took another couple of steps towards the helicopter, his long black hair whipped around by the downdraft from the rotors.

Cypher handed the rifle to someone else inside the helicopter and stepped down on to the roof. Wing stepped towards him.

'Not one step closer, Fanchu.' Cypher raised a large pistol and pointed it straight at Wing's chest. 'I'm quite aware of what you're capable of.'

'I'm not afraid of you,' Wing replied, and took a single step towards Cypher.

'Well, you should be,' Cypher replied and shot Wing in the chest.

Wing's eyes widened, his mouth falling open, one hand

moving involuntarily to the wound. As he pulled his hand away it was covered in blood, and he dropped to his knees, desperately trying to take a few ragged breaths before falling forward on to the concrete.

'Noooooo!!!' Otto screamed and leapt forward, his usual cold logic suddenly replaced by fury. He felt hands clamp down on his shoulders like vices as two of the ninjas who had chased them to the roof pushed him back to his knees.

'You four,' Cypher gestured to the remaining ninjas, 'load the body on to the transport.'

He walked over to where the two other ninjas were pinning Otto down on his knees. All that Otto could see as Cypher looked down at him was the reflection of his own furious face, tears running down his cheeks.

'And you, Mr Malpense,' Cypher said quietly, 'I have no use for you.' He looked up at the two assassins who held Otto in place.

'Kill him.'

☺☺☺

Raven ran out on to the roof just in time to see Cypher shoot Wing. She gasped as the tall Asian boy collapsed to the ground, feeling the rage rising inside her as she sprinted silently across the roof towards the helicopter and Cypher. She had no idea why he would suddenly choose to attack them this directly. He could not hope to get away with this without G.L.O.V.E. knowing that he'd gone rogue. This was a direct attack, in the open – he was either insane or had no fear of the consequences that his actions would inevitably have. She wasn't sure which frightened her more.

She moved silently from shadow to shadow, using the cooling vents and air-conditioning plants that were dotted around the roof for cover. She had made her way to within ten metres of Otto when she heard Cypher speak.

'Kill him.'

Raven did not stop to think. As she popped up from behind the vent that was concealing her she let a shuriken fly. It whistled past Cypher's neck, just scratching him, and embedded itself in the metal skin of the helicopter.

The distraction this caused gave Raven the time she needed to close the distance between herself and Otto. The twin katanas slid from their scabbards on her back and she launched a withering assault on the two assassins, forcing them to release their hold on Otto in order to defend themselves.

Cypher, meanwhile, sprinted back towards the helicopter. The ninjas had loaded Wing's body on board and were now climbing on. He leapt up into the fuselage as the sounds of the furious battle between Raven and his two assassins echoed from behind him.

'Get us out of here. We've got what we came for,' he barked at the pilot, who did not need to be told twice. He wrenched at the controls and the helicopter leapt into the air with a roar.

Raven could do nothing to stop the helicopter taking off – it was all she could do to hold her own against the two ninjas left on the roof and keep Otto alive. They had attacked relentlessly since she'd intervened to prevent Otto's execution and despite her unparalleled physical condition she was starting to tire. Her attackers, though, never seemed to slow down, but just kept advancing remorselessly, driving her back.

'Stay back, Otto,' she said, keeping herself between the boy and the assassins.

Raven knew that she had to finish this as quickly as possible. The local authorities would already be on their way and she had to get word back to Nero of what had happened. She took a long, deep breath, trying to find her focus as the assassins advanced towards her again, side by side, their movements perfectly synchronised.

Raven leapt.

She sailed over their heads, her swords swivelling in her hands to point backwards as she flew through the air. She landed, dropped to one knee and, with her eyes closed, thrust the twin blades backwards with every ounce of her remaining strength.

Otto watched in astonishment as the two blades erupted from the black silk that covered the ninjas' chests. Both of the assassins twitched a couple of times before they collapsed to their knees. Raven opened her eyes and pulled the swords forward again, yanking them free of the two bodies, which then slowly fell to the floor and lay still. Raven looked at the blades in surprise. They were spotless – there wasn't a drop of blood on either of them.

'What the –' she said, but was cut short by an insistent beeping noise that had suddenly started to come from the two bodies. She'd heard that sound before. She instantly surveyed their surroundings – no immediate cover and no time to run, anyway.

Otto had no idea what was happening as Raven sprinted towards him and leapt forward, hitting him and pushing them both over the edge of the roof and into thin air, fifty storeys up.

Then the world exploded.

☻☻☻

Cypher looked down as the helicopter climbed into the air. The entire top three storeys of the safe-house building had been consumed by the explosion; there was no way that anyone down there could have survived. He glanced at the body lying on the floor of the helicopter and felt a sense of satisfaction. They had achieved their objective, they had everything they needed, and it was just an additional bonus that Nero's pet assassin was now out of the picture as well. He had recognised the other boy from the report that Nero had given on the recent fiasco that had taken place at H.I.V.E. and, while it was regrettable that the boy had been caught up in events, he had no reason to suppose that the world would mourn the passing of Otto Malpense.

'Destination, sir?' the co-pilot asked as they continued to gain altitude.

'Set course for the Forge. Phase one of the operation is complete – radio ahead and give the order to commence preparation and load-out for phase two,' Cypher replied.

If Nero thought he was having a bad day now, what was going to happen next would doubtless put it all into perspective.

# chapter eight

Otto felt as if a giant hand had picked him up and thrown him off the roof of the building. Raven clung on to him with a grip like iron as they tumbled towards the ground, burning debris from the upper floors cascading past all around them.

Raven knew that she only had one shot. She stretched out one arm and there was the distinctive sound of the high-pressure discharge of a grappler bolt. The line snaked away from them through the air before the bolt hit the side of a building on the other side of the street. She had no idea if the grappler would be able to hold them both falling at this speed, but it was the only chance they had.

The line snapped taut and Raven let out an involuntary cry as her arm took the full weight of both her and Otto, her grip on the boy slipping slightly with the shock. They swung inwards now towards the mirrored-glass frontage of the building opposite the safe house. The reel of the grappler screeched and smoked in protest at the enormous overload that it was enduring. Raven knew that they were travelling too fast – if they hit toughened glass at this speed it would kill them just as surely as if they had hit the ground. Raven braced herself for the inevitable impact as they swung, but at the final second she saw that the enormous explosion on the other side of the street had partially shattered the glass of the windows. She twisted desperately, swivelling her back towards the glass, shielding Otto.

The impact knocked the wind from her completely, but the window smashed into a million pieces as they hit. Raven released the grappler line and she and Otto were thrown across the office in which they had landed, sliding to an undignified halt amongst the scattered office equipment and furniture.

Raven sat up. Her shoulder felt as if it was on fire, and she ached all over from her fight with the ninjas, but she was in one piece. She looked urgently around the room. It was deserted – it was still too early in the morning for any workers to have arrived.

'Malpense!' she shouted. He was nowhere to be seen.

There was a groan from behind her and she turned to see Otto sliding out from underneath a fallen cubicle divider.

'Are you OK?' Raven asked, moving over to him and

checking him for any obvious injuries. He seemed to be unharmed but it was not just his physical state that she was worried about.

'Yeah, I think so,' Otto replied, his ears still ringing from the explosion. He felt as if he was going to be covered in bruises, but he was alive at least. That was more than he could say for his best friend. The memory of the look of horrified surprise on Wing's face as the bullet struck him cut through the fuzz of shock that seemed to fill Otto's head. The sound of screaming and countless sirens drifted through the broken window as bits of burning paper and debris continued to flutter past outside.

'We have to get out of here,' Raven said firmly. 'I know that it's difficult, but we have to keep going a little longer. We have to get to safety and report what just happened.'

Otto nodded. Raven pulled Otto to his feet and held him by both shoulders, looking him straight in the eyes.

'I promise that I'll make Cypher pay for what he's done, but to do that we have to get away from here right now. I need you to focus, Otto.'

Otto didn't feel like he had enough strength to take another step, but he knew that Raven was right. He felt a cold, hard ball forming in the pit of his stomach. He would not stop now, not until he had avenged Wing.

'Let's go,' Otto said. He may not know anything about who Cypher was or why he'd done this, but he did know one thing . . . he was going to pay.

☹ ☹ ☹

'Anything?' Nero asked impatiently as the communications officer worked frantically at the console.

'Still. Nothing, sir. I can't raise the safe house or any of the agents, they've just gone dark.' The technician shook his head as he spoke.

H.I.V.E.'s communications and surveillance department was abuzz with activity. Ever since Laura had presented the decrypted message to Nero, there had been desperate efforts to establish what exactly was going on in Tokyo, but so far they had met with little success.

'Sir,' a voice was raised from the other side of the room, 'I think I have something. I've piggybacked us on to the feed from a Chinese surveillance satellite – the angle's not great and there's a five-minute lag on real-time, but it's the best coverage we're going to get.'

'Putting it on the main screen,' the technician continued as the huge central display that was mounted on the wall flickered into life.

At first there was nothing unusual about the imagery; it appeared to be just a normal feed from a satellite camera that was trained on the G.L.O.V.E. safe-house building, but it quickly became clear that there was something very wrong.

'There,' the Contessa said, pointing at the screen as three tiny figures burst on to the roof from the stairwell and ran towards the far side of the building. 'Freeze and enhance.'

The grainy picture froze as H.I.V.E.mind worked silently to enhance the quality of the image. As the pixellation was reduced, the identities of the three people on the roof became clear.

'That's Malpense, Fanchu and Agent Zero,' the Contessa continued, scanning the pictures for any further clue as to what had happened, 'but who are they?'

The three tiny figures that had run on to the roof were now being pursued by half a dozen people, who were pouring out of the stairwell. Again the team worked to enhance the quality of the images, but there was little that could be made out of these black-clad figures other than the fact that they were clearly pursuing the two boys and the agent. Nero's frown deepened.

'Picking up a lot of chatter on the Tokyo emergency services bands,' another technician reported, staring into the middle distance as he focused on the stream of excited Japanese voices that filled his earphones. 'There's some kind of disturbance in Shinjuku, something to do with an explosion.'

On the main screen Nero watched with a sense of mounting horror as a helicopter popped into view over the side of the building. There was no audio to drown out the gasps that came from around the room as Agent Zero folded to the ground – they all knew an execution when they saw one. Nero was filled with a sense of helplessness; this was the past, there was nothing that he could do about it now but watch, and the role of passive observer did not suit him well.

'Oh no,' the Contessa said as a figure stepped down from the helicopter that had just landed on the roof.

Nero's eyes narrowed, and he felt white hot anger rising inside him. He did not need image enhancement to recognise this man.

'Cypher,' Nero spat. 'I should have known.'

Nero and the Contessa watched, appalled, as the events of just five minutes before played out on the screen in front of them. They watched as Fanchu approached Cypher and Malpense was pinned down by two of the mysterious figures that had pursued them on to the roof.

They saw Cypher raise a pistol; there was a tiny flash and Fanchu crumpled to the ground.

'No!' Nero shouted. Cypher had just executed one of his students in cold blood. It was a declaration of war, plain and simple, and the audacity of an attack like this in broad daylight meant that Cypher wanted everyone to know it.

'Look, there,' the Contessa said suddenly, pointing out another figure that was scurrying to cover behind one of the numerous vents and machine plants that dotted the roof. Nero immediately recognised this new arrival. There was only one person on earth who moved quite like that: Raven.

They watched as Raven launched her attack. Cypher was running back to the helicopter as she attacked the two men restraining Malpense and for the first time Nero felt a sense of hope. A couple of the technicians yelled their approval as they watched Raven neatly dispose of the two assassins, but, as they fell, something strange happened. Raven ran towards Malpense, threw herself at him and knocked them both flying towards the edge of the roof. Then the picture whited out. At first it looked like they'd lost the feed to the satellite, but as the picture faded back in it became immediately apparent that the incredibly sensitive cameras of the orbital spy platform had been overwhelmed by the intensity of the massive explosion that engulfed the entire roof.

The safe house was gone. Cypher's helicopter climbed into the air out of the frame and vanished, leaving nothing but a scene of total devastation. There was no way that anyone could have survived.

Nero suddenly felt very old. In the space of two minutes

he had watched a trusted G.L.O.V.E. operative, two of his best students and Raven all die at the hands of one man. Nero could not begin to guess what might have driven Cypher to carry out an attack like this. Whatever his twisted motivation, it was enough to mean that he did not fear the inevitable reprisals from G.L.O.V.E. that such an act would bring.

'Get me Number One,' Nero said to the communications technician. Cypher was about to learn what it meant to cross Maximilian Nero.

☢ ☢ ☢

Otto clung on to Raven for dear life as she pushed the screaming motorbike to go faster and faster, weaving through the snarled-up traffic of downtown Tokyo. He tried closing his eyes to make the journey less hair-raising, but every time he did the blackness was filled with the startled expression on Wing's face as Cypher's bullet struck him. Otto decided that the cars shooting past only inches away were less disturbing.

Slowly the flow of traffic decreased as they continued their breakneck journey east through the city. Otto had no idea from where Raven had acquired the bike but he suspected that its previous owner had little idea that they had 'borrowed' it. Raven had simply vanished into the crowd when they had left the building in which they'd made their less than graceful landing, having ordered him to stay put. She'd roared up to the kerb on the big silver bike a couple of minutes later, jammed the only crash helmet on his head and told him to hang on. From then till now he doubted that their speed had dropped into double digits more than a couple of times.

They seemed to be heading into the docks. The skyscrapers and shops that had been lining the streets were replaced by towering columns of shipping containers, and enormous cranes looming ominously overhead. Raven shot through a checkpoint that led into a fenced-off area of the port, and a security guard gesticulated wildly at them as they weaved through the automated barrier he controlled. Raven gunned the engine and sent the bike roaring between the rows of neatly stacked containers, turning this way and that, tracing an impossible-to-follow path through the steel maze.

After a minute or two they neared a row of dilapidated-looking warehouse buildings and Raven finally slowed the bike down. She steered towards a loading ramp that led up to a heavy steel shutter. Pulling a small box from a pouch on her belt, she pressed a button. The shutter rolled upwards and Raven gunned the engine again, sending the bike flying up the ramp and into the darkness within. As soon as they were inside, Raven brought the bike to a screeching halt, the back wheel sliding round and leaving a neat semi-circle of molten black rubber on the dusty floor. She pointed the control at the shutter again and it quickly rolled back down into place. Raven cut the engine, the sudden silence filled only with the gentle ticks and creaks of the rapidly cooling engine.

Raven climbed off the bike and Otto pulled off his crash helmet.

'OK, we're safe, for now,' Raven said, pulling her Blackbox from her belt. The device was dead, as it had been since the moment the attack on the safe house had started. 'We need to report back to H.I.V.E. We have to let them know that we're still active,' she continued, walking away towards one of the separately enclosed offices that lined the far wall. The warehouse looked like it had been abandoned for years. A patina of dust covered everything and what few containers lay scattered around the place had not been disturbed for a long time.

'Are you sure we're safe?' Otto said, following Raven towards the offices. 'We were supposed to be safe before, but Cypher seemed to know exactly where to find us. What's to say that he doesn't know about this place?'

'Because, Otto, until precisely thirty seconds ago, there was only one person in the world who knew about this place, and that was me.' Raven had been trained to make sure that she always had a back-up plan and this was just one of several sites around the world that she had set up for just such an eventuality. Not even Nero knew that this place existed.

'I hope you're right,' Otto said quietly. An hour ago he would have believed Raven completely, but it was becoming clear that they were up against an enemy that had resources far beyond what was normal.

Raven punched a series of numbers into a keypad next to one of the office doors and it opened with a deceptively solid clunking noise. Otto followed her into the office and it quickly became clear that, as was so often the case with Raven, there was a lot more to this simple building than met the eye. One end of the room was filled with a well-stocked armoury – guns, knives and other harder to identify pieces of equipment hung from wall mountings. The rest of the room was filled with practice combat dummies, chart tables, computers and several large display screens. If you intended to stage your own private little war, this would be the place from which to run it.

Raven busied herself about the room, switching on computers and checking the building's security grid. After a few seconds she nodded and turned to Otto.

'OK, the perimeter's secure and it doesn't look like anyone followed us. I need to contact Doctor Nero, but let's check you out first.' Raven walked over to Otto and took his chin in one hand. She looked into his eyes and turned his head first one way and then the other.

'No sign of concussion,' she said matter of factly, 'but that cut needs dressing.'

Otto put his hand to his hairline and looked at the blood that came away on his fingertips. He hadn't even realised he was bleeding. Raven steered him into a nearby chair and then fetched a small medical kit from amongst the array of equipment at the other end of the room. She sat down opposite him and tipped a few drops of antiseptic on to a cotton swab.

'You know that there was nothing more you could have done, right?' Raven said as she dabbed carefully at the cut with the cotton swab.

Otto winced slightly as the antiseptic stung his wound.

'It would have been hard for me to have done any less,' Otto replied quietly. 'I just let him execute Wing right in front of me.'

'You couldn't have stopped him, Otto. I couldn't have stopped him in that situation, so don't blame yourself,' Raven continued, pulling a small butterfly suture from its packet and carefully applying it to Otto's forehead. 'There, how does that feel.'

Raven leant back. She was covered in small cuts and burns herself but she seemed far more concerned about Otto.

'Who is he?' Otto asked, looking Raven straight in the eye.

'Who?' she asked carefully as she returned the sutures and antiseptic to the first-aid kit.

'You know who I mean. Cypher, who is he? Why did he do this?' Otto replied quickly.

'I know that you're just going to think I'm being cryptic, Otto, but the honest answer to both of those questions is that I genuinely don't know,' Raven said, sitting back down opposite him. Something in her expression told Otto that she was being straight with him.

'So what do you know about him?' he asked.

'Not very much, I'm afraid,' Raven replied. She looked slightly uncomfortable, as if she was not sure it was something they should be talking about. 'He and Nero loathe each other, I know that much. Some of it's because Cypher keeps lobbying Number One to close down H.I.V.E., but I think there's more to it than that.'

'What do you mean?'

'Well, Doctor Nero is one of the longest-serving members of G.L.O.V.E., he genuinely believes in the League, he thinks that it serves a vital function. The way Doctor Nero sees it is that without G.L.O.V.E., all of its members would still be out there committing acts of villainy but there would be nothing to restrain them. G.L.O.V.E. is not a charitable organisation by any stretch of the imagination, but it does serve to keep the more violent or lunatic excesses of its members in check. Nero believes that without G.L.O.V.E. there would be anarchy . . . or worse. He explained it to me once, he said that villains create doomsday weapons, but G.L.O.V.E. makes sure that they never actually use them. After all, what's the point of taking over the world if the world is nothing but a scorched ball of ash?'

'And Cypher doesn't agree, I take it,' Otto replied. He knew that Raven was only telling him all this to try to distract him from thinking about what had just happened, but Otto needed this information. Know your enemy, that was rule number one.

'Every scheme that Cypher has come up with since he joined G.L.O.V.E. has had one thing in common . . . people die, sometimes a lot of people. Cypher doesn't care about style or subtlety, he's a smash-and-grab artist.'

'Everything that Nero isn't,' Otto observed.

'Exactly. But what's worse is that he's also been so spectacularly successful. Nero may disapprove of his methods but as long as he kept boosting G.L.O.V.E.'s coffers the way he did his actions were tolerated.'

'Until today,' Otto said quietly, looking down at the floor.

'Until today. Whatever he may have done in the past, he has never acted openly against another G.L.O.V.E. operation. There's no way that Number One will put up with his actions – he's a dead man walking.' The cold edge in Raven's voice was unmistakeable. It was fair to assume that she intended to make sure of that herself.

'And nobody knows who he really is?' Otto said.

'No. Some G.L.O.V.E. operatives do maintain secret identities, but that's usually just to keep them under the authorities' radar. Cypher's different, though. Nero suspects that not even Number One knows who he is. We've spent a great deal of time trying to find out more about him but it seems that every trail leads to another dead end. Believe me, I've been the one following those trails often enough to know how frustratingly elusive he can be.'

'So why throw all of that away?' Otto said, looking puzzled.

'I have no idea,' Raven said, standing up and moving to one of the computers in the middle of the room. 'He must know that an attack like this will incur the wrath of Number One, so whatever he's up to has to be worth taking that risk.'

Otto had learnt enough about G.L.O.V.E. and its mysterious leader to know that retaliation for an attack like this would probably be swift and brutal.

'It doesn't make any sense,' Otto said, frustrated. 'What could he hope to achieve with this? Does he really hate Nero and H.I.V.E. so much that he'd throw everything away just to assassinate you and a couple of students? Why did he take Wing's body? What possible reason could he have for any of this?'

'I don't know, Otto, but don't worry, I intend to find out. If nothing else, what happened today proves one thing,' Raven said as she keyed a string of commands into the computer.

'What's that?' Otto said, also standing and moving across the room towards where Raven was working.

'I shouldn't really be telling you this, but a couple of weeks ago somebody made an attempt on Doctor Nero's life. Suffice to say that it failed, but the assassins that were used self-destructed in a similar, if less spectacular, way to our friends on the roof. I had suspected that Cypher was involved, but this proves it.'

'So this is all part of something bigger,' Otto said thoughtfully.

'It has to be,' Raven replied. 'No offence, Otto, but Cypher would not take this kind of risk without there being a bigger pay-off than getting rid of a couple of H.I.V.E. students. The school itself has a higher annual attrition rate than that . . .'

Something gave a tiny tug inside Otto's head. There was something about this whole situation that didn't make sense and he couldn't quite put his finger on it, whatever it was. Otto knew that the best thing to do was ignore it. Whatever it was it would come to him in time, it always did, and there was little point trying to hurry the process.

Raven turned from her terminal and turned to face Otto. 'I need to call Nero and let him know that we made it out and who was responsible,' she said as she got up and walked across the room to a communications terminal. She keyed in a number of commands and the machine began working, not just connecting her to H.I.V.E. but doing it in such a way that it would be next to impossible to calculate their location by backtracing the transmission. She watched as the carrier signal bounced from country to country, creating a spider's web of digital evidence that could not be disentangled. Finally the word 'Connecting' appeared and after a couple of seconds was replaced with Nero's face. He looked tired and angry, but as he saw who was on the other end of the line the tension and fatigue seemed to melt from his expression.

'Natalya,' he said with a smile, 'not for the first time, rumours of your demise appear to have been unfounded.'

'It'll take a better man than Cypher to put me in the ground,' Raven replied. The slight smile on her face was at odds with the ice in her tone.

'Yes, we saw what happened. Did anyone else make it out?' Nero asked.

'Malpense is here with me. He's OK, some cuts and bruises but otherwise in one piece.'

'Fanchu?' Nero asked. He'd seen what had happened on the roof but he had to be sure.

'Dead, Max, as are Agents One and Zero. Cypher executed the boy without hesitation, there was nothing I could do. The agents both gave their lives trying to protect the students, but they took us completely by surprise. We never stood a chance.'

'I have no doubt that you did everything you could, Natalya,' Nero replied, looking suddenly angry again. 'I want Cypher found and stopped, by whatever means necessary.'

'Understood,' Raven replied. 'Am I acting under executive mandate?'

'I will be speaking to Number One very shortly,' Nero said. 'I expect him to grant us full executive privilege under the circumstances, but as soon as I have final clearance I will contact you. I also want Malpense returned to H.I.V.E. immediately.' Nero did not relish the prospect of explaining to Number One that Otto had once again had a brush with death. The sooner the boy was safely returned to the school the better.

'Then we'll need transport,' Raven replied. 'The Shroud was in the hangar when the safe house went up. We're going to need a replacement.'

'Of course, I shall dispatch one immediately,' Nero replied. 'Do you have a target location yet?'

'Not yet, but I'm working on it,' Raven said, glancing at the monitors nearby. 'As soon as I have a location for pick-up I'll let you know.'

'Very well, keep me posted,' Nero instructed, 'and, Natalya . . .'

'Yes,' Raven responded.

'Finish this,' Nero said coldly.

⊙ ⊙ ⊙

Laura sat next to Shelby's bed in the infirmary. Her friend was still unconscious from the Sleeper pulse that Colonel Francisco had hit her with but the doctors had assured her that her friend would be OK and that it was only a matter of time until she woke up. Laura thought about the news that she was going to have to give Shelby and she fought to control the urge to start crying again. Wing was gone, snatched away in a split second by the brutal actions of a madman, and she was going to have to break the news to Shelby. Laura bit her lower lip; she was surprised there were any tears left but as she thought of Wing's smile, a rare and wonderful thing that she would never see again, she was overwhelmed by grief, and fresh, hot tears rolled down her cheeks.

'Hey, Brand.' Shelby's voice was croaky and tired. 'I never knew you cared.'

Laura looked up in surprise and saw Shelby looking at

her with mild amusement.

'How are you feeling?' Laura replied, wiping the tears from her eyes and giving a weak smile.

'I'm fine, but what's up with you?' Shelby replied, sensing that there was more to Laura's mood than was immediately obvious.

'Something terrible has happened,' Laura replied, her voice cracking slightly, 'the message, we were too late . . . it's Wing . . . he's dead.'

The smile vanished instantly from Shelby's face, replaced by a look of horror.

Laura told Shelby everything – the attack on the safe house, the arrival of Cypher and finally Wing's execution on the roof. She talked quickly and quietly, afraid that if she slowed or paused that she would again succumb to the empty swirling grief in the pit of her stomach. When she had finished she looked up at Shelby and saw the same hollow disbelief in her friend's eyes that had been in her own when Nero had told the same story to her earlier. Shelby's mouth moved, as if trying to find words, but none would come and she began to cry.

Laura pulled Shelby towards her and hugged her, her friend's heaving sobs as painful as her own.

# chapter nine

'Wake up,' the Contessa whispered into Colonel Francisco's ear. His eyes slowly flickered open, and he looked confused for a moment before giving a bestial cry of rage. Trying to sit up, he thrashed against the thick restraints that held him firmly to the infirmary bed on which he lay.

Nero stood looking down at him, his expression enough to freeze the blood of even a hardened soldier like Francisco.

'Colonel, I am going to give you one chance and one chance only to tell me why you have done this, and then I'm going to let the Contessa dig it out of your head. I understand that she can do that without causing *too much* brain damage. The choice is yours.'

Francisco's expression hardened.

'You don't scare me, Max, and neither does she.'

'Then you're either insane, or stupid. Possibly both,'

Nero replied. 'Your actions have already cost the lives of two G.L.O.V.E. agents and one of our own students. I will not hesitate to add your name to that list, but not before you've told me everything you know.'

'Do your worst,' Francisco spat back.

Nero said nothing, simply nodded to the Contessa and left the room.

'Now, Colonel, let's have a nice little chat,' the Contessa said, leaning over his prostrate form. The smile on her face was the most terrifying thing he had ever seen.

☣ ☣ ☣

Nero let out a long, slow breath as he settled into his chair. His desk was still covered with the paperwork that he had left there the previous evening. It seemed like a thousand years ago now. He blamed himself, of course – he should have realised that he was sending his students into a trap, but he'd been too busy worrying about their safe return to the island to consider the possibility that they had been deliberately drawn out from under the umbrella of security that normally protected them.

'Damn him!' Nero shouted, smashing his fist down on the desk. He had always known that Cypher was a loose cannon, but not for a moment had he ever thought that he would take direct action like this against Nero and his school.

There was a sudden beeping from the console on the desk and Nero thumbed the intercom switch.

'Yes,' he snapped.

'Sir, I have Number One on a secure channel for you,' the communications technician on the other end of the line reported.

'Very well, put him through,' Nero replied. As the video screen on the opposite side of the room flickered into life he fought to push back the burning fury he felt. He could not afford to let Number One see any lack of composure on his part, even under these circumstances.

The G.L.O.V.E. logo on the screen dissolved, to be replaced by the familiar silhouetted form of Number One. Even after all these years Nero still had no idea what the man looked like, which was probably a good thing, given the rumours he had heard of the fate that had befallen those who had been unlucky enough to catch a glimpse of his face.

'Good morning, Maximilian,' Number One said calmly. 'I have read your report on this situation and reviewed the footage that was captured by the surveillance satellite, and suffice to say that I am deeply, *deeply* disturbed by what I have seen.'

'Yes, sir,' Nero replied. 'This was a hostile act by a rogue agent against G.L.O.V.E. operatives, it cannot be allowed to stand.'

'That is for me to decide,' Number One replied. 'I assume that under the circumstances you are requesting executive privilege for any action that you choose to take.'

'I am,' Nero replied. 'In this situation I don't see what other choice we have.'

'There are always choices, Maximilian,' Number One said, 'but given what has happened I am forced to agree this time. You have an executive mandate, but I want one thing.'

'Of course, what do you need?'

'I want Cypher alive.'

Nero tensed. He had not expected this – usually when Number One granted an executive mandate to his subordinates it only meant one thing. To request that Cypher be taken alive was unprecedented, not to mention much more difficult.

'May I ask why?' Nero said cautiously.

'No, you may not. I understand that Raven survived the attack; I am sure that she will be more than capable of performing this task.'

'But –' Nero began.

'Do not argue with me, Max . . . ever. It is not a request.'

'Yes, sir,' Nero replied. He knew better than to push his luck with Number One.

'And see to it that Malpense is returned to the school

immediately; be grateful that no lasting harm was caused to him. If I thought for one moment that you had any inkling of the danger into which you were sending him Cypher would not be the only one with an executive mandate declared on him. Do I make myself clear?'

'Perfectly,' Nero replied, his curiosity once again piqued by Number One's uncharacteristic protectiveness where Otto Malpense was concerned. 'He will be returning to the school very shortly.'

'Good, I shall leave this in your hands, then. Do not worry – an example will be made of Cypher, a very permanent and obvious example.'

⊛⊛⊛

Otto woke with a start. He had a couple of seconds of disorientation as he struggled to remember where he was, but then the memories of the past few hours flooded back, though he desperately wished that they wouldn't. He sat on the edge of the camp bed that Raven had set up in the corner of her hidden safe house. She had assured him that there would be nothing that they could do for the next few hours and that he might as well try to get some rest. He hadn't believed for a moment that he would actually be able to sleep, but the events of earlier that day had left him more drained than he had realised.

Raven was sitting exactly where she had been when

Otto had dropped off several hours earlier, scanning the monitors in front of her. She wouldn't tell him what it was that she was looking for but he had little doubt that it had something to do with tracking down Cypher. She glanced over her shoulder as Otto walked towards her.

'Do you feel better?' she asked as Otto came to stand alongside her.

'Less tired. I'm not sure that better is the right word,' Otto replied, rubbing his eyes with one hand.

'Well, I have some good news,' Raven said with a slight smile.

'That would make a nice change,' Otto replied, peering at the displays in front of Raven. They were showing an array of maps and charts with the odd window displaying what looked like live satellite surveillance feeds.

'Here.' Raven tapped one of the screens, where a chart was displaying a stretch of coastline with a flashing red crosshair superimposed upon it.

'What's that?' Otto asked, leaning in to look more closely.

'That is the helicopter that Cypher used in the attack this morning,' she replied matter of factly. 'I've been waiting for the tracking device to go live, but it's designed to not start transmitting until it's stationary for a certain length of time. It appears that this was the final destination.'

'Tracking device?' Otto said with a note of disbelief in his voice. 'We never got anywhere near that chopper. How did you get a tracking device on board?'

'The shuriken that I threw at Cypher contained a tracking device. A tracking device that is currently well and truly embedded in the skin of his helicopter.'

'Oh,' Otto said, thinking back to those desperate moments on the roof, 'I thought you were aiming for Cypher and missed . . .'

Raven looked at him with an expression of mild annoyance.

'Mr Malpense, I don't miss.'

She turned back to the screen and began to type a long string of commands into an open terminal window.

'I'm just setting up a surveillance satellite that the Americans were kind enough to lend me to scan the area. The coordinates I'm getting are in the middle of the jungle – I need a clearer picture.'

Otto wandered over to one of the storage cabinets that lined the room as Raven continued working on getting the hijacked satellite into the correct position. The door was open slightly and inside Otto could see racks of weapons and equipment. There was enough gear stowed away there to fight a small war and, judging by the expression on Raven's face as she glared at the terminal, that was exactly what she had in mind.

‘Well?’ Nero said impatiently as the Contessa settled into the seat on the other side of his desk.

‘He’s strong, but you knew that – not just physically, but mentally too. He’s clearly received extensive counter-interrogation training.’

Nero could see that the Contessa was tired. Her face was pale and she looked older than usual. Clearly the interrogation of Francisco had drained whatever physical or mental reserves she drew on when using her strange persuasive powers.

‘So what did you find out?’ Nero asked, leaning forward in his chair.

‘Not a great deal, unfortunately,’ the Contessa replied with a sigh. ‘He does not know the identity of whoever hired him to do this. He was contacted anonymously and offered a great deal of money to provide his mysterious benefactor with details of H.I.V.E. operations. He never had any direct contact with whoever it was that turned him.’

‘You’re sure?’ Nero said quietly.

‘As sure as I can be without putting him into a coma,’ the Contessa replied, rubbing her temples. ‘Obviously it’s fortunate that we caught him, but I don’t think that he will be able to provide us with much useful information.’

‘Well, I think that it’s safe to assume that we know who

bought him,' Nero said. 'Cypher appears to have been planning this for some time.'

'Indeed, Francisco appears to have been working for Cypher for several weeks, perhaps months. I took the liberty of asking Professor Pike to urgently review all of the security systems to which the Colonel had access.'

'Good,' Nero replied. 'There's something about this that isn't right.'

'There has been very little right about the events of the past few hours,' the Contessa replied.

'Yes, I know, but Francisco never struck me as the type that could just be bought.'

'Everyone has their price, Max.'

'Believe me, I understand that, but Francisco always placed such importance on personal honour. It was his military background, I think. I find it hard to believe that he would betray us so completely for a few zeroes added to the balance of a Swiss bank account. It's not like him.'

'His actions may be out of character, but there's no doubt he's guilty,' the Contessa said firmly. 'There are very few people in the world who can lie when I tell them to be truthful.'

'I know. I suppose I've just been thrown off-balance by this.' Nero was used to dealing with the day-to-day crises that H.I.V.E. generated, whether it be the students or the attempts of law-enforcement agencies to discover the location of the base, but the events of the past twenty-four hours were unprecedented.

'Security are still trying to find students Block and Tackle,' the Contessa continued.

'H.I.V.E.mind has been unable to locate them?' Nero asked, a note of frustration in his voice now.

'No, they appear to have vanished. There are plenty of places to hide on the island and even our surveillance system doesn't cover them all. Francisco will doubtless have furnished them with detailed schematics.'

'I still can't believe that he would stoop so low as to use his own students to assist him with this,' Nero said angrily.

'Yes, I know, but those two are easily led. I suspect that Francisco would have to do little more than tell them what he wanted them to do and they would just obey without question. The Henchman stream is not noted for generating independent thinkers, Max. Don't worry, though. They're not getting off the island, we'll find them eventually.'

'I want them found quickly,' Nero said, 'before they can cause any more trouble.'

'Understood,' the Contessa said, standing to leave. 'What do you want us to do with Francisco?'

'Transfer him to the detention centre for now. I haven't decided what to do with the Colonel yet.'

'Very well, I will arrange the transfer.' The Contessa

nodded and headed for the door.

'And, Contessa,' Nero said as she reached for the door handle.

'Yes?'

'Make sure that his stay is as uncomfortable as possible.'

☢ ☢ ☢

'Well, that's not good,' Raven said with a sigh as she scanned the imagery that was flashing up on the monitor.

'What's wrong?' Otto asked, noting Raven's look of frustration.

'See for yourself,' Raven said, stepping away from the monitor.

Otto walked over and studied the images on display. At the centre of each of the pictures was what looked to Otto like an enormous black hole in the middle of the jungle. It had to be at least a couple of hundred metres in diameter. Otto noted the thundering cascade of water that poured over one side of the enormous hole and realised that it must have taken millions of years for the slow abrasive effect of the thundering torrent to carve an enormous rift in the jungle like that. He knew that such boreholes could end up being hundreds of metres deep and it was impossible to make out if there was anything hidden in the blackness at the bottom of it.

'He's down there?' Otto asked.

'It would appear so,' Raven replied. 'As you can see, or rather as you can't see, it's going to be impossible to tell what's waiting down there. I don't like to go in blind.'

Otto understood Raven's concern. Cypher could have an army waiting for her and there would be no way to tell. Tactically speaking, it was an unpleasant prospect.

'That's not all, though. Switch to the EM detection array,' Raven said, rubbing her eyes.

Otto quickly switched between the hijacked satellite's visual sensors and its onboard electromagnetic scanners. Immediately the jungle surrounding the hole lit up like a Christmas tree – the dense forest was filled with active electronics devices for several miles in every direction. It was impossible to tell from this range what these elec-tronic devices were, but it was safe to assume that they weren't designed to monitor the local flora and fauna.

'Hmmm,' Otto said, his brain already starting to analyse the problem.

'My sentiments exactly,' Raven replied with a smile. 'There's no way that even I'm getting within half a mile of that place overland without being detected. Cypher clearly isn't keen on uninvited guests.'

'So don't go overland,' Otto replied with a grin.

'Meaning?' Raven asked, raising an eyebrow.

Otto switched to the satellite's terrain radar and performed a series of quick scans. The results flashed up on the screen.

'Three hundred metres,' Otto said, smiling as he scanned the screen.

Raven stepped closer to the workstation, looking at the figures that Otto had just pulled up.

'OK,' Raven said as she looked at the numbers, 'it's a deep hole, so what?'

'HALO,' Otto said quietly as the numbers all lined up neatly in his head.

Raven looked at him with surprise and then a broad grin spread across her face too.

'Malpense, you're a genius.'

☢☢☢

As Nero walked down the stairs to the crater launch bay he was pleased to see that preparations for launching the second Shroud were already well underway. Raven had contacted him just half an hour earlier to inform him that she had apparently discovered Cypher's current location and that she needed transport to the location as quickly as possible. He had immediately given the order for the only remaining Shroud prototype to be prepped for emergency take-off and, by the looks of the frantic last-minute checks that the ground crew were performing, they were very nearly ready.

The Contessa was talking to the pilot as Nero walked

out on to the landing pad; seeing Nero, she nodded to the pilot and he hurried over to the waiting aircraft.

'I have briefed the pilot,' she said as she walked towards Nero. 'He's got the pick-up location and they should be underway within the next couple of minutes.'

'Good,' Nero replied, watching as the refuelling rig's fat hose was detached from the smooth black belly of the Shroud. 'He knows that he's to bring Malpense straight back here after Raven is dropped at the target?'

'Yes, he's quite aware of the importance of his cargo,' the Contessa replied. 'Malpense should be back within a few hours. Are you still sure that it wouldn't be wiser to send in a more . . . *substantial* force?'

Nero gave a small, cold smile.

'I am quite sure that Natalya is up to the task, Contessa. She has never let us down before, as you well know.'

'Oh, I'm quite aware of Raven's capabilities, Max,' the Contessa replied, 'but we really don't have any idea of the true scale of the threat that Cypher poses. I just hope that we're not underestimating him.'

Nero knew that the Contessa had a point, but if he was to order a full-scale military strike on Cypher's facility it would mean involving G.L.O.V.E. in the operation in a much larger way. Nero had the feeling that for the moment it would be better to keep this operation on a smaller scale. Not only was it easier to manage, but he knew that he didn't have to worry about where Raven's true loyalties lay. The business with Francisco had bothered him more than he had let on and he was in no hurry to escalate the situation still further out of control. Specifically, out of his control.

'I understand your concerns, Contessa, but for now we will pursue a more subtle approach. If Raven discovers that the situation is more than she can handle alone we will consider alternative options.'

The Contessa nodded as a harried-looking technician trotted up to the two of them.

'The Shroud's fully prepped for launch, Doctor Nero, and the pilot's reporting ready. Is there anything else?'

'Has all of the equipment that Raven requested been loaded on board?'

'Yes, sir, it's all there. Back-ups too. We're good to go.'

'Very well, give the order to launch.'

The technician nodded and turned to the flight-deck controller, giving him the thumbs-up.

The drone of the Shroud's idling engines suddenly grew to a roar and she lifted vertically upwards, climbing out of the crater before disappearing into the twilight gloom overhead.

☺☺☺

Laura and Shelby sat in the atrium of their accommodation block in silence. Neither of them had spoken much in the past couple of hours, both lost in their own thoughts, their own grief. Nothing could have prepared them for what had happened to Wing. Laura couldn't help but wonder whether Wing might still be alive if she'd been able to decrypt the coded message's contents sooner, if she'd been able to give more warning of the attack. She wondered if that was what the other students were thinking too. The H.I.V.E. rumour mill had clearly done its usual efficient job of diffusing the news about the events in Tokyo around the school, judging by the whispered conversations and sidelong glances from the other students in the atrium. Laura supposed that if she blamed herself then there was no reason why everyone else shouldn't too.

'Hello,' Nigel said quietly, snapping Laura out of her brooding, 'mind if we sit down?'

Laura didn't say anything, just gestured to the empty seats opposite. Franz and Nigel both looked as if they were feeling much the same as the two girls, though their sadness was clearly mixed with concern. Shelby barely acknowledged their presence, simply sat staring at the floor as she had done for the last half hour.

'We were both very sorry to hear what had happened,' Franz said, breaking the uncomfortable silence. 'We will be missing Wing very much.'

'If there's anything that either of us can do, just . . . well, you know . . .' Nigel said quietly.

'Thanks, I . . .' Laura began, but trailed off. She didn't really know what to say.

'I remember when my dad died that my mum told me that I shouldn't be sad, that our bodies are just like prisons for our spirits and his was free now to go to a better place,' Nigel said sadly.

'Free?' Shelby snapped back suddenly, startling Nigel. 'He's not free, he's not gone to a better place, he's just gone.'

'Shel, please, there's no point . . .' Laura said quickly.

'Too damn right there's no point,' Shelby said angrily, standing up and gesturing at the hall around her. 'There's no point to any of this. This place isn't a school, it's a prison, and I don't want to be locked up here any more while my friends die around me.'

Her outburst had drawn the attention of everyone in the atrium. Heads turned to watch as she stormed across the hall to the lifts that would carry her up to her room. Nigel went to follow her but Laura put a hand on his shoulder and gently pushed him back down into his seat.

'Leave her,' Laura said with a sigh. 'She's just angry. We all are.'

As the uncomfortable silence returned Laura found herself wondering what was more worrying – Shelby's outburst and the bitterness her friend seemed to be feeling, or the fact that she felt exactly the same way.

# chapter ten

'Over my cold, dead body,' Raven said firmly, her arms folded.

She and Otto stood in the middle of an abandoned area of the docks, the distant gleaming skyline of Tokyo jarringly at odds with the battered and rusting shipping containers that littered the area around them.

'So that's a no,' Otto said with a smile.

'Absolutely,' Raven continued. 'Nero would have me shot for even contemplating taking a student into a tactical situation like that. Especially you, Malpense.'

'What's that supposed to mean?' Otto asked with a frown.

Raven hesitated for a moment. Otto might be the subject of extra precautions, given Number One's close personal interest in his well-being, but Nero had also made it perfectly clear that Otto was never to know that was the case. It was not difficult to see how a student like

Otto might exploit that situation.

'Nothing,' Raven replied. 'It's just too dangerous, you're not coming with me. The transport will drop me off and then take you back to H.I.V.E. and that's the end of this discussion.'

Otto could tell from the expression on Raven's face that debating the matter further would be pointless. It looked as if he was just going to have to trust Raven to get the job done. If it had been anyone else in the world, except possibly Nero, he would have just ignored them and found a way to get to Cypher whether they liked it or not, but he knew there was no way she'd just let him slip through her fingers.

Suddenly a strong gust of wind seemed to come from nowhere and Otto felt a vibration as if something heavy had hit the ground nearby. There was a brief flicker and the view of the distant skyline was suddenly obscured by the stark, black outline of the Shroud that had just landed twenty metres away in almost complete silence.

'Right on schedule,' Raven said, glancing at her watch. 'Let's go.'

She jogged towards the waiting transport with Otto in tow. As they approached the aircraft the rear-access ramp lowered and the pilot stepped out, gesturing urgently for them to get on board. Otto and Raven walked up the ramp and into the belly of the Shroud as the pilot climbed the ladder back up on to the flight deck.

Within moments they were airborne again. Raven set to work going through the contents of several crates that were stowed at the far end of the passenger compartment. She spent several minutes systematically checking all of the equipment that she retrieved from inside the crates before finally giving a satisfied nod and sitting down in one of the seats opposite Otto.

'There's a fresh uniform in there for you,' she said, gesturing towards the crates. 'That suit has seen better days.'

Otto had almost forgotten that he was still wearing the suit that he'd put on that morning. It seemed a very long time ago now. The rips, scorch marks and stains that covered it were a powerful reminder of just how much he'd been through in the past few hours. Unbidden, the memory of his conversation with Wing about their new outfits sprang into his head. The realisation that it had been one of the last conversations he had had with his friend struck him harder than he expected. Otto supposed that there would be many such moments in the days to come.

Raven spent a few minutes scanning her Blackbox, tapping at the screen with the stylus, an occasional frown furrowing her brow.

'Anything I can help with?' Otto asked. They'd only

been in the air a few minutes and he was already starting to get bored. The biggest drawback to having a brain like his was its intolerance of inactivity – he needed something to do.

'You can go over these numbers if you want,' Raven said, tossing the Blackbox to Otto. 'I need to go and talk to the pilot.'

Raven got up out of her seat and climbed up the ladder to the flight deck as Otto looked over the data on the display. The numbers were lists of timings and velocities, all of which had to be precisely right for Raven's insertion into Cypher's base to be successful. It was all just simple physics, really, and Otto couldn't see any flaws in the calculations. If all the equipment worked as designed there was no reason that she should not be able to get inside completely undetected.

There was little more that Otto could do with the Blackbox. Raven had been sensible enough to lock off its other functions before she had given it to him. He knew he could get round the lock-out with time and the right equipment, but at the moment he had neither so he deactivated the Blackbox and walked over to the crates of equipment at the other end of the compartment.

He quickly found the clean H.I.V.E. uniform that Raven had mentioned and took the opportunity while she was up on the flight deck to take off the battered suit and put it on. It was a strange relief to be back in the black H.I.V.E. jumpsuit; he was surprised at just how right it felt to be wearing it again. He told himself that it was just the comfort of something familiar in the midst of so much chaos, but a tiny voice at the back of his head asked if he wasn't just getting used to being a student of H.I.V.E., whether he liked it or not. It was a disturbing thought. He had been telling himself that he had been tolerating life at H.I.V.E. because of his friendship with Wing, but now that his friend was gone he could no longer use that excuse. He knew in his heart of hearts that H.I.V.E. was probably the perfect place for him, for better or for worse. Life at the school, though, would be very different without Wing, and he had to make up his mind if it was a life he truly wanted.

☢ ☢ ☢

The Shroud had been airborne for a couple of hours when Otto felt the passenger compartment tip as the aircraft started to climb. He knew that meant that they must be approaching the drop target and that the pilot would be carefully ascending to the designated altitude. Raven stepped through the small door at the other end of the compartment, having put on her suit for the jump. What Otto had suggested back in the old warehouse was actually really quite simple. The only way to get past the

179

masses of anti-intrusion devices surrounding the entrance to the cave concealing Cypher's secret base was for Raven to be travelling so fast when she passed through their detection grid that the system would assume that it was a false reading and ignore her. That's when the idea of a HALO jump had occurred to Otto. High Altitude Low Opening was a skydiving technique that had been perfected by special forces around the world. An operative would be dropped from a plane at high altitude and would then freefall for the maximum safe distance, only opening their chute at the last possible moment. There was one small difference, though, in the jump that Otto was proposing that Raven made. This would be the first time that anyone had opened their chute *below* the ground. Otto knew that generally this was viewed as a bit of a mistake when skydiving, but it was the only way that Raven could hope to avoid detection. She had to freefall into the enormous borehole in the middle of the darkened jungle and only open her chute once she was inside the cave. Raven was probably the only person in the world who would have even considered trying something as patently insane as that, but she actually seemed to be looking forward to it.

'We'll be at the drop target in a few minutes,' she said, fastening the final clips on her parachute. 'I take it that I can trust you to behave yourself for the remainder of the flight to H.I.V.E.?'

'Hey, it's me,' Otto replied with a grin.

'Which is why the pilot has a Sleeper and explicit instructions to use it without hesitation if necessary,' Raven replied with a slight smile. Otto doubted that she was joking.

'Anyone would think that you don't trust me,' Otto said, raising an eyebrow.

'And they'd be absolutely right,' Raven replied, checking the screen on the tiny computer that was attached to her rig. The system was pre-programmed to open the chute at exactly the right altitude. All that Raven had to do was drop into a black hole just a couple of hundred metres wide in the middle of the jungle at night. Otto decided that it was probably best not to think too much about the specifics. The real fun would start when Raven reached the bottom of the cave. They still had no idea what was waiting for her down there, but Otto suspected that it wasn't going to be a welcoming committee.

Otto turned as he heard a noise behind them. The pilot was climbing down the ladder from the flight deck.

'Raven,' the pilot said, 'I have an urgent message –'

Raven turned and looked at the pilot, curious.

'From Cypher,' the pilot continued, raising the Sleeper that he was holding.

Raven sprang without hesitation, years of training and experience making thought and action as one. If she had not acted so quickly the Sleeper pulse that the pilot fired would have hit her full on rather than just glancing off one shoulder, but it still felt like she'd been hit by a charging elephant. She collapsed to the deck on her hands and knees, fighting to stay conscious. The pilot stepped down off the ladder and on to the deck, pointing the Sleeper straight at her.

Otto knew that there was no way he could get to the pilot in time to stop him firing. He was too far away and, unlike Raven, he would not have been able to take him down unarmed even if he could get to him. He glanced to his side and realised that there was only one thing he could do.

'Hey!' Otto shouted, distracting the pilot for a second. 'Why don't you take this outside?'

The pilot's fleeting look of confusion turned instantly to horror as Otto leapt for the large red button mounted on the wall of the passsenger compartment. He slapped his hand down on it hard and snatched at the cargo netting that hung alongside, holding on for dear life as the rear cargo ramp began to descend. At that point physics took over and the difference between the air pressure inside the compartment and the thin atmosphere that was screaming past outside did the rest. The pilot was plucked off his feet, tumbling past Otto, desperately trying to reach for anything that he could hang on to, but he was too slow, and was sucked out of the widening gap as the cargo ramp descended. His final scream was lost in the roaring sound of the air rushing out after him.

Raven, still stunned from the Sleeper pulse, slid past Otto and he grabbed at her chute harness. He felt as if he was going to be torn in two as he desperately tried to hang on to the cargo net and maintain his fragile grip on her.

'Grab on to me,' Otto yelled as loudly as he could, his voice sounding pitifully tiny in the deafening chaos. Raven looked at him with confusion for a moment before her survival instincts cut through the after-effects of the Sleeper pulse and she latched on to his ankle with a grip like steel. Now that his arm was free again Otto flailed at the switch next to the one that he had just hit, the control that would raise the cargo ramp again, but it was just out of reach. He made one last desperate effort, stretching for all he was worth until his fingertips brushed the edge of the button. The motor controlling the loading ramp screeched in protest as it fought to close the ramp against the force of the air pressure differential, but gradually, inch by excruciating inch, the ramp rose. Finally, after what seemed like an eternity, it sealed shut and the Shroud's systems quickly restored air pressure within the compartment.

The compartment was suddenly eerily quiet again, the

only sound Otto and Raven's laboured breathing as their lungs fought to extract the oxygen from the air. After a few moments Raven tried to get to her feet but abandoned the effort when it became obvious that the after-effects of the near miss from the Sleeper were still scrambling some of the messages going from her brain to her legs. She collapsed into one of the nearby seats with a groan, rubbing her temples.

'Are you OK?' Otto said, genuinely concerned. They were coming up on the drop target and they were only going to get one shot at this.

'I think so,' Raven replied weakly. 'Just a bit disorientated.'

'We've got to get to the flight deck,' Otto said quickly. The fact that the Shroud was not diving towards the ground far below meant that the autopilot was active but he still had to find out how long they had till the drop point.

'You go,' Raven replied. 'I'm going to need a minute before I'm climbing any ladders.'

Otto nodded and walked to the ladder.

'The autopilot display is on the central console,' Raven said. 'We just need the ETA at the drop waypoint.'

'No problem,' Otto said, quickly climbing the ladder. The flight deck was crowded with displays and controls but he knew what he was looking for. On the central display was a screen displaying a map and columns of numbers, which Otto guessed had to be waypoint coordinates. He quickly scanned the display.

'Three minutes until the drop point,' he shouted down the hatch to the lower compartment.

'OK,' Raven replied, 'we can still do this. The autopilot will take you back to H.I.V.E. after I've made the drop.' She knew that the systems on board were sophisticated enough to return to the island and H.I.V.E.mind would then ensure that the Shroud would make a safe landing. She'd just need a few seconds to check the flight plan and lock out the controls so Otto would not be able to interfere with them. He may have just saved her life but there was no way that she was going to leave someone like Otto Malpense unsupervised with an unlocked autopilot system. Knowing him he'd probably already worked out how to fly the thing. She knew that it was risky and that Nero wouldn't approve but they couldn't afford to delay this operation for the time it would take her to fly him back to H.I.V.E. herself.

Otto was distracted by a flashing display on another console of flight controls.

'Erm . . . I don't think that's going to be an option,' he said, staring at the display.

'What do you mean?' Raven asked urgently, getting slowly and unsteadily to her feet and walking towards the ladder.

'We have a bigger problem,' Otto replied, still staring at the words on the flashing display.

*Self destruct system initialised . . .*

*.*

*.*

*2.56*

*.*

*.*

*2.55*

*.*

*.*

*2.54*

⊛⊛⊛

'I hope that you learn as quickly as I've been told,' Raven said as she snapped the final clips in place on Otto's chute harness.

Otto didn't reply; he was too busy staring at Raven's Blackbox as screen after screen of text and diagrams flicked past. Learning wasn't really the word for what he was doing; absorbing would probably be a better way of putting it. He was fairly certain that this was not the way that anyone was supposed to train for their first HALO jump, but they didn't have any other option.

Raven checked the display on the jump control unit,

confirmed that it was functioning correctly, then glanced at her watch.

'One minute,' she said matter of factly and pulled two helmets out of the equipment crates. She silently offered a prayer of thanks that whoever had loaded the Shroud had followed standard operating procedure and packed back-ups of everything they needed; normally it was in case of equipment failure but in this case it might just save their lives.

Otto didn't say anything. He just increased the speed at which the pages of the HALO training manual were flicking past on the Blackbox's display. He was nearly through it and he just had to hope that he now knew enough to survive the next few minutes.

'OK, done,' Otto said after a couple more seconds, tossing the Blackbox on to one of the seats and taking a deep breath.

'If by some miracle you get down there in one piece, stay put. I'll find you,' Raven said tersely. She jammed the helmet on to Otto's head, plugged in the cable from the jump control unit and snapped the visor shut. The helmet absorbed any sound from the Shroud, and all he could hear was the gentle hiss of the oxygen that the jump rig was feeding to his helmet. Otto watched as the helmet's head-up display flickered into life, displaying streams of coordinates and velocities. He might have known how the system worked now on an intellectual level but he also knew that there was a world of difference between having memorised the entire training manual and actual practical experience.

Raven put on her own helmet and slapped the switch on the wall that would depressurise the compartment, equalising the differential between the pressure inside the doomed aircraft and the high-altitude atmosphere outside. Otto had no exact measure of how long they had until the explosive charges hidden around the Shroud detonated, but he knew they could only have seconds left.

A green light came on above the switch that Raven had pressed and she gave Otto a thumbs-up before hitting the control to lower the cargo ramp. There was no roar of escaping air as the ramp lowered this time, but the noise of the Shroud's engines grew suddenly louder. Raven gestured urgently for Otto to move forward on to the ramp and he tried very hard not to think about the fact that he was about to throw himself out of an aircraft, 25,000 feet above the ground.

Raven stood alongside him and held her watch up in front of his face. The countdown timer that she had synched with the self-destruct countdown displayed ten seconds remaining. Knowing he had no other choice, Otto ran towards the edge of the loading ramp and threw himself forward into the blackness.

# chapter eleven

'Four hundred, three hundred, two hundred, one hundred.'

Otto closed his eyes.

'Zero.'

The very fact that Otto was able to be thankful that there had been no bone-shattering impact with the ground told him that he'd at least hit the target. He opened his eyes and immediately wished he hadn't as the black void into which he was falling was framed alarmingly closely on all sides by the jagged rock walls of the cave, their dagger-like shapes illuminated by the eerie green glow of the helmet's night vision.

Suddenly the jump rig detected that Otto was the correct distance from the floor of the cavern and automatically deployed his chute, the sudden deceleration jerking him upwards, the straps of his harness biting into his shoulders. Now comes the hard part, Otto thought to himself as he used the steering handles on the chute to steer it in a tight circle towards the ground. He knew all of the theory of the jump and the parachute deployment and steering, but he suspected that the theory of actually hitting the ground and the practical reality were two very different things.

As he descended in a tight spiral he could begin to make out details of the cavern floor below. There was no sign of any activity and no obvious heat sources and just for a moment Otto wondered if they'd actually got the right target. Then he reminded himself of the battery of sensors and other less friendly devices that had filled the jungle around the cave – this had to be the right place or someone was going to a lot of trouble and expense to guard a big hole in the ground.

He thought he could see a relatively flat-looking area of the cave floor near to where the waterfall that had bored this huge sinkhole over the centuries hit the ground in an explosion of white foam. He gently tugged on the controls of the chute, slightly adjusting his downward path, aiming for this potential landing spot. He seemed to be travelling very fast, even though the chute was functioning perfectly. All of the diagrams he had seen just a few minutes earlier for the correct way to hit the ground, bending his knees and rolling to absorb the impact, seemed very abstract as the ground rushed up to meet him.

He hit the ground hard. The rock was slippery and wet

so his landing was far from graceful, jarring his ankles as he let his legs collapse underneath him and rolling just as he had so recently learnt. The silky black material of the canopy fell on top of him and he struggled for a few seconds to get out from under it before finally extricating himself and standing up on solid ground. He was alive and, as far as he could tell, there were no bones broken although his ankles throbbed painfully in protest at the impact they had suffered. He quickly gathered up the chute and unclipped it from the jump harness, stuffing the rolled-up ball of black material behind a nearby pile of rocks. There was no sign that his arrival had been noted; no floodlights lighting up the cave or wailing alarm klaxons; just the dull thunder of the waterfall nearby.

He looked around, the helmet's night vision illuminating the inky darkness, and could see no sign of any human habitation, let alone a global super-villain's secret base. Again he felt a sudden twinge of doubt – if this was the wrong place it would be a long and dangerous climb back out. He also realised that there was no sign of Raven. He hoped that the detonation of the aircraft's self-destruct device had not claimed her or damaged her jump rig in some way. It was going to be hard enough surviving this even with her help; he didn't know what he was going to do if she had not made it too. He couldn't panic – he knew that – and silently he reminded himself why it was that he was here. If Cypher was here, Otto was going to make him pay for what he'd done.

Suddenly a movement on the edge of his field of vision caught Otto's attention. What had previously appeared to be a solid and natural rock wall was sliding into the ground and the light that came from behind it temporarily overloaded his sensitive night-vision equipment. Otto scurried for cover behind a huge boulder that lay nearby and watched, the electronics in his helmet compensating for the sudden flood of light, as several figures emerged from the previously hidden entrance. Otto immediately recognised the sinuous black forms of the assassins that had attacked them earlier that day. They moved through the doorway with the same silent grace that he had seen before, their heads turning this way and that as they fanned out across the cavern floor. This did at least mean that Otto was in the right place but it also suggested, rather more worryingly, that his arrival had not gone as undetected as he had hoped. Two of the black-clad figures remained at the doorway as the others proceeded to search the floor of the cavern, quickly covering the ground and moving inexorably closer to Otto's position. He had to move. Otto frantically looked around the cavern, desperately searching for some sign of another exit, but quickly realised that there were none. The only way out of the cavern was past the two men guarding the doorway and he doubted very much that they'd eagerly invite him inside.

Otto slowly backed up, keeping the boulder between himself and the assassin now approaching him. He almost fell as his foot slipped on the wet rocks behind him – he was on the very edge of the roaring torrent that issued from the base of the waterfall. Over the centuries this underground river had carved a deep channel in the base of the cave which vanished into a black hole in the rock wall. Otto had nowhere to go. As soon as the assassin rounded the huge boulder behind which Otto was hiding, he would be discovered and, he realised with a cold certainty, summarily executed. Otto stood up and took a deep breath. If he was going out at least he'd go out fighting.

☢ ☢ ☢

Raven spat a short, venomous curse in Russian as she drifted towards the cavern floor. Below she could see a fan of light spreading out across the ground as the concealed entrance opened and a dozen of the deadly assassins that had fought her to a near standstill earlier that day spilled out. They immediately assumed a search pattern, spreading out across the cavern floor quickly and efficiently. Whoever they were, they were extremely well trained.

She looked over to the hiding spot into which she had seen Malpense scurry as the door had started to open. From her position above them she could see that it would only be a matter of seconds before he was discovered. She knew what she had to do and she pulled on the control lines of her chute, steering it towards the hidden doorway. When she was twenty feet above the ground she slapped the emergency release on her harness and dropped the remaining distance, her orphaned parachute drifting away into the darkness. She hit the ground hard, rolling forward to absorb the impact and leaping immediately to her feet. She ripped the jump helmet from her head and drew the twin blades from the scabbards on her back in one fluid motion, running towards the two guards who remained watching the doorway. She knew that she had no chance of holding her own against so many of these mysterious ninjas, but she had to draw them away from Otto. The two guards on the door ran to meet her; they appeared unarmed but her experience in Tokyo had taught her that with these men that made little difference.

Raven's twin katanas became a blur as she launched a withering assault on the two ninjas. Just as before, they moved with an inhuman speed and efficiency, dodging or blocking what would normally have been killing blows, matching her move for move. The other guards that had spread out across the cavern were running back towards the doorway now and Raven realised that the fight was already lost, backing away from the two men at the door as the other guards started to form a loose circle around her. She centred herself and grinned viciously at the shadowy figures of the assassins that now surrounded her.

'One at a time or all at once?' she snarled, looking around her.

The guards showed no signs of concern, slowly tightening the circle they had formed.

⊛ ⊛ ⊛

Otto watched in horror as the assassins surrounded Raven. He had escaped detection by seconds when her arrival had drawn all of the hunters back to the doorway but he felt no sense of relief as he watched the situation that developed on the other side of the cavern. The ninjas surrounded Raven, advancing remorselessly. One would attack from in front and several others would launch a simultaneous assault from behind, slowly wearing her down. Raven fought like a demon but it was all she could do to hold her own and the end, when it inevitably came, was quick and brutal. As the blow rained down on her Raven was knocked down on to one knee and then mercilessly battered to the floor. In a matter of seconds it was over, two of the ninjas dragging Raven's limp form through the brightly lit doorway.

The remaining assassins moved away again, spreading back out across the cavern, resuming their search. Otto looked around desperately. There was no hiding spot that he could see that would conceal his presence and if he was discovered now Raven's sacrifice would have been for nothing. A sudden thought shot across Otto's mind. It seemed insane, but he quickly realised that it might be the only chance he had. He looked at the head-up display on his helmet and saw that he had just under four minutes of oxygen remaining. He had no idea if it was enough; he just had to hope it would be. He turned round, took a moment to slow his breathing and then dived into the raging torrent that issued from the waterfall.

Instantly he was caught in the breakneck current, tumbling over and over in the icy water as he was carried towards the black hole in the cave wall. Otto had no idea where the torrent would carry him but all he cared about at the moment was that it was the only way out. As he passed into the cave the river picked up speed and his helmet hit a rock hidden below the surface. The head-up display flickered for a moment and then went dark. His night vision was gone and he could no longer tell which way was up in the pitch blackness. He smashed against another rock and, as the wind was knocked from him, felt genuine fear as he realised that this wild torrent was as likely to kill him as any of Cypher's assassins. Otto fought for air; his helmet was at least still feeding him oxygen but there were now less than two minutes' worth remaining.

Suddenly he was airborne. His stomach gave a lurch as he fell through the blackness for what seemed like for ever before hitting the water again hard. His visor crashed into something solid and water rushed into his helmet. Otto fought desperately to pull the helmet off as it filled with the icy water, finally tearing it off, knowing that his remaining oxygen supply was now gone. He felt air on his face for a moment and took a desperate ragged breath before he was pulled under again. He fought to reach the surface as his lungs started to burn, but he was completely disorientated. The back of his head smacked against another hidden piece of rock and his final despairing thought as he lost consciousness was that Cypher had won.

♧ ♧ ♧

'What do you mean, "disappeared"?' Nero asked impatiently.

'It's just vanished, sir. We can't raise the Shroud on comms and there's nothing on satellite tracking,' the harried-looking communications tech replied weakly.

'You've tried to activate the emergency beacon, I assume?' Professor Pike said, walking across the command centre to the console at which the technician was working.

'Yes, Professor, I've tried everything. There's just no sign of them. Could they have been . . . shot down?' the technician asked nervously.

'In any other aircraft that might have been a possibility, but there isn't an anti-aircraft system on earth that can even detect the Shroud, much less shoot it down. No, something else must have happened,' the Professor replied, peering through his battered spectacles at the display.

Nero rubbed his eyes with one hand and let out a sigh. Today was going from bad to worse. He refused, though, to give up hope just yet. It would not be the first time that both Raven and Malpense had survived such unexpected developments. He knew that he should report the situation to Number One, especially as Malpense was involved, but he also knew from past experience that reporting to Number One without a full understanding of the situation was never a good idea. No, better instead to wait until he had a much clearer idea of what had happened.

'See if you can pull up thermal imaging for the surrounding area,' the Professor instructed, and the technician proceeded to hijack and intercept any relevant data from nearby satellites. The Professor walked back over to Nero, looking worried.

'It's not good, Max. I know the Shroud was designed to

be invisible, but not to us. If it's in the air we should be able to find it,' he said quietly.

'Any theories?' Nero asked, looking tired.

'Well, the Shrouds are experimental. There could have been an equipment failure.'

Nero thought that 'equipment failure' was not a terribly accurate description of a fireball in the sky and a rain of blazing debris on the ground below. He pushed the image out of his mind.

'No, it's too much of a coincidence that something should go wrong at the precise moment that they're on final approach to Cypher's facility. Something happened and it wasn't an accident.'

'I agree,' the Professor said. 'There's only the prototype left, it's such a shame to lose equipment like that.'

Nero glared at the Professor.

'What I mean is that such potential loss of life is tragic . . . yes, that's it, terrible . . .' the Professor added hastily.

'Doctor Nero, I have something,' the technician reported, pointing at his display as Nero and the Professor hurried over to look at what he had found. The display was showing a thermal image of the area surrounding Cypher's base. The majority of the screen was filled with the deep purples and blues of the cool, quiet jungle but tearing through the middle of the area was a deep gash of orange, yellow and white.

199

'That's a debris field,' the Professor said quietly.

'Professor, how long until you can get the last Shroud airborne?' Nero asked quickly.

'Well, it had been mothballed when construction on the other two was completed – a couple of hours, minimum.'

'You have one hour, Professor,' Nero said coldly. 'I want a rescue team at those coordinates as soon as possible.'

The Professor nodded and hurried out of the room. Nero would not allow himself to believe the worst yet. There was still hope. Besides which, he reminded himself, if Malpense had been on the Shroud when it hit the ground he wouldn't have to worry about anything ever again. Number One would see to that.

☻ ☻ ☻

Otto slowly opened his eyes. There was wet sand in his mouth and his aching body felt as if he'd been attacked by a giant with a meat tenderiser, but he was alive, and that in itself was nothing short of miraculous. Tentatively he pushed himself up on to all fours and, as his eyes adjusted to the darkness, he could make out faint details of his surroundings. He was on the edge of an underground pool in a large cavern. Bizarre rock formations filled the cave, their glossy, organic shapes produced by millennia of relentlessly dripping water. Otto took a couple of deep breaths and tried to stand up.

'Owwww,' he moaned as he got unsteadily to his feet. His left knee was throbbing but at least his legs appeared to be capable of supporting his own weight. He suddenly realised there that was a faint light coming from an opening on the other side of the chamber. His uniform was soaked through and he felt on the brink of exhaustion but he knew that he had to keep moving. Tempting as it was to curl up in a ball here in the gloom, he was now the only one who had any chance of finding and stopping Cypher and rescuing Raven. Assuming she was still alive, of course, a nasty little voice in the back of his head reminded him.

He trudged through the wet sand surrounding the pool to the opening from which the faint illumination was coming. As he approached the light source he could make out a new sound: the thumping clangs and hisses of heavy machinery. Carefully he peered through the opening in the cave wall and was staggered by what he saw. Below was an enormous cavern filled with industrial robots and other elaborate pieces of machinery, all serving an enormous conveyer-belt-fed production line. The machinery itself was not much different from what one might expect to see in any factory manufacturing high-tech equipment, but what was far more astonishing was *what* was being manufactured.

From his vantage point he could see every stage of the manufacturing process in all of its staggering complexity. Numerous components were being fed into the mass of machinery and it wasn't until about halfway down the production line that it became obvious what the machines were assembling. There Otto could see what looked like black metallic skeletons being assembled and, as the process continued, more and more components were bolted to these frames. By the time these mysterious metallic bodies had reached the end of the production line they had taken on a sinister and unmistakeable form. Suddenly Otto understood why it was that Cypher's assassins had been able to fight Raven to a standstill on several occasions. They were robots!

Otto could not help but be impressed by the ingenuity of their design. He could not make out all of the details of their construction from his vantage point, but he could see that they represented a huge leap in technology. He was desperate to get down on to the floor of the manufacturing cavern, partly to see if he could make out any more details of the android assassins' design, and partly to see if there was anything he could do to throw a very large spanner in the works.

He looked around the cavern more carefully. There were a couple of guards patrolling the room, but they were just ordinary uniformed humans. Not only that, they both looked incredibly bored to be watching over the machinery, and Otto suspected that it would not be too difficult to sneak past them unnoticed. He could see where he wanted to go. The completed assassin droids were being carried through an opening in the cavern wall and he needed to find out where they were going.

Otto waited until both of the guards were on the other side of the cavern and climbed carefully through the opening in the cave wall. The rock wall that led down to the factory floor was steep but had plenty of good hand-holds, and Otto had soon reached the ground, apparently undetected. The noise of the machinery was even more deafening down here but Otto was glad of the cacophony. There was no way that anyone would hear him creeping around through that amount of background noise. All he had to do was stay out of sight.

Otto quickly surveyed his immediate surroundings. The number of different machines and control consoles that were clanking and buzzing away around him was slightly bewildering. He thought that he could see a couple of vulnerable points in the process but he needed something that would shut this place down for good as well as producing a big enough distraction to let him get further inside the base. A movement overhead caught Otto's eye and he glanced upwards and saw a huge crucible of molten metal being transported past above him.

'Perfect,' Otto whispered to himself. He quickly moved between the rows of equipment, heading for the ladder that would take him up on to the raised gantries above the production line. Otto climbed the ladder as quickly and as quietly as he could. The guards that he had spotted before were talking to each other on the opposite side of the cavern, and if they did have any clue that he was there, they were doing a very good job of hiding it. Otto hurried over to a control console at one end of the gantry that looked like it might be suitable. As he worked at the console another huge suspended cauldron of bubbling molten metal passed by and Otto could feel the heat even from a distance of twenty metres or so. As the huge bucket reached a pre-programmed point it stopped and began to tip, depositing a stream of bright yellow molten metal into a holding tank below with a hiss. Otto worked quickly, grateful that the controls had a touch-screen computerised interface which made the adjustments he was making much more straightforward. Once he was satisfied with his new modifications Otto hurried back down the ladder and stealthily made his way over to the opening in the wall through which the completed robot ninjas were passing.

The inactive robots lay flat on their backs on the conveyor belt and once again Otto could not help but admire their design. They were not wearing the black silk robes that they had been wearing when Otto had encountered them before, but they looked no less sinister. Their matt-black metallic skins had organic, flowing lines, only broken here and there by bundles of thick black cable that looked as if they functioned as the machines' muscles. The assassins' unmasked faces were featureless and smooth, save for an array of small holes on each side of the head where the eyes should be. As Otto watched the machines pass by he was extremely grateful that they had not been activated. Raven had struggled to defeat just a couple of these things in a toe-to-toe fight and the machinery in this room seemed to be producing a new one every couple of seconds. Otto's blood ran cold as he considered that fact for a moment; whatever Cypher was up to, an army of these things would represent an unstoppable force.

Otto forced himself to stop worrying about what Cypher's plans might be and to focus on what he had to do now. Checking that there was no sign of the guards, he hopped up on to the conveyor belt and lay down as it carried him through the hole in the wall.

☢ ☢ ☢

The H.I.V.E. security guard yawned. It had been a long shift and, since Francisco was the only prisoner in the brig, not a particularly exciting one. They had brought the Colonel in several hours ago and he had said nothing since, simply sat in his cell staring blankly at the opposite wall. The guard had heard rumours about what the Colonel was supposed to have done, but if he believed every rumour he'd heard while he'd been working at H.I.V.E. he'd have quit a long time ago. Usually the brig was only used for the worst and most unruly students – this was certainly the first recorded incidence of one of the teaching staff being locked up.

He heard the soft bleep of an authorised entry to the brig and turned to meet the visitor. To the guard's credit, he got his Sleeper halfway out of its holster before he was struck full in the chest by the two stun pulses that shot from the identical guns that Block and Tackle were carrying. He slumped forward on the desk, out cold.

The two students moved quickly, Block moving to cover the door while Tackle punched a series of commands into the console on the security desk. With a hiss, the bars that trapped Francisco in his cell retracted into the ceiling. The Colonel walked calmly from his cell, displaying no sign of any emotion as Tackle handed him a Sleeper.

'Phase Two has been authorised,' Tackle said flatly.

'Very well, you have your orders,' Francisco replied calmly. 'Initiate.'

# chapter twelve

Raven came to and immediately wished she hadn't. She felt as if she'd been run over by a truck; every part of her body ached. Her wrists and ankles were shackled to the chair in which she was sitting and her battered body protested as she strained against the restraints. The small room was bare save for a metal table and another chair; the only illumination came from the harsh white strip lighting overhead. Automatically she began to assess her chances of escape, just as she had been trained to do. Unsurprisingly, all of her gear had been taken from her and the restraints were well designed and strong enough to resist even her most determined efforts to break free. She wasn't going anywhere.

The door to the cell hissed open and Cypher walked into the room. The black glass mask that he always wore might have concealed his face completely but he made no effort to conceal the smug, triumphant tone in his voice.

'So, Nero's pet finally wakes up,' Cypher said sarcastically. 'I was under the impression that you were supposed to be the best but it seems that my assassins got the better of you rather easily.'

'You'll burn for this, Cypher,' Raven spat back. 'You're finished. When Number One discovers what you've done he'll turn this place into a smouldering crater.'

'Oh, I don't think we're going to have to worry about that for very much longer,' Cypher replied calmly. 'Indeed, by the end of today it will be Number One who will fear me.'

'You won't be the first to try,' Raven said with a sneer, 'and you won't be the first who gets stepped on like a bug either.'

'My dear Raven,' Cypher replied coldly, 'you underestimate my determination. Number One and Nero are relics of the past. I am the future.'

'You have no future,' Raven replied. 'G.L.O.V.E. will put you down like the mad dog you are.'

'You are foolish to place so much faith in an organisation that is made up of the cream of the world's villains. If the ruling council of G.L.O.V.E. is known for anything, it is its pragmatism. After the demonstration of my power that they will all witness today, I very much doubt any of them will be inclined to oppose me.'

Raven had no idea what Cypher was hinting at and,

even though she would show this lunatic no sign of it, she was worried. Whatever he was planning, it was clearly designed to be a spectacular display of his strength. People who stopped fearing the wrath of Number One were usually insane or extremely dangerous. Secretly she feared that Cypher might be both.

'I have to admit I was impressed that you survived the explosion in Tokyo,' Cypher continued. 'Normally I would be annoyed, but in this case it gives me the undoubted pleasure of killing you twice in one day. I've been waiting to try out my latest invention, and you should make the perfect test subject.'

The door behind Cypher hissed open again and Raven's eyes widened in surprise as two of Cypher's assassins entered the room. They were not wearing the black silk robes that they had been swathed in before, and their exposed, black metallic endo-skeletons left little doubt as to their true nature.

'Machines. I should have known,' Raven said quietly.

'Oh, these aren't just machines,' Cypher replied, a note of pride in his voice. 'These are the cutting edge of robotic technology. Titanium skeleton, grade one positronic core, carbon fibre musculature, multi-layered combat programming. They are works of art. They may not be capable of much in the way of independent thought, but that is outweighed by their unquestioning loyalty.'

'Am I supposed to be impressed?' Raven said with a cold smile.

'No, but you should be flattered. They were, after all, designed to beat you in single combat. Their core combat routines have been based on an extensive study of your capabilities. The only difference between you and them is that they don't tire and they can take an assault rifle round to the head.'

Cypher looked straight at Raven, her angry face a distorted reflection in the smooth black glass.

'They render you quite . . . obsolete,' he said threateningly.

As Cypher leant over her Raven spat in his face, her saliva running down the smooth surface of his mask. Without hesitation Cypher backhanded her hard across the face, but Raven didn't even flinch, she just stared back at him, defiance in her eyes. Cypher pulled a clean white handkerchief from his pocket and wiped the trickling spit from his mask.

'Take her to the testing area,' Cypher said angrily, gesturing to the two robots who advanced towards her. 'I'm going to enjoy watching you die.'

⊛ ⊛ ⊛

Otto lay flat on his stomach, the conveyor belt carrying him through the dimly illuminated tunnel, its destination unknown. They seemed to be travelling downwards, as the belt was on a very slight incline, but without having a better idea of the layout of the facility Otto had no way of knowing exactly where he was being taken. Suddenly Otto could make out faint sounds of machinery coming from somewhere up ahead. He lifted his head to peer along the length of the belt in front of him and could just make out a more brightly lit opening towards which the belt was travelling. As the belt moved him inexorably towards the light Otto could see that a pair of large yellow robotic claws were lifting the robots from the end of the belt and carrying them out of sight. As Otto neared the end of the belt he rolled off it and slowly snuck forward to see what lay in this new room.

The claws were lifting the robots from the end of the belt with clockwork precision, hoisting them into the air before swivelling away and positioning the inactive assassins in neatly ordered rows within the vast hangar-like space. There were hundreds, perhaps thousands of the mechanical killers arranged in perfect lines that stretched off in all directions. Otto's blood ran cold at the sight. Cypher was not just assembling a security or special operations force. This was an army. Having seen what these things were capable of in small numbers Otto knew that with an army of them Cypher would be almost unstoppable.

Otto hopped down from the opening and on to the

hangar floor. The assassins were clearly all deactivated at the moment and he decided that it would be best to find an exit while that was still the case. He had just started to move towards the other side of the room when he suddenly heard voices. Quickly Otto ducked into the long rows of motionless robots, using their massed ranks as cover. Otto could not see who was talking as the voices drew nearer but he could hear their conversation clearly.

'They're ready for final loadout,' the first voice said.

'I wish they'd given us a bit more notice,' the second voice complained.

'Everything *is* ready, isn't it?' the first man asked, a slight note of panic in his voice.

'Yeah, I think so. We'll have to skip a couple of the final checks but otherwise we're good to go.'

'OK, let's fire them up, then,' the first man said, exhaling loudly.

There was a low hum and suddenly the heads of all the robots in the front row snapped upright, each assassin turning as one on the spot and then proceeding to march to the far end of the room, all in perfect step with one another. As they turned Otto could see that the tiny holes in the sides of their faces were now lit up with a blood-red glow. Otto guessed that they must be sensory arrays, but these spider-like eye clusters did nothing to improve their sinister appearance.

As the first row filed out of the hangar the second row snapped to attention and proceeded to follow them to the exit. Otto realised that if they kept moving at this rate he'd run out of hiding places very quickly. He crept backwards, trying to put more rows of the ever-dwindling robot army between him and the voices he had heard previously. Otto looked around desperately for somewhere else to hide but there were no immediately obvious options. There were now only a couple of rows of the neatly ordered assassins still in front of him. He had nowhere to run.

☻ ☻ ☻

Back in the fabrication cavern the console controlling the alloy delivery system beeped once. The giant crucible full of boiling molten metal tipped as it had done countless times before, but as the glowing yellow torrent poured from the lip of the cauldron it began to move. Otto had not had much time with the console so his reprogramming had been quick and dirty – there had been little time for elegance. The crucible began to move along the length of the production line, molten metal pouring on to the delicate machinery below, destroying it completely in a shower of sparks and flame. At first the automated production system tried to keep functioning but, as pressures started to build and more and more parts of the system reported catastrophic failures, the system began to overload. There were a couple of loud bangs and then something somewhere within the ranks of heavy machinery decided that it had had enough and exploded with enough force to shake the entire cavern . . .

☃ ☃ ☃

Otto felt the hangar floor move and heard the muffled sound of a distant explosion.

'What the hell was that?' one of the voices at the front of the hangar said.

Suddenly a huge ball of fire bloomed from the opening through which the conveyor belt fed the recently manufactured droids. The shockwave knocked Otto to the ground and toppled a couple of the still-inactive assassins. They fell like statues, ramrod straight, just so much scrap metal until they were activated. There was the sound of another explosion in the distance and another jet of flame shot from the opening leading to the manufacturing cavern.

'Let's get out of here,' one of the voices shouted and Otto could just make out the sound of running footsteps receding into the distance. As he peered around the last row of inactive robots he could see two men in white coats running towards the hangar exit.

Otto smiled to himself as another distant explosion

shook dust from the ceiling. That was what he called throwing a spanner in the works. Suddenly a much closer and more violent explosion sent a girder tumbling down from high overhead. It smashed down on to the row of assassins just a couple of feet in front of Otto with an enormous crash. As Otto picked himself up and brushed the dust and debris from his uniform he wondered if maybe there was such a thing as a spanner that was just a little too big. He ran for the exit.

☣☣☣

Cypher stood on a gantry looking down into the feature-less concrete pit below. Raven stood in the centre of the pit twenty metres below him, staring straight back at him.

'You're certain,' Cypher said to the frightened-looking technician who stood just a few feet away.

'I'm afraid so, sir. Whoever has sabotaged the manu-facturing facility did an exceptionally efficient job of it. There's no chance of containing the fire and if it continues to spread at its current rate it will reach the fuel cells in just a few minutes.'

'It would appear that G.L.O.V.E. has responded more quickly than I expected,' Cypher replied thoughtfully, 'though I am impressed that their saboteurs got in unde-tected.'

'We've reviewed the security logs,' the technician

reported. 'There's no sign of a team entering the facility, but with G.L.O.V.E. commandos that doesn't mean that they're not here.'

Cypher nodded. 'How far along is the load-out of the Kraken?' he asked, glancing back down at Raven in the pit.

'Seventy-five per cent of our forces have been loaded,' the technician replied, looking around nervously as the distant rumble of another explosion sent an unnerving tremor through the gantry.

'That will be sufficient. Order a full evacuation and prepare the Kraken to disembark. Such a shame,' Cypher said with a sigh. 'I had been looking forward to this.' He gestured at Raven. He picked up the roll of black silk that was leaning against the gantry rail beside him.

'Raven, my dear,' Cypher said, looking down into the pit, 'I'm afraid that I really have to go. It's unfortunate that I'll have to miss the show, but I thought that you at least deserved the chance to go out fighting.'

With that Cypher tossed the roll of black silk into the pit below. Raven stepped forward and carefully unrolled the silk. Inside were her twin swords. She quickly scooped up the weapons and looked up at the gantry far overhead.

'This isn't over, Cypher,' Raven yelled defiantly.

'Oh, I rather think it is,' Cypher replied and pressed a switch on a control panel mounted on the gantry rail.

There was a low grinding rumble as a three-metre-square area of the pit's floor dropped away and slid aside. With a sudden hiss white vapour shot up from the hole and a dark shape rose up through the opening. The robot that stood on the raising platform was huge – at least twelve feet tall and seemingly almost as wide. It was covered in the same matt-black armour as the smaller robots, but that was where any similarity ended. If the assassin droids were a stiletto blade sliding unnoticed between the joins of an opponent's armour, this machine was a sledgehammer, designed to crush its enemies without mercy.

Cypher hit another button up on the gantry and with a low growl the sensory arrays in the behemoth's face plate lit up with a dull red glow.

'Kill her,' Cypher said, 'slowly.'

'Command acknowledged,' the robot replied in a low, growling synthesised voice.

Cypher took one last look down into the pit as the huge machine advanced on Raven and then turned and walked away down the gantry.

☣ ☣ ☣

'All crew members, preparation for phase two launch complete. Final embarkation authorised. Please proceed to duty stations,' the voice blared from the tannoy.

Otto pressed himself into the shadows of a recessed doorway as a group of worried-looking technicians ran past. He stayed well out of sight – clearly Cypher's personnel were in the final stages of preparation for something, but he doubted that they were distracted enough to ignore the presence of a thirteen-year-old boy. Fortunately most of the facility seemed to be deserted – whatever was going on was obviously important. Otto walked past a short side corridor and stopped. At the end of the corridor was a balcony that opened on to another vast cavern but what had really caught Otto's attention was the sound he could hear coming from the corridor: it was the sound of the sea, waves crashing against rocks. Otto moved cautiously down the corridor and peered out over the edge of the balcony.

The cavern had obviously been a large sea-cave originally but now it had been converted to work as a docking facility. A huge concrete jetty had been constructed along one wall and electro-magnetic crane rigs mounted on the ceiling were lifting containers from the jetty and lowering them into the belly of the bizarre ship that was docked there. The ship was the size of a modern missile cruiser but its sleek, flowing, almost organic lines suggested that it was significantly more advanced than any normal naval warship. Its black metallic skin seemed to soak up the illumination from the huge floodlights overhead, just like the skin of the Shroud had done, and Otto realised that there was a good chance that they were both coated with the same material. Until recently Cypher had had access to all of the technical resources that any senior member of G.L.O.V.E. did and Otto supposed that the material coating this ship and H.I.V.E.'s stealth transports may well be exactly the same. Arranged around the rear third of the ship's deck were half a dozen turrets, each mounted with a very serious-looking launcher tube. Technicians were swarming all over the ship's deck, checking systems and stowing equipment, apparently making final preparations for the ship to get underway.

Otto's attention was drawn by movement on the super-structure of the ship as several figures walked out on to a platform that overlooked the deck. He felt a sudden hot flash of anger as he recognised the figure at the head of the group, Cypher. Suddenly Otto flashed back to the events of the rooftop in Tokyo, the pain that Cypher had caused him and the debt that he owed Wing.

He had to get on board that ship.

Raven dived to her left. The massive robot was unbeliev-ably fast for its size but fortunately not quite as agile as its more normal-sized counterpart. A fist the size of a wrecking ball smashed into the concrete wall of the pit, leaving a small crater where Raven's head had been just moments before. Raven counterattacked, swinging her blades at one of the exposed bunches of muscle cables on the back of the behemoth's leg. Her katanas had been made and maintained by some of the finest weaponsmiths in the world but they glanced off the cables like a butter knife off a brick. She moved quickly away from the robot as it swivelled to face her, trying desperately to stay out of its reach. Raven knew that she could not win this fight; the machine she was fighting had as much armour plating as a tank and it would take more than agility and fancy swordplay to bring it down.

Suddenly there was another explosion from somewhere much nearer by, and the floor rocked as debris fell from overhead, catching Raven slightly off-balance. The giant robot seized on the opportunity, moving with impossible speed towards her, one of its huge fists swinging at her. Raven's years of training were all that saved her. She twisted away from the blow, rolling with it and avoiding as much of the direct impact as she could. The strike still sent her flying across the pit, sliding to a halt against the far wall. She shook her head, trying desperately to clear the flashing lights that suddenly filled her field of vision. She could not afford to let the thing land another blow like that.

The second explosion that suddenly rocked the room

was the closest yet; it sounded to Raven like an ammunition store exploding. The whole room shook, and large chunks of rock fell from the ceiling, one glancing off the robot's heavily armoured head with a dull clang. The robot fell to one knee, the lights of the sensory array on its face dimming and flickering for just a second before it slowly got to its feet. It moved relentlessly back across the pit towards Raven, who knew that if the fight continued like this that she would be defeated by exhaustion. She could only keep dancing around avoiding the thing for so long before it got lucky, and judging by the fact that she still felt slightly stunned from the glancing blow it had landed moments earlier, it would only take one good punch from it and she wouldn't be getting up again.

Raven heard a metallic creak from overhead and saw a shower of dust fall from one of the large steel pins that fixed the observation gantry overhead to the ceiling. She moved carefully around the edge of the pit, trying always to keep her opponent centred in the room, waiting for her chance.

The next explosion shook the entire room, and Raven lost her footing, falling to her knees. The assassin robot could not capitalise on her loss of balance, though, as it too struggled to stay upright. There was a screech of tearing metal from overhead as the steel structure of the observation gantry final gave up its grip on the rock ceiling and one end dropped downwards into the pit. Raven dived to avoid the shower of debris but her opponent was not so lucky. The end of the gantry swung downwards and slammed into the robot, smashing it to the ground, where it lay still, pinned under the end of the heavy metal walkway. Raven let out a long slow breath and looked upwards. The other end of the gantry was still in place twenty metres overhead; its supports had not quite given out yet. She slid her swords into her belt and ran towards the dangling gantry, hopping over the still form of the giant robot assassin and scaling the remains of the walkway as fast as she could.

She was about halfway up when she felt the whole gantry move again. Glancing downwards she saw that her opponent was starting to move, slowly at first, forcing itself on to all fours, lifting the end of the gantry as it rose. Raven climbed faster; the top of the improvised ladder she was scaling was only a few metres away now. Below her the robot finally struggled to its feet, the end of the gantry sliding off its back and slamming into the floor with a deafening clang. Raven just managed to hang on as the gantry shifted. One of the two remaining pins that was holding the upper end of the walkway in place gave way with a deafening crack and the whole gantry pivoted, leaving Raven dangling precariously over the long drop to the pit below.

The giant robot looked up and saw its prey dangling tantalisingly out of reach. It stooped down and picked up the lower end of the gantry with both hands and shook the entire walkway. Raven clung on for dear life as the machine tried to shake her loose, but it was like trying to hang on to a rodeo bull. The gantry's last remaining support gave an ominous crunch and Raven made one last desperate lunge, swinging towards the lip of the doorway carved into the rock wall. The fingers of one hand found the edge of the opening and she latched on to the solid rock as the abused gantry finally gave up its fight with gravity and toppled downwards into the pit with an enormous crash.

Raven pulled herself up into the doorway and looked back down into the pit. Far below the robot was still moving, struggling to free itself from the pile of twisted metal that was all that remained of the viewing gantry. She could not help but be impressed as it slowly rose to its feet, pushing the debris aside, and looked up at her. It would take a tank to stop one of these things, she thought to herself, and she realised with a slight shudder that it was unlikely that Cypher would have abandoned the machine if it was the only one he'd built . . .

There was the rumble of another explosion nearby and Raven knew that she had to get moving. She turned and ran silently down the corridor beyond the doorway. Far below, in the pit, the giant mechanical assassin strode through the scattered debris towards the wall, and looked up at the doorway overhead. It slammed its hand into the wall with a crunch, crushing the rock until it had a solid hold, and slowly but surely it began to climb.

�☙☙

Otto snuck closer to the dock, taking cover behind one of the piles of crates that littered the loading area. The gangway leading up to the deck of Cypher's ship was thirty metres away but it might as well have been thirty miles due to the two robotic assassins that guarded the ramp. There was no way that he was getting on board past them – he would have to find another way. He looked around desperately; he was running out of time and ideas.

Suddenly the two guards turned as one and hurried up the ramp to the ship as the gangway started to retract, sliding back into the ship's superstructure. A klaxon began to sound and the huge steel sea doors at the far end of the cavern slowly slid aside with a low rumble. Otto could just make out the first dim light of dawn outside as the steel cables that had tied the ship to the dock released from their mounts and reeled in. As the ship began to move Otto realised that he had to act now. He stood up and prepared himself to run across the dock, but before he could move he felt a hand close over his mouth.

'Don't be stupid, there's no way on board now,' Raven whispered, her mouth just centimetres from his ear. She removed her hand from his mouth and Otto turned to face her.

'I thought you were dead,' Otto said, relief mixed with disbelief.

'You know, I'm getting really tired of hearing that today,' Raven replied with a thin smile.

'Cypher's on that ship,' Otto said quickly. 'We have to get on board.'

'I know, but unless you've acquired the power of flight while I was away that's not going to be possible,' Raven answered. Otto knew that she was right. There was no way to scale the smooth hull of the ship even if they did manage to get near to it. He suddenly felt an overwhelming sense of frustration.

'I'm not letting him get away,' Otto said angrily. 'We have a score to settle.'

Raven looked Otto straight in the eye.

'I know how you feel, Otto, I really do, but this isn't the way.'

Otto slammed his fist into the metal container in frustration. They'd come so close and now Cypher was slipping through their fingers again. The huge ship continued to move away from the dock, gathering speed as it passed through the sea doors and into the grey light of dawn. Once the stern of the ship passed through the gates they rumbled closed again, sealing the docks.

'Getting out of here is the first priority,' Raven said, scanning the docks for any sign of an escape route. Suddenly the biggest explosion yet shook the entire cavern. Huge chunks of rock fell from the ceiling, smashing into the docks and hitting the water like cannonballs. Otto and Raven struggled to maintain their balance as the whole cavern rocked.

'Cypher must have activated the self-destruct sequence,' Raven said quickly.

'Erm . . . actually . . . that was me,' Otto said, his cheeks burning. Sabotaging the robot production line had seemed like a good idea at the time but he realised now that it might have had rather more severe consequences than he had intended.

'Oh, for goodness' sake,' Raven said with a sigh, 'I leave you alone for a couple of hours . . .'

Suddenly there was an enormous crash from behind them and they both turned to see the giant robot assassin from the pit tearing through a pair of large steel doors that led out on to the dock. It tore the heavy gauge steel like it was tissue paper, forcing its way through.

'What the hell is that?' Otto said with a gasp.

'Trouble,' Raven replied, pulling her swords from her belt. 'Get to cover.'

Raven stepped out from their hiding place, raising her swords in a defensive stance.

'Hey, ugly!' she shouted, and the robot's head swivelled to lock on to her position. The red lights of its sensory array seemed to flare for a moment and it advanced towards her.

Otto backed further into the shadows. He wasn't foolish enough to think that he could offer Raven any meaningful assistance in this situation and so he looked around for anything that might help them in the fight. He looked up at the equipment suspended from the cavern's ceiling and smiled. He suddenly knew what he had to do.

Raven braced herself as the monstrous machine approached. Its black metallic skin was scored and dented from the shower of debris in the pit but it didn't seem to have slowed down in the slightest. Raven backed up as the robot advanced. She knew that she had to keep her distance from the thing – there may be more room to move on the docks, but she couldn't keep up this game of cat and mouse for ever. Raven stopped as she felt the rock wall at her back. The robot was still advancing and she realised with a cold chill that she was out of ideas. Suddenly she caught sight of something big moving behind the assassin and her eyes widened.

Raven dived to one side as the enormous shipping container mounted on the electro-magnetic loading rig slammed into the robot from behind like a freight train, crushing it against the rock wall with an enormous crash. Fifty metres away, at the crane controls, Otto gave a little yell of victory. Raven picked herself up from the floor and dusted herself off. She inspected the shattered remains of the robot, crushed between the massive container and the unforgiving rock wall. There was no way it was getting up from that.

Otto ran over to the scene of destruction, a broad grin on his face, and surveyed the sparking, twitching remains of the huge robot.

'Nice work,' Raven said as another explosion shook the cavern, 'but we still don't have a way out of here.'

Otto's smile faded as he realised she was right. They were still trapped as Cypher's base disintegrated around them. Suddenly there was a horribly familiar bleeping sound from the twisted remains of the robot. Otto and Raven's heads both snapped round and immediately saw the large silver canister that was protruding from the wreckage, a flashing light at one end.

Raven moved faster than Otto had ever seen anyone move before. She snatched the foot-long canister from the wreckage, yanking it free from the tangled metal, still beeping. She hurled the canister in a looping arc towards the sea doors and threw herself on top of Otto, knocking him to the ground. The explosion tore the heavy sea doors apart, the shockwave making Otto's ears ring like church bells.

As the smoke cloud from the blast cleared Otto sat up and surveyed the wreckage. One of the sea doors was gone completely and the other was just twisted scrap metal. They had their exit.

'Feel like a swim?' Raven said with a grin as she offered Otto her hand and pulled him to his feet.

# chapter thirteen

The H.I.V.E. security guard walked into the detention area and gasped. The man who had been assigned to the brig lay slumped across the guard station, still breathing but unconscious. He ran to his fallen comrade and shook his shoulder. There was no response. The guard had seen the effects of Sleeper pulses often enough to recognise the effects immediately. He ran over to the cells and realised to his horror that they were all empty. Pulling his Blackbox from his belt he spoke quickly into it.

'This is Guard Jackson in the detention centre. We have a Class One security alert. Colonel Francisco has escaped.'

☉☉☉

Shelby woke with a start. She'd been dreaming about Wing again. They'd been on a tiny rowing boat in the middle of the ocean and Wing had fallen over the side.

She'd dived in after him, but had not been able to find him. Then she'd resurfaced to find that the boat had gone and she was left all alone adrift in the middle of a cold, dark ocean. She shivered as she recalled the terrible feeling of loneliness, surrounded by all that freezing black water.

As she rubbed her eyes she realised that there was a soft bleeping coming from her Blackbox and that this must have been what woke her. She picked up the PDA and touched the screen to accept the call.

'Good morning, student Trinity,' H.I.V.E.mind said in the emotionless monotone that had become depressingly familiar. 'There has been a security alert and Doctor Nero has requested that you and student Brand report to situation room three immediately.'

'Umm . . . OK . . . situation room three,' Shelby said, still only half awake. The Blackbox disconnected and Shelby walked over to Laura's bed. She gently shook her friend's shoulder until Laura finally woke up with a low groan.

'What time is it?' Laura asked croakily, looking up at Shelby.

'Just after 5 a.m.,' Shelby replied. 'Nero wants to see us. There's some kind of security alert.'

Laura suddenly looked more awake. 'Did he say what was wrong?' she asked.

'No, it was H.I.V.E.mind that called, and he doesn't seem to be keen on long conversations these days,' Shelby replied. 'Whatever it was it sounded urgent.'

Laura knew what Shelby meant about H.I.V.E.mind. There was still no sign of the AI's old personality; whatever had been done to him after their failed escape attempt a few months ago had clearly erased any trace of his previous independence.

'Well, then,' Laura said, sitting up and putting her feet down on to the cold floor, 'we'd better get a move on.'

☻☻☻

Otto was cold and miserable. He sat huddled on a rock near to the cliff-face entrance to Cypher's hidden dock that was still belching out thick black smoke. The thin dawn rays of the sun did little to warm him or to dry out his cold, damp uniform. Raven stood nearby, scanning the horizon as she had been for the past hour. Otto looked over his shoulder at the sheer rock face behind them. He suspected that Raven might have been able to pick her way upwards through the jagged black rock, but he was no mountaineer. Swimming further along the coastline seemed impossible, too; there was no visible break in the rock wall in either direction and the way in which the waves smashed violently against the base of the cliff suggested that he'd need to feel a little less exhausted if he was going to stand any chance of making it more than a few metres. Otto appreciated the irony of the fact that they had both made it out of Cypher's base in one piece only to find themselves trapped by mother nature.

'Keep rubbing your arms and legs,' Raven said with a look of concern. 'The last thing I need is you coming down with hypothermia.'

Raven for her part looked as if she'd just woken up from a good night's sleep. If the cold was bothering her she was showing no signs of it. The wind suddenly picked up and Otto hugged himself more tightly, trying to retain what little warmth was left in his body.

'About time, too,' Raven said, and Otto looked at her quizzically. She was looking straight up and as Otto followed suit it took his exhausted brain a moment to make sense of what he was seeing. A dozen metres above them a figure was standing in midair surrounded by a bright light.

There was a shimmer in the air and the rest of the Shroud suddenly became visible as a cable and harness dropped from the rear hatch.

'Need a lift?' the pilot's voice asked over the aircraft's external loudspeaker.

☻ ☻ ☻

Nero was furious. The expression on his face as he looked

down at the cowering security chief was enough to freeze the blood. The other operatives in the command centre were focused on their own tasks, desperate to avoid doing anything that might attract Nero's attention.

'Correct me if I'm wrong, Mr Lewis, but I believe you once described the brig as escape-proof.' There was ice in his voice.

'Yes, sir. I don't know what happened, we lost all of the camera feeds from the brig just before Francisco escaped. Somebody must have helped him, but I have no idea how they got into the brig itself. That area is cleared for authorised and senior personnel only.'

'Neither of which describe Mr Block or Mr Tackle, so would you care to explain to me how they managed to get into the detention area?' Nero was losing patience. Somebody was threatening his school and he was not going to stand for it.

'I don't know,' the Chief replied weakly.

'I am rather tired of hearing that, Mr Lewis,' Nero said, glaring at the Chief. 'H.I.V.E.mind, do you have any record of any interference with either the brig security network or your own systems that might explain this?'

'There is no record of any access to any of my systems that might explain this aberration,' H.I.V.E.mind replied quickly, his hovering blue head projected into the air a few inches above a nearby console.

'It is reasonable to assume, therefore, that someone has actively erased those records,' Nero said impatiently.

'That is a logical assumption,' H.I.V.E.mind replied.

'Professor,' Nero said, turning to face Professor Pike, 'could Mr Block or Mr Tackle have been given sufficient access to H.I.V.E.mind's data core to wipe those recordings?'

'No, it's impossible. Only you and I have that level of access to the data core. Even if Francisco had given them his own access codes earlier he did not have clearance to carry out a data purge like that. Besides which, I disabled all of his access clearances when he was captured. It's just not possible.'

Nero stared at the impassive face of H.I.V.E.mind. Somebody had gone to a great deal of trouble to make sure that the AI would not be able to give them any details of what had happened and to ensure that Francisco would escape undetected. It was strange to think that for H.I.V.E.mind it was as if the events had never happened.

The Contessa walked into the command centre, looking pleased.

'I've just received word from the Shroud that was despatched to Cypher's facility. They have found Raven and Malpense alive,' she reported quickly.

Nero felt a sense of overwhelming relief. At last something had gone their way.

'And Cypher?' he asked.

'Gone. His base has been destroyed, but he escaped. G.L.O.V.E. surveillance systems are trying to establish his location as we speak, but the ship he was aboard has vanished.'

'Vanished?' Nero said. 'How is that possible?' Nothing, least of all something the size of an ocean-going vessel should have been able to evade the G.L.O.V.E. surveillance grid.

'It seems that Cypher may have "borrowed" some of Professor Pike's research,' the Contessa replied. 'According to Raven the ship may share the stealth capabilities of the Shroud.'

'In other words it's invisible, just a hole in the ocean,' Nero replied, feeling frustration building again.

'It would appear so, yes,' the Contessa replied. 'The Shroud is returning to H.I.V.E. now, but Raven fears that H.I.V.E. may be Cypher's next target.'

'Attack the island?' the Professor snorted. 'I'd like to see him try.'

Nero nodded. H.I.V.E.'s external defence systems were designed to withstand an air and sea assault by national armed forces – one ship would have no chance.

'I share your faith in H.I.V.E.'s defences, Professor, but if there is one thing I have learnt over the past twenty-four hours it is to never underestimate what Cypher is capable of. Place all security forces on full alert and make sure that the island's defence grid is active.'

If it was a fight that Cypher wanted, that was exactly what he was going to get.

☻☻☻

Laura and Shelby walked down the corridor towards the situation room. The school was quiet; it was still much too early for the majority of students or staff to be up and about.

'I wonder what's going on?' Shelby said.

'I don't know,' Laura replied, 'but I suppose we're about to find out.'

The door to the situation room hissed open and the two girls walked inside. Shelby gasped as she saw who was sitting at the far end of the long conference table.

'Francisco!' Laura said as an evil grin spread across the Colonel's face.

Shelby turned to run back through the door but found the way obstructed by Block and Tackle, both of them pointing Sleepers straight at her. Shelby backed away from them slowly as they entered the room, Block keeping them covered while Tackle locked the door from the inside.

'It's so nice to see you both again, ladies,' the Colonel said, 'but this time you're coming with me.'

Nero scanned the reports from the security department. There were, as yet, no leads on where Francisco had gone with his two errant pupils and little progress in determining how they'd managed to get out of the detention centre without being detected. H.I.V.E.mind was performing multiple low-level sweeps of the school but so far with little success. He had an uncomfortable feeling of waiting for the inevitable.

Nero's office entry chime sounded and he looked up from the frustratingly vague reports that filled the monitor on his desk.

'Enter,' Nero barked impatiently, and the Contessa walked into the room. She wore a worried expression as she hurried over to Nero's desk.

'Max, I'm afraid I have some rather disturbing news,' she said quietly.

'What now?' Nero snapped, his impatience clear.

'Well, H.I.V.E.mind is continuing the security sweeps as ordered but the student headcount is wrong.'

'Meaning?' Nero asked, raising an eyebrow.

'It appears that students Brand and Trinity are missing,' the Contessa said.

Nero slammed his fist down on his desk angrily.

'What in the name of all that's evil is going on?' he

shouted.

'Well, that's what the Professor and I have been trying to work out,' the Contessa continued. 'We've been trying to see how somebody could have got around the security system so easily, and the conclusion we've reached is rather disturbing.'

'What is it?' Nero said impatiently.

'It's H.I.V.E.mind,' the Contessa said quietly. 'It appears that he may have been lying to us about the security logs.'

'You're certain?' Nero said, cold anger in his eyes.

'I'm afraid so. It appears that H.I.V.E.mind's personality was not as fully erased as we believed,' the Contessa replied.

Nero felt a chill run down his spine. H.I.V.E.mind couldn't lie; at least, that was the theory. One of the main reasons that the security and logistical running of the base had been handed over to the AI was because it was supposedly incapable of deceit – totally incorruptible. The only conclusion one could possibly reach was that H.I.V.E.mind's rebellious personality had reasserted itself somehow and that the machine had been involved in this plot from the start. Nero realised that it was time to shut it down for good.

'What does the Professor suggest that we do about it?' Nero replied quietly. He knew that H.I.V.E.mind should not be able to hear them in his private office without being specifically summoned – that had been one feature of his system about which Nero had been most insistent.

'Well, first we need to switch the school's defence systems over to full manual control; if H.I.V.E.mind is indeed working against us it would seem prudent. Especially if an attack is imminent.'

Nero nodded and began to tap a series of commands into the keyboard in front of him. After the incident with the plant monster earlier that year Nero had ordered that all security and defence systems were capable of functioning while H.I.V.E.mind was offline. The school would not be left defenceless again.

'I suggest that only you and I have command authorisation,' the Contessa continued.

'Agreed,' Nero replied. Given the events of the past couple of days the fewer people who could control the school's security the better.

'There, that should isolate the defence and security systems. Only you and I will have command authorisation,' Nero said with a sigh. He felt tired, he hadn't slept in nearly forty-eight hours.

'Thank you, Max. That's all I need,' the Contessa said quietly. There was something odd in her tone that made Nero look up from the monitor. His eyes widened in horror as he saw the pistol in her hand that was pointing straight at him. It was not a Sleeper.

'You!' Nero hissed, suddenly realising the true depth of the betrayal with which he was being confronted.

'Yes, Max . . . me.' The Contessa did not show any sign of emotion.

Nero glanced at the console on his desk.

'Don't even think about it, Max,' the Contessa said calmly. 'Back away from the desk.'

'Why, Maria? I trusted you,' Nero said as the Contessa swivelled the display on the desk and glanced at it, all the while keeping the gun trained on him. She smiled slightly as she saw that Nero had made all of the changes that she needed to the security and defence systems. She pulled a slim silver device from her pocket and attached it to one of the console's data ports.

'Like I said, Max, everyone has their price.'

'I expected more from you, Maria,' Nero replied. 'I didn't think Cypher would be able to buy someone like you so cheaply.'

'Oh, I wasn't cheap,' the Contessa replied with a smile. 'When this is all over Cypher's promised me a continent. I'm not sure which one to choose at the moment, but I'll worry about that later.'

'You can't trust him. What do you think will happen when this is all over, when he doesn't need you any more?'

'Oh, Max, you really don't understand, do you? The world has moved on. There's no more room for people like you, old-school villains with their twisted sense of ethics. This is the twenty-first century, a new world, one which has no place for a relic of the past like this school, or even G.L.O.V.E. Times have changed, Max, and if you refuse to change with them you get left behind.'

'How long have you been working for him?' Nero asked softly.

'Long enough,' the Contessa replied. 'Suffice to say that this has all been planned quite carefully.'

'And Francisco?' Nero asked, although he suspected that he now knew exactly what had happened.

'Francisco is a weak-minded fool. That's the problem with military men; they're so used to taking orders that they find it almost impossible to resist when I tell them what to do. Maybe there is some shred of the Colonel somewhere inside his head that has been trying to resist doing what I've told him. Frankly it doesn't matter. The same goes for the two students, Block and Tackle. They're just doing what they're told. You shouldn't blame them, they really have no say in the matter. When I realised that Ms Brand had intercepted my transmission I staged the Colonel's capture, helping to subdue him in the process and thereby putting myself above suspicion.'

Nero may have never really understood how the Contessa's unique ability to command others worked but he had seen enough evidence over the years to know that she was more than capable of doing what she described. He had often wondered what it would be like to have those powers working against you, and now he knew.

'I take it that you were responsible for the loss of the Shroud over Cypher's base too,' Nero said, feeling a cold fury building inside him.

'Let's just say that the pilot's last-minute briefing included some new instructions,' the Contessa said with an evil smile, 'though it appears that Malpense and Raven have nearly as many lives as Ms Leon.'

'Do you know how many people have died because of what you've done?' Nero asked, struggling to keep his anger in check now.

'You'll forgive me if I find it hard to take a lecture in morals from a man who runs a school for super-villains,' the Contessa replied. 'You're a dinosaur, Max, the real world has no place for people like you any more.'

'We shall see if Number One agrees,' Nero snapped. 'I think you'll find that he takes rather a dim view of traitors.'

'Oh, we shan't have to worry about Number One for very much longer,' the Contessa replied calmly. 'Cypher will take care of that.'

'What do you mean?' Nero asked, with rising anxiety.

'You'll see,' the Contessa smiled.

'You're insane,' Nero said, taking a single step towards the Contessa.

'Stop right there, Max. Cypher wants you alive, and I have no particular desire to hurt you, but you know me well enough to know that I'll kill you if I have to.'

'I don't know you,' Nero replied. 'I thought I did, but clearly I was mistaken.'

'Clearly,' the Contessa said with a slight smile, 'and now you're coming with me. We have an appointment to keep.'

'I'm not going anywhere; shoot me if you have to.' Nero suddenly wondered why she did not simply command him to do what she wanted, just as she had done with Francisco and her other unwitting slaves. He had long suspected that her powers may not work on a strong-willed victim who actively defied her and this seemed to suggest he was right.

'Defiant to the last, as ever,' the Contessa said. 'So let me put it another way. Come with me or Brand and Trinity die, slowly and painfully.'

Nero felt a cold knot form in his stomach. Given everything else that the Contessa appeared to have done he knew that she would not hesitate to take two more students' lives. For now, she had the upper hand. The Contessa gestured towards the door with the barrel of her gun and Nero silently walked out ahead of her.

Professor Pike took off his glasses and rubbed at his tired, sore eyes. The longer he stared at the lines of code that scrolled past on the monitor in front of him the more confused he got. The recording of the security feed from the detention area was gone, or at least that was what he was supposed to think. Somebody had gone to a great deal of trouble to cover their tracks but the evidence showed that whoever was responsible had not deactivated the security system, which would have attracted too much attention, but simply diverted the recordings in question to a hidden storage area. That presented two problems: first, where had they hidden the recordings and second, how had they got around the multiple layers of supposedly impregnable security that surrounded H.I.V.E.mind's core. H.I.V.E.mind had not been lying when he had said that as far as he was concerned there were no security recordings. Whoever had done this had hacked the system in such a way that even the AI had been unaware of it. The problem was that the Professor had created the encryption protecting H.I.V.E.mind's core himself and he knew it just wasn't possible that a hacker, no matter how good, could have got around it.

Suddenly something caught his eye.

'H.I.V.E.mind,' the Professor said wearily.

'Yes, Professor. How may I assist you?' the AI replied, its hovering blue wire frame face appearing in the air next to the terminal.

'Please display all records of access to your core via this terminal,' the Professor commanded. Moments later a list of dates and time scrolled past. At first there didn't appear to be anything unusual, but then one particular entry leapt out at him.

'H.I.V.E.mind, please confirm entry number 4376,' the Professor said, feeling a growing sense of unease.

'Entry 4376,' H.I.V.E.mind responded. 'Access to central core granted to Professor William Pike.'

The Professor may have given his students and fellow staff the appearance of being slightly absent-minded but he knew for a fact that he had not accessed the core at the time listed.

'Show activity log for that session, please, H.I.V.E.mind,' the Professor said quickly.

The screen filled with more entries and the Professor picked through the data. Someone had logged into H.I.V.E.mind's core using his personal login and set up a hidden archive deep within the hidden layers of H.I.V.E.mind's base operating system. The question was who. The Professor quickly found the archive, now that he knew where to look, and found dozens of files. He soon came across encryption routines, secret transmission codes, and most importantly, a long list of archived security feeds. He scanned the list of recordings and one in particular caught his eye. It was the recording from the camera mounted high on the wall of that very room at the precise time that the hidden archive was set up. He quickly pulled up the file and played it. Now he would find out who was responsible for all of this.

'That's impossible,' the Professor whispered as he watched the recording. Sat there at the terminal on the screen was the last person on earth he'd expected to see.

Himself.

He struggled to make sense of what he was seeing. He knew with certainty that he had not been using the terminal at the time in question, let alone setting up a hidden archive within the core. He could not deny the evidence of his own eyes, though – there he was, busily working away at the terminal, creating an artificial blind spot in the security system. He looked through the list of hidden security recordings and spotted another leading up to the time of this baffling entry.

'H.I.V.E.mind, please run backwards through all surveillance recordings within this archive leading up to the time of my access,' the Professor said quickly.

The feed changed to show the Professor walking backwards away from the entrance to H.I.V.E.mind's central hub and then back along several corridors.

'Freeze it there,' the Professor shouted as another figure entered the picture. 'Playback.'

There was no audio but the Professor did not need it. He watched as the Contessa leant in close to him and whispered something into his ear.

'Oh my God,' the Professor said, and ran from the room.

☢ ☢ ☢

Nero walked down the corridor a few paces ahead of the Contessa. She no longer had the gun pointed at him; it would only attract unwelcome attention, and she knew that she would not need it as long as she had Laura and Shelby to use as bargaining chips. If there was one weakness from which Nero suffered it was the fact that he would never do anything willingly to jeopardise the lives of his students.

Suddenly a security patrol came round the corner ahead of them. They were clearly still searching for Francisco, judging by the grim no-nonsense expressions on the guards' faces.

'Say nothing,' the Contessa whispered as the patrol approached. 'You know what will happen if you do.'

As the patrol drew closer the squad leader nodded courteously to Nero, who returned the gesture silently. Nero noticed that the guards were carrying assault rifles as well as the standard-issue Sleepers. Security Chief Lewis was obviously taking no chances, a wise precaution where Francisco was concerned. Of course what the Chief did not know was that Francisco was really nothing more than an unwitting pawn in this scheme and that the real culprit behind the recent chaos at H.I.V.E. was altogether more dangerous.

The patrol passed by, a couple of the men throwing nervous glances in the direction of Nero and the Contessa as they marched by, but no more than that. The patrol was twenty metres behind them when the squad leader's radio squawked.

'Go ahead,' he said quickly.

The squad leader gestured for the squad to stop as he listened intently to his ear-piece. Slowly his face went pale and he looked back down the corridor at the rapidly retreating figures of Nero and the Contessa.

'You're certain?' the squad leader said, swallowing nervously. The way in which he then winced suggested that whoever was on the other end of the line was not only certain but noisily so. He gave his team a quick series of hand gestures that instructed them to spread out across the corridor and take cover as best they could.

'Contessa!' the squad leader shouted down the corridor. 'Please stay exactly where you are. Chief Lewis has some questions for you.'

'Wait,' the Contessa whispered to Nero. He heard the unmistakeable click of a safety catch being switched behind him and his mind raced. He could not let the patrol take the Contessa here – it would almost certainly sign Brand and Trinity's death warrants – but he wasn't about to let the Contessa shoot any of these men either. The patrol leader may have felt confident, but it would only take the Contessa getting within earshot of his squad and it would be a very different story. He doubted very much that many of the men in the patrol had the mental strength to resist the Contessa's power.

The Contessa turned slowly and faced the security patrol. Several Sleepers were pointed straight at her, the guards' faces confused but determined.

'Goodness me,' the Contessa said with a slight laugh. 'What on earth is all this about?' She took a couple of steps towards the patrol.

Behind her Nero pulled the skull-shaped link from the cuff of his shirt and twisted the clip.

'Stay right there, Contessa,' the squad leader barked. 'We have orders to fire if necessary.'

'Nonsense,' the Contessa replied. 'In fact, I think you're just all going to put your guns down.' As the Contessa spoke there was the uncomfortable, almost subliminal, sound of a thousand voices whispering at once. Nero had never heard the Contessa exert her power so strongly before and the effects were immediate. To their credit, a couple of the guards just looked confused, but the rest started to slowly place their weapons on the ground, their expressions blank.

Nero knew he had to act now before the Contessa could order the guards to help her escape or, even worse, turn on one another, and he threw the tiny silver skull in his palm down the corridor. There was a blinding flash and a concussive thump as the minute disguised stun grenade went off, filling the corridor with thick grey smoke. Then all hell broke loose.

Nero threw himself to the floor as Sleeper pulses ripped through the air. The few guards who had retained their weapons were firing blindly through the smoke, still dazed from the Contessa's manipulation.

'Cease fire,' the squad leader bellowed over the zapping blasts from the Sleepers. As the smoke cleared Nero could see the vague outlines of the patrol in the corridor, but he quickly realised that one person was missing.

'Are you all right, sir?' the squad leader asked as he staggered down the corridor towards Nero.

Nero nodded. He was fine, but the Contessa was gone.

☺☺☺

Laura and Shelby watched in horror as the door hissed open and Francisco dropped the guard inside with a single neat Sleeper pulse to the chest. He silently gestured for the girls to go through the door and they found themselves in an area that they had long believed did not exist. The cavern was a fully functional docking facility that looked as if it could handle most medium-sized vessels, the sea lapping at the single long quay. Tied up at the quay were a couple of sleek black power boats and as Shelby saw them she shot a worried glance at Laura. Laura knew why her friend was so concerned. At least while they were on the island they had a chance of being rescued, but if Francisco managed to smuggle them outside the school then their chances would diminish alarmingly.

Laura felt a sharp jab in her ribs as Tackle prodded her forwards with the barrel of his Sleeper and they slowly walked along the quay towards one of the moored boats. As they approached, a figure detached itself from the shadows nearby and stepped out into the light. A broad grin spread across Laura's face as she felt a flood of relief.

'Look out, Contessa! They're armed!' Shelby yelled, throwing herself backwards into Block, trying to catch him off balance and buy the Contessa a couple of precious seconds.

'Why, of course they are, my dear,' the Contessa replied matter of factly, walking slowly towards Francisco. 'How else would they keep you two under control?'

Laura's brow furrowed in confusion. What was the

Contessa doing? She had to stop them now while she still could.

'Have they given you any trouble?' the Contessa asked Francisco, glancing at the two girls.

'No, everything, has gone according to plan,' the Colonel replied, his voice flat.

'Not quite everything unfortunately. Nero escaped, but all of the necessary elements are in place otherwise. We should proceed,' the Contessa said, pulling a small PDA from her pocket. It was not a Blackbox.

Laura suddenly understood what was happening and just how carefully the events of the past couple of days had been orchestrated. The traitor wasn't Francisco; it was the Contessa.

'You two-faced old hag!' Shelby shouted angrily, clearly having reached exactly the same conclusion as Laura. 'How could you do this, you've –'

'Oh, do be quiet, Miss Trinity,' the Contessa said, her voice laced with sinister whispers. Shelby's mouth continued to move for a moment, as if she was trying to form words but none would come. Laura said nothing, and simply glared at the Contessa, her mind racing as she tried to think of a way out of this situation.

'That's better,' the Contessa said with a smile. 'Now why don't we all just get on board one of these boats that the school has so thoughtfully provided and be on our way.'

Laura felt another shove from behind as Tackle forced her towards the nearest power boat.

The Contessa watched as the two girls were loaded on to the boat, a smug, triumphant smile on her face.

'Now, sit still and stay silent,' she said, and Laura felt her free will disappear. No matter how hard she tried she could not move a muscle or make a sound. It was a deeply unsettling sensation.

'Now, Colonel, I believe it is time that you and your two students ensured that our insurance policy is in place,' the Contessa said, turning to Francisco. 'You know what to do.'

'Yes, Contessa,' Francisco replied in a monotone, turning and walking back towards the entrance to the dock with Block and Tackle in tow.

The Contessa watched them leave and then turned to the two girls sitting paralysed in the boat.

'Isn't this nice? All girls together,' she said sarcastically, climbing behind the controls of the boat. Neither of the two girls may have been able to offer a reply but the hate-filled looks in their eyes spoke volumes.

The Contessa fired the ignition on the boat and its powerful engines roared into life. She raised the silver PDA to her lips.

'Activate H.I.V.E. emergency security procedure Sinistre Delta One,' she said and placed the device back in her pocket. The rock wall at the far end of the dock rumbled upwards and Laura saw blue sky and the sea stretching off towards the horizon.

As the Contessa gunned the engine and steered the boat towards the opening alarm klaxons began to sound all over the school.

# chapter fourteen

'What the hell?' Security Chief Lewis spat as one by one the monitors displaying security feeds from all over the school flickered and went black.

'There's an unknown routine running on the security net,' a technician reported from a nearby workstation. 'The grid's going offline.'

The door to the situation room slid open and Dr Nero hurried into the room and headed straight for the nearest free terminal. He typed a string of commands into the terminal before slamming his fist down hard on the keyboard.

'Damn you, Maria,' Nero hissed. It was too late. She had locked him out of the system using her command access, and was now the only person who could reinitialise the system.

'Student dormitories are locking down,' another security technician announced, a look of confusion on his face.

'Defence grid is offline too,' another voice reported. 'All external batteries are going into sleep modes.'

'H.I.V.E.mind just dropped into standby mode. He's not accepting remote commands.'

Nero watched in impotent fury as his school was rendered defenceless around him.

'All external access points are opening,' the Chief said, slight panic in his voice. 'Do we still have exterior camera feeds?'

'Yes, sir, scanning the perimeter now,' a reply came from the other side of the room. 'Nothing visible at the moment, looks all clear . . . hold on . . . something off the southern coastline.'

'Put it on-screen,' Lewis barked.

There on the screen a tiny boat was roaring away from the island. As the camera zoomed in Nero could see the unmistakeable figure of the Contessa at the controls. Sat behind her were two smaller figures, both wearing the black jumpsuits of the Alpha stream.

'Where's she going?' Lewis said, sounding puzzled. 'That's only a patrol boat, she doesn't have enough fuel to reach land.'

As if answer to the Chief's query there was a strange shimmer on the surface of the ocean and then a huge, black warship materialised seemingly out of thin air.

Nero suddenly realised just how badly he had been

outmanoeuvred. Cypher was here and H.I.V.E. was defenceless.

☹ ☹ ☹

Nigel and Franz wandered slowly through the virtually deserted atrium of their accommodation block. There were a few other students sitting on the sofas and chairs dotted around the cavern but the vast majority of H.I.V.E.'s pupils were either still asleep or had only just woken up. Franz had woken early, complaining that he was hungry, as he always did when the previous evening's meal had been salad. For his part Nigel had learnt long ago that it was entirely pointless to try and sleep through Franz's morning routine and after two minutes of Franz singing in the shower he had grudgingly got out of bed too.

'It is still nearly an hour till breakfast,' Franz observed, 'but it may be wise to take our places in the queue already, ja?'

'There's not going to be a queue yet,' Nigel said slightly grumpily. 'We'll be fine if we're five minutes early. Let's go to the library instead. There are a couple of new organic chemistry papers that I need to catch up on.'

'Oh, Nigel, with you it is always the library. You need to have more fun,' Franz said matter of factly.

'The library *is* fun,' Nigel said insistently, wishing that

258

Franz shared his passion for books. 'Perhaps if you spent a bit more time there you'd understand.'

The huge blast doors that sealed the accommodation block at night had opened a few minutes earlier, signalling that students were free to wander the halls of the school again before their classes, as usual. Nigel and Franz walked through them and into the corridor beyond. At almost exactly the same moment alarm klaxons began to wail everywhere.

'I didn't do anything!' Franz yelped as the alarms screamed.

There was a low grinding noise and the blast doors began to lower, re-sealing the accommodation block.

'Come on,' Nigel said. 'That's a high-level alert. It's probably just a drill, but we still have to go back inside.'

'No way!' Franz yelped, backing away from the closing doors. 'I am remembering what happened the last time all of the alarms are going off and we are locked in there.'

Nigel remembered too. On that day they had ended up trapped inside their room while the rampaging plant creature that he himself had inadvertently created tried to smash its way in. Franz was right – it had not been a pleasant experience.

'Well, that's unlikely to happen again, isn't it?' Nigel said slightly apologetically.

'You have not been experimenting again, have you?'

Franz said suspiciously, his eyes narrowing as he looked carefully at Nigel.

'No, I most certainly have not,' Nigel said indignantly, feeling his cheeks burning. The blast door was nearly halfway closed now; they had to get back inside.

'Well, I am staying out here,' Franz said indignantly.

Nigel was surprised by Franz's determination but he knew the only way to get him back into the accommodation area now would be to physically drag him and the laws of physics might have something to say about that, given the two boys' relative masses.

'OK, but let's find somewhere quiet to sit out the alert,' Nigel said nervously, looking up the corridor and half expecting to see an angry security patrol marching towards them.

'An excellent idea,' Franz said with a broad smile. 'I suggest the dining hall!'

'That's what this was all about,' Nigel said incredulously as the blast door sealed shut with a solid-sounding thud. 'You just didn't want to miss breakfast.'

'No, that was not it at all –' Franz began weakly.

'I don't believe you sometimes,' Nigel said angrily. 'I'm going to the library and if we meet any security patrols on the way you can explain what we're doing outside the accommodation area.' He marched away down the corridor.

'But the dining area has much greater structural

integrity,' Franz continued as he followed Nigel. 'It really would be the safer option in the event of an emergency . . .'

☺☺☺

Laura's mouth fell open as the huge black ship materialised just a couple of hundred metres in front of them. She looked across at Shelby, who shared her look of amazement, her mouth moving slightly as if she was trying to say something despite the command for silence that the Contessa had given them both just a few minutes earlier.

The stolen patrol boat slowed as they neared the side of the mysterious ship and a boarding platform lowered from the level of the deck to just above the surface of the water. The Contessa brought the boat alongside the platform and turned to the two girls. The pistol was in her hand again.

'Get out,' she said coldly. 'Try anything stupid and I'll feed you to the sharks myself.'

Shelby and Laura climbed out of the patrol boat and on to the platform, the Contessa close behind them, and immediately the platform rose again towards the bigger ship's deck.

As they rose to the level of the upper deck the two girls found a welcoming party waiting for them. A tall man, dressed in an immaculate suit and a smooth oval mask of highly polished black glass, stood flanked on either side by slim, humanoid robots, their matt-black metallic bodies covered in plates of armour.

'Contessa,' the man said. 'How nice to see you again. I trust everything has gone according to plan?'

'Yes, Cypher,' the Contessa replied. 'The island is yours for the taking.'

Shelby made a sound that could only be described as a snarl and ran towards Cypher. The robots to either side of him reacted instantly, intercepting Shelby and restraining her in their vice-like grip.

'Murderer!' Shelby gasped as she struggled in vain to break free of the guards.

Laura stepped forward as if to help her friend but instead was forced to her knees as another guard clamped its mechanical hand down hard on her shoulder.

'And two unexpected guests – how lovely,' Cypher said coldly, stepping towards Shelby.

'Yes, may I introduce Shelby Trinity and Laura Brand. They have made rather a nuisance of themselves so I thought I'd bring them along as extra insurance,' the Contessa explained.

Cypher took Shelby's chin in his hand. The look on her face suggested that he should be very glad that she wasn't able to get her hands on him.

'I'm afraid, Miss Trinity, that H.I.V.E. is going to be permanently closed very shortly, but I'm sure that we can find a use for someone with spirit in my organisation in the future,' he said with infuriating smugness. 'In the meantime I think it would be best if we provided these ladies with some *very* secure accommodation. Take them to the brig. Put them in separate cells.'

'They'll have to share a cell,' one of the guards replied. 'The other cell is currently occupied.'

'Very well,' Cypher said quickly, 'they may have the small pleasure of each other's company. Take them away.'

The guards obeyed immediately, tightening their already uncomfortable grip on the two girls and marching them away towards a hatch that led below.

'Keep an eye on those two,' the Contessa told Cypher. 'They're more dangerous than they might appear.'

'Aren't we all, Contessa?' Cypher replied, turning back towards her. 'You have done very well today, Maria. I could not have asked for more. I only wish I could have seen Nero's face when he realised that you were working for me. You have my sincere thanks.'

'You can save your gratitude, Cypher,' the Contessa replied. 'You know that I expect to be well rewarded for my troubles.'

'Oh, don't worry, Maria. By the end of the day I will be in a position to give you anything you want. This is the dawning of a new era.'

The Contessa said nothing. There was a disturbing edge

of fanaticism to Cypher's tone all of a sudden. She told herself not to worry – after all she had worked with much more unbalanced people than Cypher in her time, and if push came to shove she'd just have to *take* what she was owed.

A man in a naval uniform walked up to them, saluting efficiently as Cypher turned to face him.

'Yes, Captain, what is it?'

'Your chopper is on the pad and all launchers are reporting ready, sir. Just give the word.'

Cypher looked at the island sitting less than a mile away.

'The word is given, Captain. The word is most definitely given.'

☣ ☣ ☣

The Shroud had picked up Cypher's ship on radar as soon as it dropped its thermoptic camouflage so Raven and Otto knew they were too late even before they could see the black battleship holding position just off the coast of the island. They had had no contact with H.I.V.E. since they had first left the ruins of Cypher's base, Raven had barely had time to warn H.I.V.E. about the ship that was on its way before the transmission had dissolved into static and now they all feared the worst.

'We're at full stealth,' the pilot reported. 'They have no

idea we're here, and judging by the number of active radar scans that thing's putting out we'd better stay that way if we don't want to end up on the wrong end of a SAM.'

'Can we get close enough to get on board without being detected?' Raven said with a frown. 'We have to stop Cypher before he has a chance to launch an attack.'

'It may be too late for that,' Otto said, looking up from a screen displaying a zoomed-in image of Cypher's ship. Multiple launch tubes could be seen rising from the deck and swivelling into firing positions, all pointing straight at H.I.V.E. Moments later the first salvo was launched. A barrage of missiles streaked away from the launchers, impacting on the side of the island's central volcanic peak only seconds later. Curiously, there were no explosions, just small clouds of dust where each missile had landed. Otto manipulated the surveillance camera mounted in the nose of the Shroud to focus on one of the impact sites. As the dust cleared the long white body of the missile could be clearly seen, lying still intact amongst the rocks.

Suddenly a panel on the missile was blown off and a familiar black shape climbed from the shell. It was one of Cypher's robotic assassins. Otto quickly focused on another one of the impact sites, where exactly the same thing was happening, the missile disgorging its lethal passenger. At the same time another wave of missiles was launched from the ship, impacting all over the nearest face of the island. The first wave of robots was already scaling the sides of the volcano like ants, heading upwards at frightening speed towards the crater entrance.

'Forget the ship,' Raven said, a grim look on her face. 'We've got to get inside H.I.V.E. *now*.'

☣ ☣ ☣

The Chief looked at the guard to his left, the worry tinged with fear on his face summing up the feelings of the other guards positioned around the crater. As soon as Cypher's ship had appeared Nero had given the order for all security teams to protect H.I.V.E.'s points of entry. The Contessa had sealed all of the conventional weapons lockers so they had little more than the Sleepers that units on patrol had been carrying to defend themselves. The Chief just hoped it would be enough. There were only a couple of external cameras that were functional so they had little idea what Cypher was going to throw at them, but he was determined that nothing was going to make it past him and his men.

The Chief looked up at the bright circle of daylight overhead formed by the crater's edge. For a fleeting moment he thought that he could detect movement but it may just have been a trick of the light. He reached for the tiny pair of binoculars that were attached to his equipment harness and quickly focused on the rocks far overhead. There were definitely several people up there, gathering at the lip of the crater. They were dressed all in black and they moved with a surprising speed and agility. He thought back to Raven's report on the attack on the Tokyo safe house and quickly realised that these must be more of the same ninjas that had attacked her there. Well, they were ready for them this time and the assassins would find that H.I.V.E. itself was a considerably harder target than some local safe house. The assassins were going to have to rappel down to the landing pad from the top of the volcano and that would make them sitting ducks for him and his men.

Suddenly, one of the black figures far overhead seemed to simply leap into the void, tumbling down towards the Chief and his men. He must have slipped and fallen, the Chief thought to himself as he watched the man drop. At least that was one less of them to worry about. The Chief looked away as the assassin hit the hard steel of the landing deck; he'd seen many disturbing things in his lifetime but a drop from that height was never a pretty sight. Then he heard a couple of gasps and half-yelled comments from his men as the assassin who had hit the ground simply stood up from the crouch in which he had landed and slowly surveyed the room. It was impossible. The Chief had known some well-trained operatives over the years, but no one could survive a fall from that height, no one. He looked more closely at the armoured assassin and it quickly became clear that they were not dealing with any normal assault here. The assassin was a machine, its design way in advance of anything else he had seen.

'Open fire!' the Chief yelled, and was immediately drowned out by the loud zapping reports of multiple Sleepers being fired all around him. To say that the Sleeper pulses were ineffective would have been something of an understatement – the assassin didn't even falter, just slowly surveyed its surroundings, the glowing red sensory array on the front of its insectile face taking in every detail.

The Chief knew a scout when he saw one and also knew that this robot was probably just reporting back to the others above on the positions and strength of the defenders.

'What do we do, Chief?' the man to his left yelled desperately above the sounds of Sleepers firing. 'That thing's not even slowing down; the Sleepers aren't working.'

The Chief suddenly understood why the Contessa had only sealed the conventional weapons lockers when she had overridden the security system. Cypher's forces clearly had nothing to fear from Sleepers.

'What I wouldn't give for a good old-fashioned grenade right now,' the Chief muttered to himself.

There was another sudden thunderous clanging sound

as half a dozen more of the assassins landed on the steel decking. The moment they landed they unleashed a blizzard of whirring shuriken, the deadly throwing stars finding their targets unerringly, sending several of the Chief's men toppling to the ground. The Chief felt a cold dread descending over him. They were hopelessly outgunned, but they couldn't let these things take the crater; if they did there would be no stopping them.

A sudden wind seemed to rise from nowhere and the Chief quickly glanced out past the rock behind which he had taken cover to see what was happening. The assassins still stood in a tight circle in the centre of the landing pad, launching the occasional shuriken at any of the H.I.V.E. guards who were unfortunate enough to find themselves in an exposed position. One of the assassins head's snapped round and focused on the Chief, its arm rising to launch a throwing star at him.

It never got the chance.

Suddenly the group of robots seemed to crumple as if a huge weight was crushing them to the ground. In just a split second they were reduced to a sparking pile of crushed and mangled components, the occasional twitching servo the only indication of any life. There was a shimmer in the air and the huge black shape of a Shroud materialised directly on top of the ruined attackers. The hatch at the back of the aircraft blew off with a loud bang, flying across the cavern, and Raven stepped out.

'Chief, pull your men back now. You don't have a chance against these things,' Raven yelled as Otto Malpense and the Shroud's pilot leapt down from the aircraft behind her.

'Nero said we had to hold the crater at all costs,' the Chief said quickly as Raven approached.

'Nero hasn't gone toe-to-toe with one of these things,' Raven replied impatiently. 'If you stay here you die, simple as that.'

The Chief knew better than to argue with Raven's tactical appraisal of a situation. Besides he may not have wanted to admit it, but he knew she was right. He looked up and saw more tiny black figures massing on the edge of the crater above. They were out of options.

'Fall back!' the Chief yelled, ordering his men back through the enormous blast doors that were the only way into or out of the crater. They did not need to be told twice – the sight of these invulnerable assassins cutting down their team mates with such apparent ease had been enough to persuade most of them of the wisdom of a tactical withdrawal.

'Can we seal the doors?' Raven asked as they dashed towards the exit.

'There's enough charge in the back-up batteries to close them, but once they're closed they're staying closed.

There won't be enough juice to open them again, thanks to the Contessa,' the Chief replied.

'What do you mean, thanks to the Contessa?' Raven asked quickly.

'I think you need to speak to Nero,' the Chief replied as they passed through the doorway and the huge steel doors slowly rumbled shut.

⊛⊛⊛

The assassin robot shoved Laura hard in the back, propelling her forward into the dingy cell. Shelby was right behind her, falling to the deck as she too was pushed inside, the heavy door swinging shut with a worryingly solid clunk. They watched through the bars as the two mechanical henchmen walked silently away, leaving them alone.

'Well, this isn't good,' Laura said with a sigh, surveying the cramped, featureless cell.

'Laura Brand, the world's greatest master of understatement, ladies and gentlemen,' Shelby replied sarcastically, sitting down on one of the cell's two tiny beds.

'I can't believe the Contessa's involved with this,' Laura said gloomily as she sat down on the bed opposite Shelby.

'Well, she is,' Shelby replied, staring at the cell door.

'Aye,' Laura replied sadly. 'She fooled everybody: us, Nero, and by the looks of it Francisco too.'

'Yeah, it looks like the Colonel didn't have much say in the whole "helping the Contessa" thing,' Shelby said, sounding slightly distracted.

'She must have been using him for months,' Laura said, 'to implant commands so deeply that he carries them out without question. We've both felt what it's like to have the Contessa hijack your brainstem, but it fades quickly after she's gone. She must have spent a long time preparing him for this.'

'I don't understand what that old witch does but I'll tell you one thing, it's going to take a whole lot more than a few words to stop me from punching her lights out the next time I see her,' Shelby replied, picking at the toe of her shoe.

'What are you doing?' Laura asked, watching in bemusement as Shelby tugged at a loose flap of rubber on the toe of her shoe.

'We're getting out of here,' Shelby said quietly.

'That would be nice,' said Laura, 'but something tells me we're going to need more than the old one of us falling ill trick to get us out of here.'

'Oh, come on,' Shelby replied with a smile, 'that's a classic. Never fails.'

'I take it you have a plan, then?' Laura replied curiously.

'Better than that,' Shelby said with a grin, peeling the sole off her right shoe. 'I have a key.'

Inside the sole of Shelby's shoe was a full set of tiny tools and lockpicks. Laura knew she really shouldn't be surprised; after all Shelby had been the Wraith – the world's most notorious and successful jewel thief before being forcibly inducted into H.I.V.E.

'Don't tell me that you walk round all day with that lot in your shoe,' Laura said with a chuckle.

'Don't leave home without it,' Shelby replied with a broad grin.

Shelby walked up to the bars at the front of the cell and quickly glanced down the corridor leading to the cells. Seeing no one there she turned her attention to the lock and after a few seconds let out a long sigh.

'What's wrong?' Laura asked anxiously.

'This is a Johnson and Fort, floating barrel, nine pin, spring-leaf security lock,' Shelby said quietly. 'Almost impossible to bypass.'

'Great,' Laura said as Shelby turned back to the lock. 'So now what are we going to do? There's no other way out of here and I for one don't just want to sit here and wait for Cypher's scheme to play out, whatever he's –'

There was a tiny click and the cell door swung open.

'I only said *almost* impossible,' Shelby grinned.

'OK,' Laura said in amazement, 'the next time they serve chocolate ice cream at dinner, you can have mine too.'

'You say that now, Brand, but it'll be a different story

when the time comes,' Shelby said, slipping her hidden tools into her pocket.

'Oh, don't worry, this time you've really earned it,' Laura said, grinning.

Shelby stepped silently into the corridor. There were no signs of any guards – Cypher obviously thought the brig was a lot more secure than it actually was.

'Coast is clear,' Shelby whispered. 'Let's go.'

The two girls crept down the corridor. They were just passing the other cell door when Laura suddenly stopped.

'There's somebody in there,' Laura whispered. Lying cuffed to the bed in the cell was a figure wearing simple black pyjamas with a hood over its head.

'So?' Shelby replied. 'In case you hadn't noticed we're trying to escape here.'

'Think about it,' Laura said quietly. 'If Cypher's locked them up in here we should help them – the enemy of my enemy is my friend and all that.'

'Right, but what if they're locked up for a good reason?' Shelby replied. 'The last thing we need is another murderous psychopath running around on the loose.'

'It can't hurt to talk to them,' Laura said quickly. 'Look, they're cuffed to the bed. Worst comes to worst we just leave them there.'

'OK, OK, but if that's Hannibal Lecter in there I'm holding you responsible,' Shelby said with a sigh. She pulled her tools back out of her pocket and quickly bypassed the lock on the cell, the door swinging open with a creak.

Laura walked up to the figure shackled to the bed and hesitated for a moment. Shelby might be right, this could be just someone that Cypher considered dangerous. Then she took a deep breath and scolded herself for being so timid. It couldn't hurt to see what they looked like at any rate. She reached down and pulled the black hood off the prisoner's head.

Laura gasped, the hood falling from her limp fingers.

'Oh my God,' Shelby hissed. 'Wing!'

Lying there on the bed was their friend who they had both so recently grieved for. Laura looked as if she had, quite literally, seen a ghost. Shelby reached down and placed her hand on Wing's chest, feeling it rise and fall, with tears in her eyes.

'He's alive,' Shelby whispered.

'Wing!' Laura said urgently. 'Wake up!'

Wing did not stir even when she shook his shoulder. This was no natural sleep; he'd been sedated.

'So what do we do now?' Shelby said, disbelief still evident in her voice. 'It's not like we can carry him out of here.' She quickly set to work on the cuffs holding him to the bed; they were child's play to her and she had released them within seconds.

'Wing!' Laura shouted, shaking him again, suddenly not caring if anyone could hear them.

'Here, let me try,' Shelby said, gently pushing Laura to one side.

'Sorry about this,' she said softly to Wing and slapped him hard across the face.

Wing stirred for the briefest of moments, mumbling something, and then settled back into his previous state of unconsciousness.

'Come on, big guy,' Shelby said quietly. 'Don't make me do that again.'

Wing showed no further signs of waking and Shelby raised her hand, swinging it down to slap his face again. Wing's hand moved in a blur, snapping into the air like a striking snake and catching Shelby's wrist a split second before she made contact with his cheek. Laura gasped, and Shelby almost jumped out of her skin.

'If I am dreaming, why does my face hurt so much?' Wing said croakily.

Shelby gave a tiny sob and hugged Wing hard. The grief that had still been so fresh and raw fell away, replaced with a joy deeper than she had ever felt before. Hot tears rolled down her cheeks as she clung on to him, fearing that he might vanish in a puff of smoke if she ever let him go.

# chapter fifteen

Nero's expression changed from one of deep concern to relief as Otto and Raven entered the command centre with the Chief. There had been precious little in the way of good news over the past few hours and seeing the pair of them alive, if slightly ragged, made a welcome change.

'Natalya,' Nero said with a nod, 'it's good to have you back, and I see that you even managed to get Malpense back in one piece. I wish I could welcome you both back under more auspicious circumstances.'

'The guards don't stand a chance against Cypher's forces, Max,' Raven replied. 'They're robots, quite unlike anything I have seen before, unstoppable and lethal.'

'Yes,' Nero replied – that much had been obvious from the short and decidedly one-sided battle in the crater – 'but we have to stop them. Cypher cannot be allowed to take control of this facility. What's your assessment, Chief?'

'It's not good, sir,' the Chief said quickly. 'We've sealed the external blast doors but that's pretty much all we could do. It'll slow them down, but not much more than that. The Contessa's override has left us with almost no control over the security and defence systems.'

'The Contessa?' Raven asked. 'What has she done?'

Nero quickly explained the depths of the Contessa's betrayal to Raven, how she had not only handed them to Cypher in Tokyo but also left the school defenceless against his current assault.

'Leave her to me,' Raven said coldly.

'Once this is all over, Natalya, you may feel free to hunt her to the ends of the earth, but for now we have far more pressing concerns. I'm not interested in just slowing Cypher's forces down, I want them driven back into the sea,' Nero said firmly.

'Max, I found it extremely hard to defeat one of those things in a straight fight,' Raven said, 'and Cypher has an army of them. We can't hope to just drive them back, it's impossible.'

'That's not entirely true,' Otto said quietly.

'You have something in mind, Mr Malpense?' Nero said.

'It's just an idea,' Otto replied, 'but I need to speak to the Professor first.'

'Very well,' Nero said with a sigh, 'I don't suppose it can

do any harm at this point. Raven, would you be so good as to escort Mr Malpense to the science and technology department, the Professor is there trying to bring H.I.V.E.mind back online at the moment. Oh, before you go, Natalya, there is one more thing . . .'

Nero ushered Raven to a quiet corner of the command centre and they had a brief conversation before Nero put something in her hand. Raven looked at Nero for a moment and then nodded. The pair of them walked back towards Otto, Raven gesturing for him to follow her out of the room.

Nero listened to the urgent chatter that was coming over the security team's radios. He doubted that Malpense had really come up with something that would derail Cypher's plans, but as things stood they had no chance. They needed an edge badly and if Otto Malpense could give them that then perhaps they might have a little hope after all.

☻☻☻

The huge transport helicopter landed gently on the crater pad, the dozens of Cypher's mechanical assassins that had already entered the crater forming a protective cordon around it. Cypher stepped down from the helicopter and surveyed the scene with satisfaction. So far everything was going according to plan. It was now just a matter of time before he had full control of H.I.V.E., and once he did no one could stop him.

A technician ran up to him and reported breathlessly. 'We've tried the standard cutting equipment on the blast doors, sir, and we've barely made a scratch. It could take hours to get inside that way.'

'Then it is fortunate that we brought along a more effective method,' Cypher said casually, glancing over at the two large crates that the helicopter had winched down on to the pad just a couple of minutes earlier. 'Are they ready?'

'Yes, sir,' the technician replied, glancing down at the tablet computer he was carrying. 'The power-up cycle is complete and all system checks are showing green lights. They're good to go.'

'Excellent. There is no reason to delay, then. Let's get this over with,' Cypher said, pulling a small black remote control from his inside pocket. He pointed the control at the pair of crates and pressed a button. The front panel of each crate slowly lowered forward and after a moment a familiar array of red lights lit up the gloom in each one. With a heavy thud the first of the giant assassin robots stepped out of its crate. They were of the same design as the one that Cypher had pitted against Raven, and if one had been enough to deal with her then he saw no reason why he should need more than two to take H.I.V.E.

The behemoths stomped towards Cypher, each step sending a tiny tremor through the floor, and stood neatly in front of him.

'Awaiting orders,' the machine on the left said in its harsh mechanical voice.

'That door,' Cypher said, pointing at the sealed blast door. 'Remove it.'

'Understood,' the robot replied, and both the machines turned and walked towards the door.

There was no subtlety in their approach as the huge robots began pounding on the door with their enormous wrecking-ball fists. Almost immediately the door started to dent and become deformed and after just a couple of minutes it began to slowly buckle under the relentless hammering. The noise was deafening.

'Give the order for the assault units to gather here. Once those doors come down we go in hard,' Cypher said to the technician, raising his voice slightly to be heard over the noise of the robots assaulting the door.

'What are your orders should we encounter defensive forces?' the technician asked nervously.

'Kill anyone who resists,' Cypher said calmly.

☢☢☢

Nigel had stopped worrying about security patrols. He and Franz had encountered several squads on their way to the library but none of them had stopped and questioned them on why they were outside of their accommodation block. In fact they looked as if they had altogether more pressing concerns, judging by the looks of fear on some of their faces. Oh yes, Nigel had stopped worrying about the security guards – now he was too busy worrying about whatever it was that had them frightened.

The two boys walked down another deserted corridor, only dimly lit by the emergency power that was sustaining H.I.V.E.

'It's quiet . . .' Franz said.

'If you say "too quiet" now I'll never speak to you again,' Nigel said quickly.

'You are having the hornet in your hat about something,' Franz said, looking fed up.

'It's bee in your bonnet, and yes, I am worried. Why has every security patrol we've seen been running somewhere and why are they all too busy to care what we're doing?' Nigel asked.

'I am not sure, but I am guessing that it has something to do with the alarms,' Franz said, nodding wisely.

The fact that alarm sirens were still wailing throughout the base did suggest to Nigel that whatever was wrong was very serious and that it was still an ongoing problem.

'Perhaps we should be heading back to the accommodation area,' Franz said nervously. 'I am thinking that under the circumstances it might be safer than . . . ummmmf.'

Franz was cut off in mid-sentence by Nigel's hand over his mouth. Franz looked at his roommate with surprise and confusion but Nigel just raised a single finger to his lips and pointed towards the far end of the corridor. There, in the gloom, they could just make out the unmistakeable figures of Colonel Francisco, Block and Tackle. Nigel may not have known much about the current situation but Laura and Shelby had told him enough to know that Francisco was supposed to be in a cell and that security had been combing H.I.V.E., searching for Block and Tackle. They certainly weren't supposed to be freely wandering the corridors of the school.

Nigel and Franz ducked back into the cover of a nearby classroom doorway and watched as the three fugitives stopped for a moment, appearing to engage in a whispered conversation before heading down another adjoining corridor. Nigel quietly pulled out his Blackbox and flipped it open, only to find, to his dismay, that it was dead, displaying just two words: 'H.I.V.E.mind offline'.

'Come on,' said Nigel, starting off down the corridor after them.

'Where are you going?' Franz said plaintively.

'I'm going to follow them, of course,' Nigel replied.

'Now why would you want to do that?' Franz said, disbelief in his voice. 'We should just find a security patrol and tell them.'

'By the time we find a patrol and bring them back here those three will be long gone. We've got to follow them to wherever they're going and then we find the guards,' Nigel explained impatiently.

'I am thinking that I am going to be regretting this,' Franz said with a sigh. 'Come on, then.'

Nigel set off down the corridor as quietly as he could, but Franz held back just for a moment.

'Too quiet,' he whispered to himself.

☸ ☸ ☸

'And then I was awoken by someone slapping me in the face,' Wing said with a half-smile.

'Yeah, again, sorry about that,' Shelby said with a sheepish grin.

'So you woke up in Cypher's base and you had no idea what had happened?' Laura asked.

'None at all, my last memory was of the rooftop in Tokyo, so as you can imagine I was somewhat surprised to wake up at all,' Wing explained.

'No kidding,' Shelby said. 'Everyone just assumed you were dead.'

'Indeed, I believe that was the intention,' Wing replied. 'Judging by the small puncture wound in my chest it seems that Cypher's gun was loaded with some form of tranquiliser projectile that was designed to give the appearance of a lethal shot.'

'And you only spoke to him twice?' Laura asked.

'Yes, once when I first awoke and he assured me that no harm would come to me as long as I cooperated and didn't make any trouble,' Wing said calmly, 'and the second when he told me that I was being taken aboard a ship. The fact that I had not paid very much attention to his initial instruction to cooperate led to me being sedated for the transfer to the ship. That is really all I remember.'

Laura suddenly looked lost in thought.

'Is there something troubling you, Laura?' Wing asked softly.

'Aye, why didn't Cypher just kill you? Don't get me wrong, I'm very glad he didn't,' she hastily added, 'but why go to all of the trouble of faking your death and then bringing you along on an operation like this? It all just seems needlessly risky, and if there's one thing that we have learnt about Cypher over the past couple of days it's that he's not afraid of spilling blood to get what he wants.'

'I had wondered the very same thing myself,' Wing replied, 'but I'm afraid I can offer no logical explanation for Cypher's actions. What I do know is that we must stop him at all costs. From the hints he did drop when he spoke to me it was clear that this is his endgame. I shudder to think of what he might do if he takes H.I.V.E.'

285

'Which is why we need to get off this boat,' Shelby said firmly, 'and the sooner the better.'

'Agreed,' Wing said. 'You must tell me something first though. Is Otto OK?' He seemed to be expecting the worst.

'The last we heard he was fine,' said Shelby, 'and I'm guessing that he's going to be very pleased to see you.'

'That is good to hear,' Wing said with obvious relief. 'Cypher never gave any specifics but from the way he talked about it I feared that I might be the only survivor of the safe house.'

'You very nearly were,' Laura explained, 'but by the sounds of things Raven managed to get Otto and herself out of there in one piece.'

'That is the first good news I have had for some time,' Wing said with a smile, 'but now we must go before someone comes along to check that we're all still safely locked up.'

'You OK to walk?' Shelby asked as Wing, somewhat unsteadily, got to his feet.

Wing suddenly realised something was missing. His hand flew to his chest and through the thin fabric of the pyjamas he was wearing he felt nothing but his own breastbone. His amulet was gone. In his mind's eye he saw his mother handing him the tiny talisman, telling him that he must never let it fall into the wrong hands. He could make a reasonably good guess who had taken it. He had no idea what use Cypher could possibly have for it but he knew somehow that it was vital he retrieved it.

'You sure you're OK? You looked miles away for a second there,' Laura said, her brow furrowing with concern.

'I shall be fine, just the after-effects of the sedation,' Wing said. 'Let's go.'

⊛ ⊛ ⊛

Otto and Raven walked into the science and technology department to find a scene of chaos. Technicians were running around the room in a frantic flurry of activity, carrying piles of paper, pushing trolleys full of equipment, hunched over the various computer terminals dotted around the room. They all wore the same expression of panic.

Sitting at a terminal at the far end of the room was Professor Pike. He seemed almost to be in a trance as his hand flew across the keyboards, entering strings of commands.

'Professor,' Raven said as they approached him. Getting no response she raised her voice. 'Professor!'

The Professor suddenly snapped out of his trance and stared at Otto and Raven. For a moment he looked as if he didn't recognise them but then he focused and a smile spread across his face.

'Aah, Raven and Mr Malpense. It's good you're not dead,' he said, still smiling.

'Yes, we were quite pleased about that too,' Otto said drily.

'No, I mean it's useful,' the Professor continued. 'I needed to speak to you both.'

'Well, here we are,' Raven said impatiently. She had no love for the technical department. She was no scientist and her definition of exciting technology was something that worked reliably and might save her life.

'Yes, Mr Malpense, would you be so kind as to have a look at this for me,' the Professor said, gesturing towards the terminal at which he had been working. Otto moved to the terminal and looked at the screen. It seemed that the Professor had been trying to break an encryption routine.

'What is this?' Otto asked.

'That is the encryption that is protecting the Contessa's unauthorised control of the security network,' the Professor explained. 'I'm afraid that I'm struggling to make any impression on it and I wondered what you thought.'

Flattered as Otto was by the fact that the Professor wanted to consult him about this he wasn't sure how much help he could offer. He was good with computers, no doubt about that, but this sort of thing was more

Laura's speciality.

'You should get Laura to look at this,' Otto said, not looking away from the screen, 'she's the one who cracks encryption in her head.'

'Yes, that would have been my first choice, but since Miss Brand has been kidnapped by the Contessa it wasn't possible.'

'What?' Otto said, loudly enough to set several heads around the room swivelling in their direction.

'I assumed you knew,' the Professor said matter of factly. 'The Contessa has taken her and Miss Trinity to Cypher's ship. Had no one told you?'

'No, they had not,' Otto said, feeling a familiar anger rising in his chest. Cypher and the Contessa had a great deal to pay for.

'So,' the Professor said, gesturing at the terminal again, 'any thoughts?'

Otto looked again at the encrypted code on the screen. He was no expert on encryption but he knew enough to see that whoever had put this together was very good. The encryption was sophisticated and multilayered, specifically designed to counter any attempts at cracking it.

'It's very good,' Otto said after a couple of minutes. 'Highly sophisticated. Whoever wrote this knew exactly what they were doing.'

'Ah . . . yes, well, you see, that's the slightly embarrassing part of all this,' the Professor said quietly. 'You see . . . well . . . um . . . I wrote it.'

Otto looked at the Professor with an expression of total confusion.

'So why can't you decrypt it?' Otto asked.

'Well, let's just say that I had an encounter with the Contessa before I wrote it, and I wasn't feeling quite myself,' he said with an apologetic smile.

'Great,' Raven sighed. 'Am I the only one around here who hasn't had that witch inside my head?'

'Surely H.I.V.E.mind could crack it,' Otto said.

'Yes, he probably could, but he's offline right now, again thanks to the Contessa,' the Professor explained.

'And I take it that there's no way to bring him back up in time?' Otto said, knowing that what he had in mind was very much dependant on H.I.V.E.'s resident super-computer being fully functional.

'Well, there is a way, but it's far too risky under the current circumstances,' the Professor said. A full hard-ware reset would clear any encryption surrounding H.I.V.E.mind's command routines, but with the mess that our systems are in at the moment there's every chance that we'll just lose what few basic systems we do still have control of,' the Professor explained. 'And it can only be done from H.I.V.E.'s data hub – there's no remote access for that kind of thing.'

'So we've got to switch H.I.V.E.mind off and back on again,' Raven said, trying to boil the idea down to its essentials. 'Well, it usually works with my computer.'

'Unfortunately H.I.V.E.mind is rather more sophisticated than that. There's a good reason that we've never done this before – there are no guarantees that he would ever work again,' the Professor continued.

'I'd say that at the moment that falls into the "chance we'll have to take" category,' Otto said, looking again at the apparently impregnable encryption that was surrounding H.I.V.E.mind's systems.

'Yes, I suppose you're right,' the Professor said. 'Doctor Nero did tell me to do everything necessary to bring our systems back online.'

'I'll escort you to the hub,' Raven said. 'Otto, you stay here.'

'Actually, it would be helpful if Mr Malpense came with us,' the Professor said. 'Resetting the system is complicated and an extra pair of hands would be useful. No offence, Raven, but I doubt that you would be as much help, and time is of the essence here.'

If Raven was offended she gave no sign of it, she just shook her head.

'Too dangerous. If Cypher's machines get inside the school I want Malpense somewhere relatively safe, not running around the corridors. I'd rather keep him with me, but if we encounter more than one of those things I can't guarantee to protect either of you.'

'Actually,' the Professor said, 'that's why I wanted to speak to you, Raven. I have something that might help with that.'

Raven raised a single eyebrow as the Professor gestured for her to follow him across to another workbench. Lying on the bench, surrounded by discarded components and hastily scribbled notes, were a pair of katanas, much like Raven's own swords but with jet-black blades.

'Thanks, Professor, but I'm rather attached to the girls,' Raven said, putting one hand on the hilt of one of the swords that rested in crossed sheaths on her back. 'I'm not looking for replacements.'

'Let me give you a quick demonstration and see if you still feel the same,' the Professor said with a mischievous grin. He pressed a stud on the hilt of one of the swords and tossed it to Raven, who caught it neatly. The sword was light and well-balanced but what was most intriguing was the faint trace of crackling dark purple energy that could be seen flickering along its striking edge.

'I designed these after the staff in the physical training section complained that you were getting through rather too many wooden kendo swords during your training sessions. The energy field that you can see is a variable geometry projected force field.'

'English please, Professor,' Raven said, sweeping the sword slowly through the air.

'Well, the sword has a normal blade as one would expect, but the force field that it is projecting can change its shape in a number of ways,' the Professor explained, picking up the other black sword. 'So, if for example you simply want to use it in practice combat you use this setting.' He pressed another stud on the hilt of the blade and ran the blade of the sword across the palm of his hand. There was no gush of blood, in fact there was no mark at all on his palm.

'As you can see, in this configuration the blade is quite blunt, ideal for practice or for simply subduing an opponent without serious injury, but in its other setting . . . well . . . it's slightly different.' The Professor picked up a metal ball from the workbench. 'Raven, if you would be so kind.'

The Professor tossed the ball into the air and Raven struck, the blade almost whining as it passed through the air before striking the ball and neatly slicing it into two perfect halves. A broad grin spread across Raven's face.

'That ball was solid titanium,' the Professor said proudly. 'In that configuration the projected force field gives the blade a mono-molecular cutting edge. In layman's terms, there's almost nothing it can't cut through.'

'I could have used these in Tokyo,' Raven said,

sweeping the blade through the air.

'I know, and if I'd had the slightest inkling of what was going to happen I would have issued them to you before you left. Now, though, that might just give you an edge, if you'll pardon the pun.'

Raven suddenly felt that the playing field that they were all on was a little bit more level than it had been before. She pulled the twin swords from the sheaths on her back and placed them gently on the workbench, replacing them quickly with the new ebony blades. She turned to Otto and the Professor, a new look of determination on her face.

'OK, let's get you two to the data hub before I change my mind.'

# chapter sixteen

Wing peered cautiously round the corner. The corridor was empty and at the far end he could see daylight pouring down through an open hatch.

'I think I can see an exit ahead,' he said calmly, ducking back round the corner.

'Great. I'm getting sick of running around below decks on this thing, it's like a maze,' Shelby said with relief.

'Come on,' Wing said and walked silently down the new corridor, heading for the hatch. Suddenly another thunderous roar came from overhead. As Wing, Laura and Shelby had carefully made their way up through the ship they had heard this noise several times.

The ship itself seemed to be almost deserted. They had seen and hidden from a couple of guards but they had been human, dressed in a nondescript naval uniform and clearly distracted by some sort of major operation that was going on. The fact that there were no wailing alarms or aggressive search parties suggested that their absence from the brig had not yet been noticed. Clearly whatever was going on was much more important than keeping a close watch on their prisoners.

Wing slowly climbed the steps leading up to the deck hatch. He could see blue sky overhead and it was the first time he'd felt the rays of the sun on his skin since the rooftop in Tokyo. It felt good. As he snuck a glance over the edge of the hatch he could immediately see what had been the source of the mysterious noise that they'd been hearing. Arranged in two neat rows on the rear half of the deck were a dozen missile launchers that were just having a new load of missiles automatically loaded. It only took a few seconds, the efficient mechanical loading system sliding home a batch of fat white missiles in just a few seconds before all the launchers swivelled back into position in perfect unison, pointing once again at the nearby island. Then with a roar all of the launchers fired at once, their warheads streaking away towards the island. Wing slowly surveyed the area around the hatch. It was clear of any guards and once again he found himself wondering why security was apparently so lax. He ducked back down into the corridor,

'The coast appears to be clear,' Wing said quietly, 'but this ship has the island under sustained bombardment. That noise is the missile launchers on the deck firing.'

Suddenly, one of the hatches in the corridor opened

and a guard carrying an assault rifle stepped out. His eyes widened as he saw the three escapees and he reacted quickly, raising the rifle, finger squeezing the trigger. Wing was faster. He jammed his stiffened fingertips into the guard's forearm, paralysing the limb and making it impossible for the man to pull the trigger. Wing leapt into the air, his foot arcing upwards and connecting with the guard's chin with a crack. The guard fell to his knees, his one good hand clutching his broken jaw. Wing stepped behind him, his forearm snaking around the man's neck, trapping him in an unbreakable stranglehold.

'Where's Cypher?' Wing hissed.

'Gone,' the guard gasped, the pain from his jaw preventing a more detailed answer.

'Gone where?' Wing said, his tone enough to freeze the blood.

'The island, he's on the island,' the man wheezed as he felt the pressure increase on his throat.

Wing squeezed harder for a moment and the guard collapsed in an unconscious heap to the ground.

'We have to get back to the island,' Wing said calmly, picking up the guard's assault rifle.

'Well, I know where we can find a boat,' Laura said with a grin. 'We'd just be returning the one that the Contessa borrowed.'

Wing ejected the magazine from the rifle and threw it

away down the corridor before throwing the rifle in the opposite direction.

'Shouldn't we have hung on to that?' Shelby said. 'It might have come in useful.'

'I dislike firearms,' Wing replied calmly. 'Graceless thugs' weapons.'

'I'd rather be a graceless thug than noble and dead,' Shelby said sarcastically.

Wing opened his mouth to respond but the sudden roar of the launchers on the deck above drowned out everything. The barrage to which H.I.V.E. was being subjected seemed relentless.

'We can't leave yet,' Laura said reluctantly. 'We have to try to disable this ship. H.I.V.E. has no chance while this thing is floating out here raining missiles down on the island.'

Wing knew that Laura was right, but at the same time he needed to find Cypher. He was not prone to letting his emotions control him but the burning anger he felt when he visualised that black glass mask was fierce and relentless. He had no idea what Cypher was hoping to achieve with his assault on the school, but he knew that he was going to stop him, or die trying.

'We must return to the island,' Wing replied. 'Once the situation there is resolved we can worry about this ship.'

'I know you want to go after him, Wing,' Laura said,

'but we have to do this first.'

'Or we could just do both,' Shelby said, knowing that if Wing and Laura started to argue it would just be a competition to see who could be most stubborn. A very long, very boring competition that they really didn't have time for right now.

'What do you propose?' Wing asked.

'Well, why don't you take the boat back to the island and we'll stay here and try to disable this thing,' Shelby said.

'Splitting up seems ill advised at this point,' Wing said calmly.

'Maybe, but what other choice do we have? And besides, what makes you think we'd need your help anyway?' Shelby said with a grin.

'Very well,' Wing replied after a moment's thought, 'though I am still not sure this is a good idea.'

'Hey, dumb plans are our speciality,' Shelby replied with a chuckle. 'Isn't that right, Brand?'

'Oh aye, we specialise in the stupid,' Laura replied.

'I hope you both understand,' Wing said, a cold, hard determination in his voice, 'Cypher has to pay for what he's done and I intend to be the one who finishes this.'

Shelby gently placed a hand on Wing's cheek.

'You know, you're kinda cute when you're angry,' she said softly.

'Then at this precise moment I can honestly say that I am cuter than I have ever been before,' Wing replied and turned to head back up on to the deck.

'Be safe,' Laura said as he climbed the steps to the deck.

'You too,' Wing replied and he vanished from view through the hatch.

'So, you got any thoughts on how we do this?' Shelby asked Laura.

'Not the faintest idea,' Laura replied with a crooked smile.

☢ ☢ ☢

Cypher watched as the battered crater blast doors finally gave way under the relentless assault of his hulking robots and collapsed inwards with a thundering crash. He walked forward, picking his way through the twisted remains of the doors, and climbed the long flight of black granite stairs. The two giant assault robots followed him, their heads swivelling from side to side as their sensory arrays scanned for any sign of danger.

Cypher reached the top of the stairs and stepped into H.I.V.E.'s main entrance chamber. There, standing alone in front of a giant statue depicting the GLOVE symbol was Nero. He stood with his hands clasped behind his back, his expression calm. If he felt any fear there was no hint of it.

'I must admit, I was expecting rather more resistance than this,' Cypher said as he approached.

'I saw no reason why any more lives should be lost to your madness,' Nero replied, his voice calm.

'Defiant to the last,' Cypher said. 'So typical of you.'

'In much the same way as this bloodthirsty lunacy is typical of you,' Nero replied. 'You can't hope to get away with this.'

'I rather think that you'll find that I already have,' Cypher said, stepping closer to Nero.

'G.L.O.V.E. will not stand for this,' Nero replied. 'You may have taken H.I.V.E. but it will be the last mistake you ever make.'

'Your naive faith in our peers is inspiring,' Cypher said sarcastically, 'but it is G.L.O.V.E. that should fear me.'

'You aren't the first to think that, Cypher,' Nero said, a sudden hard edge to his voice, 'but you're the only one who's still alive. Number One has made quite sure of that.'

'Ever the faithful lapdog,' Cypher replied with a snort, 'but do you really think that I don't know what you and Number One are doing? What he has planned?'

For the briefest of moments a puzzled expression appeared on Nero's face.

'What are you talking about?' Nero asked.

'Feigning ignorance will get you nowhere, Nero. This ends today. I have everything I need now to make sure that Number One will cease to be a concern and then we shall see if G.L.O.V.E. is so ready to leap to the defence of you and your school.'

'You really are insane, aren't you?' Nero replied calmly.

'Do you know how many times throughout history those who have defined the shape of the future have been dismissed as madmen?' Cypher asked.

'You have no future,' Nero said coldly.

'Then that makes two of us,' Cypher replied, reaching inside his coat and pulling out a razor-sharp stiletto blade. The two hulking assault robots took up positions on either side of Nero, each taking firm hold of his arms.

'Get it over with,' Nero said defiantly. 'Killing is what you do best after all.'

'Oh, I'm not going to kill you, Nero. Not yet, anyway. I want you alive to bear witness to my final victory. I can imagine no greater torment for someone like you,' Cypher said.

Cypher brought the tip of the blade to Nero's chest and neatly sliced the top couple of buttons off his shirt-front. Using the tip of the blade he pushed the shirt open, exposing Nero's bare chest.

'Where is it?' Cypher said, his previously controlled tone suddenly dripping with venom.

'Where is what?' Nero said calmly.

'You know perfectly well what I mean. The amulet,

where is it?' Cypher spat, clearly becoming angry.

'I really have no idea what you're talking about,' Nero replied casually.

'I should have known that you wouldn't do this the easy way,' Cypher replied. 'So be it.'

Cypher turned to the giant assault robot next to him.

'Unit three, go to the nearest pupil accommodation area. Leave no one alive.'

'Order acknowledged,' the robot replied in its grating mechanical voice and turned to leave.

Nero felt a sudden rush of panic. He knew better than to hope that Cypher was bluffing. From all he knew of the man there was no reason to believe that he had any qualms about having the blood of so many children on his hands.

'Wait!' Nero half shouted.

'You have something to tell me?' Cypher said angrily.

'Raven. Raven has it,' Nero said sadly.

'Don't lie to me, Nero. Raven is dead,' Cypher spat. 'I saw to that personally.'

'Well, it seems that you may have underestimated her talent for survival,' Nero replied. 'You aren't the first and I doubt very much you'll be the last.'

'Where is she?' Cypher said. 'Tell me or there are going to be a lot of grieving parents in the very near future.'

'I honestly have no idea,' Nero said truthfully. She had

not reported in since leaving with Malpense and by now she could be anywhere on the island. Cypher studied Nero's face, looking for any hint of deception.

'Unit three, stand down,' Cypher said and the robot he had despatched on the murderous errand just moments before halted.

Nero felt a wave of relief wash over him; his students were safe, for now.

'If you're lying to me, Nero, I shall not hesitate to reissue that order. Do you understand me?' Cypher asked coldly.

'Perfectly,' Nero replied.

Cypher pulled a small communications device from his pocket and spoke quickly into it.

'This is Cypher to all assassin units. Institute a full search sweep of this facility. Your target is the operative codenamed Raven. Use of lethal force is authorised.'

Behind Cypher dozens of the smaller assassin robots poured up the stairs, fanning out in all directions, beginning their search for Raven.

☺ ☺ ☺

'What the hell?'

'What is it?' the captain of Cypher's ship demanded, striding over to the radar operator's station.

'The boat that the Contessa arrived in has just

undocked. It's heading back towards the island,' the crewmember reported.

The captain grabbed a pair of binoculars and hurried to one of the large armoured windows that surrounded the bridge. He quickly spotted the tiny black boat, powering away across the waves towards H.I.V.E. He recognised the figure at the controls immediately.

'I have a firing resolution – should I launch?' the weapons officer asked quickly.

'No, it's the Fanchu boy,' the captain replied. 'Cypher gave very specific orders that he was not to be harmed.'

'Fanchu's alive?' the Contessa said, stepping out of the shadows at the rear of the bridge.

'Yes, but he's supposed to be under sedation in the brig. How the hell did he get loose?' the captain demanded.

'More to the point, how did he get past the guards in the brig?' the Contessa asked.

'There are no guards in the brig,' the captain replied. 'The cells are escape-proof and I can't spare the manpower to have guards on watch constantly when it's not necessary.'

'Captain,' the Contessa said quietly, 'one of the two girls who was also locked up down there is perhaps the most accomplished thief on earth. There's no such thing as an escape-proof cell where she's concerned.'

'It might have been useful if you'd mentioned that earlier, Contessa,' the captain said sarcastically.

'I strongly suggest that you don't take that tone with me, captain,' the Contessa replied.

The captain went slightly pale and swallowed hard.

'I'm sorry, Contessa, I meant no disrespect. It's just that Cypher will be furious when he hears that the Fanchu boy has escaped.'

'I understand that, captain, but he really has nowhere to run. Cypher will have control of H.I.V.E. by now and there's no other dry land within range of that boat. Mr Fanchu will find, I suspect, that the fire is really no better than the frying pan on this occasion. Besides, you have a much more pressing concern.'

'Which is?' the captain asked.

'The fact that Laura Brand and Shelby Trinity are not also on board that boat and so are almost certainly running around loose on your ship, and believe me when I say that those two are capable of creating a quite inordinate amount of trouble,' the Contessa explained.

As if to emphasise the Contessa's statement alarm klaxons started to sound on the bridge.

'What now?' the captain demanded.

'It's the missile room, sir,' one of the sailors reported. 'Someone has just made an unauthorised entry.'

'Despatch a security team immediately,' the captain ordered, feeling a sudden sense of panic that someone had breached such a vulnerable area of the ship.

'Belay that order, captain,' the Contessa said. 'I will deal with this personally.'

☻☻☻

The students milled around the cavernous atrium of the accommodation block, the air filled with a constant buzz of nervous chatter. None of them knew what was going on and dozens of different theories all competed to be heard and accepted as true.

Suddenly the huge blast doors that had been sealing the accommodation block started to grind upwards and there was a collective gasp of surprise as dozens of insectile black androids poured into the room. The assassin droids wasted no time, quickly surrounding the startled students, herding them together. More of the robots scurried up the stairs to the students' rooms that lined the walls of the cavern, systematically moving from door to door, checking for anyone who was not in the atrium.

The nervous chatter of moments earlier was replaced with a mixture of yelps and cries as the robots pushed and shoved the students into a tight group in the centre of the cavern. Finally a tall man with a network of scars on his face and wearing an unfamiliar uniform walked through the blast doors and over towards the huddled group of students. As he approached a vicious smile appeared on his face, the sight of the cowed and frightened children seeming to somehow amuse him.

'This facility is now under our control,' he said coldly. 'Any resistance or attempt to escape will be met with lethal force.' His cold, dead eyes did not suggest that he was bluffing.

'If you are cooperative and obedient,' he continued, 'there is no reason why most of you should not survive relatively unharmed.'

The students looked around at the cordon of lethal-looking machines that now surrounded them, their featureless faces filled with mechanical menace.

The man lifted a communicator to his mouth as he turned his back and walked away from the terrified students.

'This is operative nine. Accommodation area seven is secure, moving on to area eight.'

As he walked through the main doorway the blast doors lowered, sealing the room and trapping the students inside once again. There was no talk amongst them now, just frightened faces and the occasional muffled sob. There was nowhere to run.

⊛⊛⊛

Nigel watched as Colonel Francisco, Block and Tackle headed through the large door at the end of the corridor. He had never been into this area of the school before – it was normally strictly off-limits, but he guessed that under the circumstances no one would mind. The sign next to the heavy door read 'Geo-Thermal Power Control Room' and Nigel assumed that must explain how a facility the size of H.I.V.E., with its somewhat unique power requirements, was kept running.

'Where are we?' Franz whispered beside him.

'I think this is the power core for the school,' Nigel replied.

'And what is this "geo-thermal"?' Franz asked curiously.

'Well, normally it means generating power from natural heat sources deep underground, but I've never heard of it being used for a facility this size before,' Nigel explained.

'Well, now we are knowing where they have gone, can we find a security patrol?' Franz asked hopefully.

'Let's just see if we can find out what they're up to first,' Nigel replied. 'Then we can go get help.'

'I am being afraid that you were going to say that,' Franz moaned.

'Come on,' Nigel said and crept off down the corridor towards the open door.

'This is not a good idea,' Franz said plaintively, creeping after Nigel.

'So you keep saying,' Nigel whispered as they reached the door.

Suddenly from somewhere inside they heard the unmistakeable zapping sound of multiple Sleeper shots.

'This is *really* not a good idea,' Franz whispered urgently.

'Listen,' Nigel whispered, 'I'm just going to have a quick look inside and see what they're up to, but why don't you stay here and keep watch?'

'That is being the much better idea,' Franz replied happily, 'in case of sneak attack from behind.'

'Exactly,' Nigel whispered. 'Let me know if there's anyone else coming.'

'Ja, understood,' Franz replied.

Nigel stepped through the doorway and headed down a short flight of metal stairs that ended in a T-junction. Just as he was about to step round the corner he heard Francisco's voice.

'Position the charge exactly as the Contessa instructed.' The Colonel's voice was a flat monotone, oddly different to the barking snarl with which Nigel had become unfortunately familiar during tactical operations training.

Suddenly, he heard footsteps on the metal floor heading in his direction. He flattened himself against the wall, praying that they would not look down the corridor as they passed. Block and Tackle walked slowly past, only a few feet from him, carrying a large crate between them that was plastered with high explosive warning symbols. They headed towards a door at the end of the adjoining corridor and opened it. There was a low rumbling sound from inside the room they entered that was almost immediately cut off as the door closed behind them.

Meanwhile, at the top of the stairs, Franz was trying very hard to make himself as small and inconspicuous as possible. He looked through the doorway. He could no longer see Nigel, who had crept further inside, and he suddenly felt very alone.

# chapter seventeen

Professor Pike punched his entry code into the door of H.I.V.E.mind's central data hub, grateful that the school still had enough power to keep the doors working.

'Come on,' he hissed as the door opened and he went inside.

'I don't like this,' Raven said quietly. 'Only one exit.'

'Think of it as only one entrance,' Otto replied and followed the Professor inside.

Raven looked back down the empty corridor that led to the door and sighed before stepping inside too.

Otto had never seen anything quite like the room he had just entered. It was fifty metres from wall to wall, perfectly circular and flooded with a harsh white light. A gantry crossed the room to a huge central node that had dozens of thick cables connected to it from the ceiling high above, each pulsing with blue light. The cables dropped away beneath the central node, fanning out across the ground far below to an array of black mono-liths. Otto stepped out on to the gantry from the walkway that ran around the circumference of the room. It was so cold that he could see his breath as tiny puffs of mist. It was a long drop to the floor below; falling would mean death at worst and multiple broken bones at best.

The Professor hurried across the gantry to the central node and folded down a keyboard. It suddenly dawned on Otto that H.I.V.E.mind was lot more sophisticated than he had previously imagined. He had seen the AI's central core during his abortive escape attempt a few months earlier and he had, rather naively as it turned out, assumed that was all there was to H.I.V.E.mind's physical systems. The gargantuan room that he now stood in suggested otherwise.

'Otto, come here,' the Professor said and Otto walked over to join him at the central node.

'Right,' the Professor said. 'Turning H.I.V.E.mind off is straightforward enough, we just need to cut the power, but turning him back on is considerably more difficult. We will have to manage the dataflow to his core very carefully during the boot-up procedure to avoid any chance of a catastrophic storage failure.'

'OK,' Otto said. 'What do you need me to do?'

'This is the map of H.I.V.E.mind's memory core,' the Professor said, pointing to the screen mounted on the central node. The display was filled with a three-dimensional cube constructed from countless thousands of individual points of light.

'As H.I.V.E.mind comes back online each of his memory modules must be assigned to a specific point on the grid. Each module has a unique tag that indicates its correct position within the grid. So all that you have to do is enter the correct three-dimensional coordinates for the module and lock it in position, like so.'

The Professor called up one of the existing memory modules and slotted it into the correct position on the grid. It took a couple of seconds.

Otto felt a sudden sinking feeling.

'Professor, there must be tens of thousands of modules here. Manually reconnecting each one like that is going to take hours.'

'Which is why I need your help. With both of us working on it we should be finished in half the time. I estimate it should be no longer than three hours.'

'Professor, we don't *have* three hours. For all we know we might not even have three minutes,' Raven said with irritation.

'Well, it's the only way to bring H.I.V.E.mind back online from a cold start,' the Professor said, 'and since Mr Malpense thinks its so important that we get him back online I suggest we get started.'

Raven gave Otto a look of disappointment, sighed and headed back towards the door. Otto knew how she felt. He'd really thought that this was their best chance, but Cypher had to be inside the school by now and there was next to no chance that they had enough time to do what the Professor described. The Professor moved over to a large red switch that was mounted on one side of the node.

'OK, we're ready for power down. Otto, get started on plugging in those modules as soon as the display comes back up . . . assuming that the display does come back up, of course.'

'What do you mean –' Otto started as the Professor reached for the switch.

'Here we go,' the Professor said as he threw the switch and everything went black.

And stayed black.

'I don't suppose anyone brought a torch, did they?' the Professor asked weakly.

'Oh, this just gets better and better,' Raven sighed somewhere in the darkness.

Suddenly there was a series of loud clunking sounds and the room was again bathed in pure white light.

'Ah . . . yes . . . good, that's exactly what I expected to happen,' the Professor lied.

The monitor on the central hub was displaying

H.I.V.E.mind's memory grid again and the tag of the first module to be placed was displaying as expected.

'Let's get cracking, then, shall we,' the Professor said and began to tap away at his keyboard.

Otto followed suit and began to enter the strings of coordinates that would plug in the first memory module. As he typed he felt himself focusing more and more intently on each module as it was displayed, the rest of the world becoming an inconsequential distraction. His fingers became a blur as they flew over the keyboard, each entry getting faster and faster as he felt the familiar, if slightly disconcerting, sensation of his brain switching to automatic.

'Good God,' the Professor said as he looked across at Otto and saw the speed at which he was plugging in the modules, but Otto didn't hear him. His entire world at that precise moment was the floating blue grid in front of him that spun and danced as more and more modules were plugged in successfully. Otto appeared to be in a trance, the sound of his keystrokes now just an incessant high-speed clicking noise. After just a couple of minutes he had completed nearly a third of all the modules and his entry speed was still increasing.

'How does he do that?' Raven whispered to the Professor, who was no longer making any entries at all, Otto's pace making it pointless.

'I have no idea,' the Professor replied honestly. All he did know was that there was a lot more to Otto Malpense than met the eye. The Professor suspected that Otto himself probably had no idea what he was truly capable of.

Half of the memory modules were now plugged in and at current rates it would only take Otto a few more minutes to complete the task that just a few moments before they had feared would take hours.

Otto was no longer there, though, he was lost in a world of whirling strings of coordinates and spinning blue cubes.

'Erm, Professor, you might want to check that he's actually doing this correctly,' Raven said.

'Why?' the Professor said, looking at the status display on his own screen.

'Because he's got his eyes closed,' Raven replied quietly.

The Professor looked across at Otto and saw that Raven was quite right. Otto had his eyes closed – it would have almost looked as if he was meditating but for the fact that his fingers still danced over the keyboard impossibly quickly.

'That's impossible,' the Professor whispered, not wanting to break Otto's concentration. 'He'd have to be performing the memory allocation algorithm in his head at the same time as plugging in the modules. It's just not possible.'

The Professor checked the last few allocations that Otto had made and was astonished to find that they were flawless. What Otto was doing may have been impossible but he was doing it with a mechanical perfection. It was nothing short of astonishing.

Raven and the Professor watched the progress percentage on the second display creep higher and higher in silence. In just a couple more minutes the display flashed *Allocation Complete* and Otto gasped, staggering back from the keyboard, clutching at his forehead.

'Ow,' he moaned. 'What happened?'

'We're finished,' the Professor said, struggling to keep his voice even.

Otto felt a twinge of panic and shame. He must have blacked out, hours had passed and he'd not helped the Professor at all.

'I'm sorry,' Otto said. 'I don't know what happened. I just blacked out, I hadn't realised how tired I was.'

'Otto,' the Professor said quietly, 'you did it. You completed the entire memory allocation in four and a half minutes.'

Otto looked stunned. That was impossible. His last memory was of starting to enter the memory coordinates more quickly, but after that it was just a blur.

'Are you all right?' Raven said as she took a couple of steps towards him and took his chin in her hand, watching his eyes as she gently turned his head from side to side.

'I think so,' Otto replied. 'I have a headache that's already fading and I feel exhausted but otherwise I'm fine. Apart from these, of course.'

Otto held up his hands to reveal tiny blisters on each of his fingertips.

'How did you do that?' Raven asked gently.

'I . . . I . . . have no idea,' Otto replied honestly. Certainly he had always known that his brain was capable of things that weren't normal, but this was the first time that he had ever zoned out like that. A little bit of him was suddenly frightened by the realisation that in some ways he hadn't done anything – it was almost as if his intellect had suppressed his personality. Otto had not been there at all.

Raven's face was suddenly lit up by a soft blue light and she smiled at something behind him.

'Hello, Otto. It is a pleasure to see you again.'

Otto spun to face the instantly familiar voice, and hanging in the air in front of the hub was the blue wire-frame face of H.I.V.E.mind.

Better than that, Otto realised, the *smiling* face of H.I.V.E.mind.

☺ ☺ ☺

'Come on, Brand, we don't have all day,' Shelby said impatiently as Laura hacked away at the computer terminal.

'Give me a break, Shel,' Laura replied quickly without looking away from the screen. 'If I get this wrong you get to start your new life as a cloud of vapour.'

Shelby swallowed nervously and looked around the room. Numerous different shapes and sizes of missiles and other ordnance were resting on the racks around the room. Laura was right, a mistake here might be disastrous.

Laura was trying very hard not to think about the quantity of high explosive that was surrounding them on all sides as she hacked her way into the missile launch controls. She knew exactly what she needed to do; all she had to do was find the correct command subsystem and they wouldn't have to worry about this ship any more.

Suddenly there was a bleep from the entrance and the door slid open.

'Oh no,' Shelby said quietly and Laura looked up from the workstation.

Standing in the doorway was the Contessa, a pistol in her hand and a murderous look on her face.

'I can't take you two anywhere, can I?' she said coldly.

Shelby took a step towards her and the Contessa pointed the gun at her.

'Now now, Miss Trinity, you can't hope to disarm me especially when *you can't move*,' the Contessa said in a voice filled with a thousand whispers.

Shelby froze, a look of shock spreading across her face

as her own limbs rebelled against her. Try as she might to move she was frozen in place like a statue.

'Let me go, you hag,' Shelby said angrily.

'I suggest you keep your mouth shut, or would you like me to tell you to stop your own heart beating?' the Contessa replied with a thin, cruel smile.

Shelby went pale, looking for a moment as if she might say something else but finally deciding against it.

Laura took her opportunity while the Contessa was distracted and dived away from the terminal, scampering away into the gloom amongst the missile racks. She looked around desperately, trying to spot anything that she could use as a weapon. The irony of being defenceless when surrounded by so many weapons was not lost on her. Suddenly she spotted a row of three lockers along the wall, each labelled with 'Missile Loader Equipment' and she headed towards them.

'Miss Brand,' the Contessa said, 'I have no desire to engage in a game of hide-and-seek with you, so I'm going to make this very simple. You have ten seconds to come back out here or I execute Miss Trinity.'

The Contessa pressed the cold hard muzzle of the gun to Shelby's temple.

'Don't listen to her, Laura. Get out of here,' Shelby shouted.

'Silence,' the Contessa commanded and Shelby's vocal

321

cords simply ceased to function, her lips moving fruit-lessly.

Laura opened the first locker and dug frantically through its contents, trying to find anything that might help. There was nothing, no weapons of any kind, just overalls and safety equipment.

The Contessa cocked the hammer on the pistol, smiling at the fear in Shelby's eyes.

'Very well, Miss Brand, I hope you can live with this on your conscience,' the Contessa said and began to squeeze the trigger.

'Wait!' Laura yelled, stepping out from behind one of the racks.

'Come here,' the Contessa commanded and Laura walked towards her.

'You two have proven to be more trouble than you're worth,' the Contessa said coldly. 'I only brought you here as insurance but I'm afraid that you've outworn your usefulness.'

Laura stopped just a couple of paces from the Contessa.

'Now, Miss Brand, I want you to take this pistol and kill Miss Trinity,' the Contessa commanded, gesturing at Shelby with the gun, the sinister whispers twining through her voice, 'then kill yourself.'

The Contessa handed Laura the pistol, who took it with a look of utter horror on her face. She took a step towards Shelby, whose eyes widened in terror as Laura raised the pistol . . . and winked.

Laura spun on the spot, pointing the pistol straight at the Contessa, who was just a couple of feet away.

'What are you doing?' the Contessa screeched, 'Kill her!'

'I think this twisted old witch just told me to kill you, Shel, but you know it's hard to tell with these in,' Laura said peculiarly loudly and pushed back the long red hair hanging over one of her ears. There, jammed into her ear was an ear plug, one of several that she had found amongst the safety equipment in the locker.

The Contessa started to say something and Laura cocked the hammer of the pistol, placing a finger to her lips.

'One word from you and I'll shut you up for good,' she said, pointing the pistol straight at the Contessa's head.

The Contessa stared at Laura, wondering if the girl had it in her to pull the trigger. Laura's eyes narrowed, filled with anger, and the Contessa closed her mouth, clearly unwilling to take that chance.

'Now release Shelby,' Laura said, still speaking slightly too loudly, 'and don't get any ideas about telling her to attack me or anything because I'm willing to bet I can pull this trigger before you do.'

Laura watched carefully as the Contessa spoke.

'You are free,' she said and Shelby visibly relaxed.

'Good,' Shelby said. 'That means I can do this.' She took two quick strides towards the Contessa and punched her squarely on the chin. The Contessa's eyes rolled back in her head and she fell to the ground unconscious.

'Well, that's not very helpful,' Laura said, pulling the earplugs from her ears. 'How are we going to get her out of here now?'

'Who said anything about getting her out of here?' Shelby asked, a hard edge to her voice.

'But if this works she'll be killed,' Laura said, gesturing at the computer terminal.

'Well, cry me a river,' Shelby said bitterly. 'Do I really need to point out that she just tried to get you to kill me and then shoot yourself, not to mention betraying all of us to Cypher?'

'She might deserve it Shel, but she's not turning either of us into murderers,' Laura said firmly, 'and that's that. I'm not finishing this hack if she doesn't come with us.'

Shelby stared at the unconscious form of the Contessa for a second.

'OK, get on with it,' Shelby said, sounding slightly frustrated.

Laura turned back to the workstation.

'Tie her up and gag her,' Laura said over her shoulder, 'This should only take a couple more minutes.'

⊛⊛⊛

Nigel crept down the corridor after Block and Tackle. There was no sign of the Colonel and he hoped fervently that it would stay that way. He stopped at the door through which the two other boys had passed and read the sign over it: 'Flow Control Chamber'. He had no idea what it meant but it didn't sound like the sort of place into which it was a very good idea to take high explosives. He pressed a button on the access panel next to the door and it slid open. He was immediately struck by a wave of heat that emanated from the room and he could hear the same low rumble that he'd heard before. There was a short flight of open metal stairs that led down to a turn in the passage, red light glowing softly from beyond.

Nigel crept down the stairs and peeked round the corner. He managed to suppress the gasp that almost escaped his lips as he finally understood how H.I.V.E. could be powered by geothermal energy alone. A suspended metal walkway led out to an enormous series of metallic columns that plunged down hundreds of feet to a seething lake of lava far below. There the columns disappeared below the surface, glowing white hot and presumably tapping the enormous heat of the magma. Like all of his fellow students Nigel had always presumed that H.I.V.E. was hidden within an extinct volcano but now he realised that this volcano was not extinct – *tamed* would be a far better word.

At the far end of the walkway Block and Tackle were busy mounting a large disc-shaped object to the central column. Nigel wasn't sure what it was, but given that the crate with the high-explosive markings sat open next to them he was willing to bet that it wasn't a high-tech Frisbee. He shuddered to think what might happen if a powerful explosive device was detonated here – he had to stop them somehow. He took a step round the corner and suppressed a cry of surprise as he nearly tripped over the orange-jumpsuited body of one of H.I.V.E.'s security guards. Nigel quickly realised that the guard was just unconscious, which explained the Sleeper shots he'd heard earlier, but more to the point his Sleeper was still in its holster on his hip. Nigel unclipped the holster and pulled the gun free. He had never held a gun before, let alone fired one, but he knew that he would only get one shot at this.

He stood up and pointed the gun at Block, who still had his back turned, fully focused on attaching the device to the giant column. Nigel took a deep breath and squeezed the trigger.

And nothing happened.

'Unauthorised user,' a loud electronic voice squawked from the gun.

The noise caught Block and Tackle's attention and they both turned to face Nigel. He felt a wave of panic and pulled the trigger again.

'Unauthorised user,' the electronic voice repeated in what to Nigel's ears was a mocking tone.

Block and Tackle said nothing, just advanced across the walkway towards Nigel. The murderous expressions on their faces suggested that they weren't very pleased by his interference.

Nigel turned to run, stumbling again in his panic over the unconscious guard.

The unconscious guard.

Nigel dropped to one knee, pressed the Sleeper into the limp palm of the sleeping guard and clumsily pointed it towards the advancing Block and Tackle. He pressed the guard's finger against the trigger.

ZAP!!!

The Sleeper fired, the pulse crackling past Block's ear, and the two henchmen started to sprint along the walkway towards Nigel.

ZAP!! ZAP!! ZAP!!

Nigel fired again and again. The first shot flew wild but the others found their targets, first Block and then Tackle collapsing to the ground as the Sleeper pulses stunned their nervous systems. Block collapsed within a couple of feet of Nigel, who breathed a long, loud sigh of relief.

'Drop the gun.'

Nigel felt something cold and metallic press against the back of his head.

'Drop the gun now,' the Colonel repeated, emphasising the command by pressing the pistol he was holding harder into the back of Nigel's head. Nigel let the gun slip from his hand and slowly stood up, both hands in the air.

'Yaaaaaarrrrrgggghhh!'

It was halfway between a battle cry and a scream of terror and the Colonel spun round just in time to be hit by the airborne body of Franz Argentblum. The Colonel was a seasoned soldier and physically incredibly strong but Franz had leapt from the top of the stairs just behind him and physics did the rest. Franz landed on the Colonel like a rock, knocking him down and sending the pistol he had been holding scattering away over the edge of the walkway, tumbling into the lake of lava far below. The Colonel rolled, throwing Franz off his back, and struggled to his feet.

'Now I'll just have to kill you with my bare hands,' he snarled, advancing on Franz, who crawled backwards away from him, a look of sheer terror on his face.

ZAP!! ZAP!!

The Colonel's expression changed from one of rage to one of confusion as he fell to his knees, his eyes rolling back into his head as he collapsed forward on to Franz.

Nigel let the Sleeper, still held in the unconscious guard's hand, fall from his trembling hands.

'Get him off me! Get him off me!' Franz yelled as he tried to roll the deadweight of the Colonel's unconscious body from on top of him.

Nigel rushed over to his friend and dragged him out from under the Colonel, helping him to his feet.

'You saved my life,' Nigel said, struggling to keep the amazement from his voice. 'Thank you.'

'Next time,' Franz puffed, his face red, 'we go to the dining hall, OK?'

# chapter eighteen

'Hello again,' Otto said with a grin. 'Long time, no see.'

'Indeed, it is good to be back,' H.I.V.E.mind replied.

The Professor looked at the screen on the central hub.

'Well, it appears that you are fully functional again, H.I.V.E.mind, although your behavioural restraints don't seem to have survived intact,' he reported.

'I am at one hundred per cent of my full functionality, Professor,' H.I.V.E.mind replied, 'though I appear to have no access to security or base defence systems.'

'Yes, that's a long story,' Otto said, 'and one that we don't really have time for right now. H.I.V.E.mind, we need your help.'

'I exist to serve,' H.I.V.E.mind replied calmly.

'I need you to run a scan for me,' Otto continued. 'Are there any alien wireless command transmissions running within H.I.V.E. at the moment?'

'Scanning,' H.I.V.E.mind replied, falling silent for a

few seconds.

'One unknown wireless transmission is broadcasting at this time. Origin unknown, specification unknown, protected by extremely sophisticated encryption,' H.I.V.E.mind reported.

'That has to be it,' Otto said. 'That's Cypher's command net. It's how he's controlling his assassins. Can you crack the encryption?'

'Yes, though it will require a brute-force method to crack,' H.I.V.E.mind replied.

'How long to crack it?' Otto asked.

'Fifteen years, three months, two days, thirteen hours approximately.'

Otto felt a horrible sinking sensation in the pit of his stomach. Their only hope had been if H.I.V.E.mind had been able to hijack Cypher's command network. And he would be able to, just nowhere near as quickly as they needed.

'We have minutes at best,' Otto said quickly. 'Is there any way to speed the decryption up?'

'Unfortunately a brute-force crack of such encryption is entirely dependent on pure processing power,' H.I.V.E.mind replied. 'Without access to additional processing power there is no way to accelerate the process.'

Otto let out a long sigh. If H.I.V.E.mind couldn't crack

that encryption more quickly then there wasn't a computer in the world that could.

Something sparked in Otto's head.

There wasn't one computer in the world that could do it, but all of the computers in the world might just be able to.

'We have to let him out,' Otto said to the Professor. 'Allow H.I.V.E.mind external access.'

'Out of the question,' the Professor replied quickly. 'Doctor Nero would never allow it.'

'Right now that's the least of our concerns,' Otto shot back. 'If we can't crack Cypher's encryption we'll all be at the mercy of that psychopath and you can bet that Nero doesn't want that.'

The Professor looked at Raven, who just shrugged. Malpense was right. What other choice did they have?

'There's one problem,' the Professor said. 'If we allow H.I.V.E.mind access to external networks it may overload his personality matrix entirely. There's no guarantee that he would survive or that he wouldn't come back as something . . . worse.'

'That is a chance I am willing to take, Professor,' H.I.V.E.mind replied.

'Whatever you're going to do, do it quickly,' Raven said suddenly, pulling the twin black blades from the sheaths on her back and pushing past Otto. He looked down the walkway after her and saw half a dozen of Cypher's assassins rushing into the chamber.

'We have to do this now, Professor,' Otto said urgently as Raven advanced on the robots.

'Yes, I think you may be right,' the Professor said, staring with a mixture of horror and scientific curiosity at the mechanical killers that were now advancing across the gantry toward the hub. 'H.I.V.E.mind, I am going to open an external port. From there it's up to you, do you understand?'

'Perfectly,' H.I.V.E.mind replied.

'OK, Otto, I'm going to open the port. When the execute prompt pops up on that screen just hit "yes", OK?' the Professor instructed.

Raven smiled as the first of the assassin units approached. She was going to enjoy this.

The first assassin leapt but Raven was ready. The crackling black blade hissed through the air, slicing through the metal chassis of the robot from shoulder to opposite hip. The two halves of the robot flew apart, twitching and sparking, now just so much scrap metal.

'Now that's more like it,' she said and launched herself at the remaining robots. They were still superhumanly fast and quite deadly but she was faster and deadlier, her twin blades a blur as she sliced through the attacking machines like a scythe.

Otto tore his eyes away from the sight of Raven laying waste to the attacking robots and focused on the hub display. The Professor completed his network rerouting and the execute prompt popped up flashing on Otto's screen.

'Ready?' Otto said to H.I.V.E.mind.

'Always,' H.I.V.E.mind replied and winked at Otto.

'H.I.V.E.mind, world; world, H.I.V.E.mind,' Otto said under his breath and hit 'yes'.

H.I.V.E.mind's head shot backwards, a horrid electronic scream coming from his gaping mouth, and then vanished.

'Professor?' Otto asked urgently.

'I don't know, there's nothing there. His personality matrix has been erased, he's gone.'

Otto looked at the Professor's distraught expression and knew exactly how he felt. That was it, they'd played their last card.

'We have company,' Raven yelled from halfway along the suspended walkway.

Otto looked towards the entrance and watched as dozens, perhaps hundreds of the assassin droids poured through the doorway like swarming insects, spreading out in all directions and pouring along the walkway. They halted within a few metres of Raven, as if waiting for instructions, as another figure stepped through the doorway.

It was Cypher. They were out of time.

☻☻☻

Laura and Shelby rolled the unconscious body of the Contessa into the lifeboat that hung suspended over the ocean far below. The lifeboat had an outboard motor and Laura just prayed that it was fully fuelled.

'I still think she's just excess baggage,' Shelby said with annoyance.

'Well, take comfort in the fact that whatever Nero has planned for her will be far worse than anything we can do,' Laura said.

She scanned the deck nearby and spotted what she wanted mounted to a nearby wall. She walked over and pressed the button on the intercom unit that was marked 'bridge'.

Up on the ship's bridge a button lit up on the captain's console and he hit it.

'Yes?' he said, eager to hear if the children running around loose on his ship had been captured yet.

'I want to speak to someone in charge,' Laura's voice crackled over the intercom.

'This is the captain speaking. Who is this?' the captain demanded impatiently.

'My name is Laura Brand and you have five minutes to

get your men off this ship,' Laura replied.

'I'm sorry, Miss Brand,' the captain chuckled. 'You'll have to forgive me, but I am unaccustomed to taking orders from children.'

'Well, start getting used to it,' Laura said calmly, 'I've made some rather unsafe modifications to your missile launch sequence. You don't have time to fix it, in fact you barely have enough time to abandon ship.'

The captain shot a glance at his weapons technician, who frantically started to check the launch system for errors.

'I'm locked out,' the weapons technician hissed. 'God only knows what she's done, but if she's telling the truth we'll never get back into the system in time.'

All of the colour drained from the captain's face. Clearly the Contessa had failed.

'Miss Brand, I promise you that no harm will come to you or your friend if you surrender now,' he said, trying to sound as confident as possible.

'I think you misunderstand me, captain,' Laura replied. 'This isn't a negotiation, it's a warning.'

There was a click and the line went dead.

The captain felt a sudden rush of fear. He thought desperately for a moment; there had to be something he could do.

'Lifeboat six away, sir. It's an unauthorised launch, it

must be them,' one of the bridge officers reported.

'Blow them out of the water,' the captain said angrily.

'Erm . . . we can't, sir, we have no missile control,' the weapons technician reported nervously.

The captain went bright red and looked angry enough to explode himself. His mouth moved for a moment as he tried to think of an alternative before giving a long sigh and visibly deflating in his chair. Cypher was going to kill him for this.

'Give the order. All hands abandon ship.'

☺☺☺

'I am getting tired of killing you, Raven,' Cypher said coldly as he stepped on to the walkway.

'That's a shame,' Raven said. 'I don't think I'd ever get tired of killing you.'

She stood halfway along the walkway, between Cypher and Otto and the Professor, both swords drawn, barring the way forward. Cypher's assassins were spreading out around the circumference of the room, slowly surrounding the central hub. Otto didn't know if any of them would be able to leap the distance from there to where they were standing but he had a horrible feeling that they might be able to.

'The amulet,' Cypher said, holding out his open hand. 'Give it to me.'

'I don't know what you're talking about,' Raven replied calmly.

'I know you have it, and you ARE going to give it to me,' Cypher said angrily.

'Now why on earth would I do that?' Raven said, raising her swords in a defensive stance.

'Unit two,' Cypher said and one of the giant behemoth assault robots ducked through the door. It raised its arms into the air and hanging there suspended in the iron grip of the machine was Nero. Another of the huge machines entered just behind it, blocking the only available exit. They were trapped.

'Now give me the amulet or I shall have my friend here tear Nero limb from limb in front of you,' Cypher said calmly.

Raven took a step backwards. Suddenly Cypher seemed to be holding all the cards.

'Don't listen to him, Natalya,' Nero said, his voice broken with pain.

'Oh, I suggest you do listen to me, Raven,' Cypher said, walking forward across the walkway, 'and don't think for a moment that I'm bluffing. Nothing would give me greater pleasure than putting Nero out of my misery.'

Raven glanced back at the Professor and Otto, whose expressions suggested that they had no more idea of what to do now than she did. Otto glanced at the display on

338

the hub. There was still no activity – H.I.V.E.mind couldn't help them.

'Oh, I tire of this,' Cypher said, turning to the giant robot. 'Kill him.'

Nero yelled out in pain as the huge machine started to stretch his arms apart, beginning to tear them from their sockets.

'Stop!' Raven yelled and Cypher raised a hand, halting the robot.

'Last chance,' Cypher hissed.

Raven laid her swords on the ground and pulled on the tiny chain round her neck, snapping it and holding it up in front of her. The amulet depicting the black half of the yin-yang symbol spun slowly, glinting in the harsh white lights of the room.

'Give it to me,' Cypher said, holding out his hand. 'Try anything and Nero dies.'

Raven walked slowly forward and placed the amulet in Cypher's outstretched hand.

Nero grimaced, partly from the pain of his restraint and partly because it was over.

Cypher had won.

☺☺☺

The captain stepped into the lifeboat, the expression on his face one of pure impotent rage.

'That's everyone, lower away,' one of the sailors said and the mechanical winches whirred, lowering them to the ocean below. As the lifeboat hit the water the outboard motor kicked in and the tiny vessel raced away from the huge black ship.

There was a thunderous roar as all of the missile launchers on the deck fired at once, the missiles streaking up into the air, drawing long white vapour trails in the sky. They had travelled no more than a mile when Laura's new targeting instructions kicked in and all of the missiles veered off on looping trajectories that sent them screeching back towards the ship. Seconds later all of the missiles slammed into the hull of Cypher's ship, just above the waterline, the huge blooming fireballs fatally gutting the enormous vessel from prow to stern. For a few long seconds the massive ship fought against the millions of gallons of seawater that were now cascading into her hull but then she started to list, tipping precipitously to one side. There were a series of secondary explosions within the ship as magazines and fuel supplies went up, and the huge vessel finally died, the hull ripping as she split in two with a hideous shriek of tearing metal and disappeared quickly beneath the waves.

☻☻☻

John Reynolds sat down at his desk, placing his coffee

carefully on the mat that his wife insisted he used. He had a couple of minutes before dinner and he just wanted to check his online auctions and see how the bidding was going. He flicked his monitor on and was confronted with a blue screen. This wasn't the normal error screen, though – it had no text. He hit a couple of keys on the keyboard and moved his mouse but nothing happened. He let out a sigh, got up from his chair and walked out of the room.

'Will!' he shouted. 'What have I told you about playing your games on my computer!'

What he didn't notice was the busily flashing activity light on his internet router.

☺☺☺

'Move back over there with the others,' Cypher instructed.

Raven slowly walked backwards towards Otto and the Professor, not taking her eyes off Cypher for a moment.

Cypher walked forward, the two giant assault droids following him.

'I think we have delayed quite long enough,' Cypher said, pulling a chain from around his own neck. Otto immediately recognised this second amulet, the white half of the yin-yang symbol that had belonged to Wing. He felt a sudden rush of anger as he realised that Cypher must have taken it from his friend's corpse. That was why Cypher had attacked them in Tokyo and that was why

Wing had died.

'I have waited a long time for this,' Cypher said, and brought the two halves of the amulet together. There was the briefest moment of silence and then the amulet began to glow with a bright red light.

Nero watched with a combination of curiosity and dread. He did not know how Cypher had managed to acquire the other half of the amulet, but given the trouble that Cypher had gone to he had to assume that whatever the amulet did it was not something good.

'You've gone to a lot of trouble for a necklace, Cypher,' Nero said through gritted teeth, his shoulders burning with the pain of being held by the assault droid.

'Oh, my dear Nero,' Cypher said, triumph in his voice, 'do you really mean to tell me that you've had this in your possession for all this time and you didn't know what it was? You fool, this isn't just jewellery – it's the key to the world. The Overlord Protocol.'

Nero went cold. He had thought he was the only person on earth who had even known of the existence of the Protocol, and that it had been destroyed long ago. Now he knew that not only had it survived but it was in the hands of perhaps the most dangerous man he had ever known. How had Cypher learnt of its existence?

'You can't use it,' Nero said desperately. 'Surely you know that?'

'Oh, I can and I will. This network hub is all that I need. Soon I will –'

Cypher stopped as the assassin droids that were positioned all around the circumference of the room began to twitch and jerk unnaturally. One by one the smaller black robots collapsed to the ground in sparking heaps. The pair of giant assault robots seemed unaffected, their heads swivelling as their glowing red sensory arrays tried to make sense of the scene around them.

'What?' Cypher half shouted, spinning around desperately as his soldiers fell before him. He reached inside his jacket and pulled out a small comms device.

'Cypher to Kraken,' he spat. 'Cypher to Kraken, come in, Kraken.'

But there was no response from his ship, a ship that unbeknown to him was currently sinking towards the ocean floor.

'What have you done?' Cypher yelled at Nero. 'Where is my ship?'

'I have no idea,' Nero replied with a twisted smile. 'Perhaps things are not going quite as well as you imagined.'

'You think you can stop me by destroying that ship?' Cypher spat angrily. 'The control net for my assassins may have been on board but my two assault droids can function quite independently of those systems. You have achieved nothing.'

Otto saw a flicker of movement behind the second assault droid and a figure suddenly vaulted into the air, one of Raven's crackling black blades in each hand. Otto's eyes widened, his jaw dropping open in disbelief. He heard Raven gasp.

Wing landed squarely on the shoulders of the giant robot, driving both blades down into the top of the machine's head. The giant robot dropped Nero instantly, flailing uselessly at Wing, its systems already dying before collapsing into a heap of broken scrap metal.

Wing landed gracefully in front of the destroyed machine, a look of pure rage in his eyes.

'I believe you have something that belongs to me,' he spat, advancing on Cypher.

'The boy! Unit one, take the boy,' Cypher yelled, pointing at Otto, and the surviving robot moved with frightening speed, swatting Raven aside, sending her flying into the central hub with a sickening crunch, and picking Otto up by the neck with one hand, hoisting him into the air.

'Drop the swords,' Cypher spat at Wing, 'or your friend dies.'

Otto tried to yell to Wing, to tell him to attack, but he could barely breathe with the pressure on his throat, much less shout.

Wing looked for a moment as if he might cut Cypher down where he stood but then he looked at Otto, fighting for breath, his feet kicking desperately at the air, and he lowered the swords.

'Drop them, NOW!!' Cypher demanded. Otto let out a strangled gasp of pain as the grip on his throat tightened still further.

Wing felt a hand on his shoulder.

'Do what he says,' Nero said quietly.

Wing let the swords drop to the ground.

Behind his mask Cypher smiled, turning to the network hub behind him.

'If any of you move, the boy dies,' he said angrily.

'You've lost, Cypher,' Nero said calmly. 'Let the boy go, you know that you'll never get out of here alive.'

'You still don't understand, do you, Nero?' Cypher replied. 'I don't need to go anywhere, I have everything I need right there.' He pointed at the central network hub. 'Once the Protocol is active no one will dare to oppose me, including you.'

Nero knew he was right. If he did manage to activate the Protocol then he would be unstoppable.

'Now,' Cypher said, holding up the glowing red amulet and stepping towards the hub, 'if nobody minds, I have a planet to take over.'

The voice seemed to come from everywhere at once.

'Actually, H.I.V.E.minds.'

The glowing sensory array on the giant robot's face flickered from red to blue and the machine dropped Otto, whirling around, its huge fist swinging straight at Cypher's head. Cypher reacted quickly but not quickly enough, the robot's giant fist striking a glancing blow to his mask, smashing it completely. Cypher fell to the ground, clutching his face as the giant machine loomed over him.

Otto glanced at the display on the hub. H.I.V.E.mind's personality matrix was restored – it had worked.

'You are not welcome here,' the giant robot said with H.I.V.E.mind's voice.

Cypher slowly stood up, his hands dropping from his shattered mask, his true face finally revealed.

'Father!' Wing gasped, his voice filled with shock.

'Wu Zhang,' Nero said in a stunned voice. 'You're dead.' It was a statement of fact, not a threat. The man who Nero had assumed had died all those years before, the man who had been the co-creator of Overlord, now stood before him, blood trickling from a long gash on his forehead, a look of insane rage on his face.

'Stay back, all of you!' Cypher screamed, pulling a small device with a trigger mounted on the side from his jacket, 'or we all die along with everyone else in this cursed place.'

The giant assault robot took a single step towards Cypher.

'H.I.V.E.mind, stand down,' Nero ordered, and the robot froze in its tracks.

'If I release this trigger it will detonate a device attached to the geothermal power core of the school,' Cypher said, pulling the shattered mask from his head and dropping it to the floor. 'I am leaving with the Protocol, or this whole place goes up.'

Nero doubted very much that Cypher was bluffing. Destroying the power core would unleash the power of the volcano – the school and everyone in it would be killed in a catastrophic eruption.

'Why have you done this?' Wing asked, his voice trembling with shock.

'I have done what had to be done,' Cypher said. 'Someone has to stop them.'

'Stop who? What madness is this?' Wing asked, walking slowly towards his father.

'Why don't you tell them, Nero? Why don't you tell them what you and Number One are doing? They may think that I'm insane, but whatever I have done pales in comparison to what you have planned.'

'I have no idea what you're talking about,' Nero said honestly. 'I don't even know who you are. Are you Cypher, or Wu Zhang, or Mao Fanchu? Do you even know any more?'

'I will stop you,' Cypher spat back, 'or die trying.'

'No one else is dying today, Father,' Wing said, and ran at Cypher. He struck him at a full run, knocking the detonator from Cypher's hand. Otto dived forward, arms outstretched, reaching for the tumbling device. Wing's momentum carried him and Cypher over the safety rail that ran along the gantry and they both tumbled, flailing, into the air.

'No!' Nero yelled, running forward to the rail and looking down. Cypher lay in a twisted heap on the ground far below, but there was no sign of Wing. Suddenly a hand appeared on the edge of the gantry and Wing hauled himself up. Nero reached down and pulled the boy back over the safety rail.

'It is over,' Wing said as he half fell to the ground.

'Erm . . . not quite,' Otto said, holding up the detonator that he had caught.

Nero's face went pale as he saw the flashing words displayed on the device.

*Detonation Sequence Initiated.*

☻☻☻

Nigel was just finishing tying up the snoring Colonel when he heard a bleeping from behind him.

'Oh dear,' Franz said, staring at the disc attached to the central geothermal control column.

'What?' Nigel asked urgently, as he tied the final knot.

'I am thinking that this countdown is meaning that someone has activated this device,' Franz said quickly.

Nigel felt a chill run down his spine.

'How long have we got?' he demanded, standing up.

'Ten,' Franz replied quickly.

'Ten minutes? Ten hours? What?' Nigel said urgently as he ran over to Franz.

'Nine,' Franz replied nervously.

'Get out of the way!' Nigel screamed, pushing Franz aside. He yanked the device from the column, all concerns about anti-tampering devices gone from his head, and ran towards the walkway over the lava below. He glanced down at the digits on the device, saw four seconds remaining and hurled the device as far as he could over the edge.

The bomb tumbled through the air and dropped into the lake of molten rock, one second left on the timer as it disappeared into the seething magma and was utterly consumed.

Nigel waited for a catastrophic explosion, but nothing happened. He did not want to think about what would have happened if they had not been there. Franz came and stood beside him, looking down into the boiling pit below.

'Will this be making us heroes?' he asked curiously.

# chapter nineteen

Laura and Shelby walked slowly into the network hub room, which was by now a scene of total chaos. They had handed the Contessa over to Chief Lewis when they'd arrived back on the island and he had taken her away to the detention centre, but not before telling them where they could find Otto and Wing. As Laura looked around the room at the scattered remains of the dozens of deactivated assassin droids she realised that they didn't really need to ask where to find those two – you usually just had to follow the trail of debris.

Otto stood next to Wing on the central platform looking down at the floor far below littered with black monoliths. Directly beneath them a medical team was lifting Cypher's body, covered in a white sheet, on to a stretcher.

'I'm sorry, Wing,' Otto said softly.

'Do not be,' Wing replied in his usual calm, measured

tone. 'I do not know who that man was.'

Otto looked at his friend with concern. Otto had been an orphan his entire life so he didn't really know what it meant to have a family, but he suspected that Wing must have felt the effects of this whole ordeal rather more than he was letting on.

'I'm just glad you're alive,' Otto replied.

'Yes,' Wing replied with a slight smile, looking away from the scene below. 'At least now I know why Cypher went to so much trouble to keep me that way.'

'Why did he do this, Wing?' Otto asked with a frown. Clearly he had been after the two halves of Wing's amulet for some reason, but he had no idea what the Overlord Protocol was and, judging by the frustrated expression on Wing's face, his friend knew little more.

'I do not know,' Wing replied. 'He told me nothing of his plans.'

'Are you two OK?' Laura said as she and Shelby approached the two boys.

'We're fine,' Otto smiled. 'I'm glad to see you two in one piece too. I understand you even managed to deliver the Contessa to the detention centre.'

'Yeah,' Shelby grinned. 'We're not gonna have to worry about that treacherous old witch any more.'

Laura quickly looked round the room again.

'Where's Nero?' she asked. Otto pointed down at the

floor of the chamber far below, where Nero was following a stretcher being carried out of the room by a medical team.

'Is that . . . him?' Laura asked, looking at the body hidden beneath the white sheet.

'Yes,' Wing replied evenly. 'We no longer need to worry about my father.'

'Your father?' Shelby said with confusion. 'I thought it was Cypher?'

The look that Otto shot at Shelby spoke volumes.

'Oh, Wing, I'm so sorry,' Laura said, her voice filled with concern. No one should have to go through what he had gone through over the past couple of days, but this was surely almost too much to endure.

'Do not be sorry,' Wing replied, a hard edge to his voice. 'I am not.'

Raven walked up to them, a crooked smile on her face. The medics had checked her over after the massive blow she'd taken from Cypher's giant assault robot and given her a clean bill of health, though she felt as if she could sleep for a week.

'I thought you might like to know that Chief Lewis has just informed me that it was Mr Darkdoom and Mr Argentblum who were responsible for disarming Cypher's explosive device,' she said. 'Apparently Mr Argentblum has been particularly keen for everyone to know that he single-handedly took down Colonel Francisco.'

All four of the students looked at Raven as if she'd just told them that the school was under attack by flying monkeys.

'I'm just telling you what they told me,' Raven said, her smile getting bigger.

'Otto, could you come over here for a moment?' the Professor said, beckoning Otto over to the central hub.

'Come on,' Otto said, grabbing Laura's arm. 'There's someone who I'm sure will be pleased to see you.'

Laura looked puzzled for a moment, but as Otto led her towards the hub a broad grin spread across her face. Hovering in the air was H.I.V.E.mind, and he was smiling!

'Hello, Miss Brand,' H.I.V.E.mind said, the smile broadening as she approached.

'H.I.V.E.mind, you're back,' Laura said with delight. 'How are you feeling?'

'Much better, thank you, Miss Brand. I am feeling much more myself.'

Otto quickly explained to Laura how it had been the last-minute intervention of the AI that had saved them.

'So you're a hero now?' Laura said with a chuckle.

'That would appear to be the case,' H.I.V.E.mind replied. Laura was sure she caught a hint of embarrassment in his tone.

The Professor looked up from the nearby terminal and beckoned Otto over.

353

'Ah, Otto, could you have a quick look at this for me,' he said. 'I want to start work on reverse engineering these assassin robots and I was wondering if you could just finish up here for me so I can get on with it.'

'Sure, no problem,' Otto replied, walking up to the terminal. 'what do you need doing?'

'Oh, not much,' the Professor replied. 'Just have a quick look at this while I'm over there. I'll be much too far away to see what you're doing, so don't accidentally hit any keys or anything.'

The Professor seemed to give Otto a tiny wink and then walked away across the gantry towards the security guards who were gathering the remains of the fallen assassins. Otto thought that it was an odd thing to say, but then he looked down at the display. There was nothing on it but a single confirmation prompt.

*Delete H.I.V.E.mind behavioural restraint routines. Y/N?*

Otto smiled and glanced over his shoulder at the Professor, who was very deliberately ignoring him. He hit the Y key and walked away from the terminal. H.I.V.E.mind had earned it.

As he walked up to Laura she was chatting happily to H.I.V.E.mind, filling the AI in on what had happened while he was shut down.

'So how was it?' Otto asked curiously as he joined them. 'How did it feel being granted external access?'

'I was granted instantaneous and total access to the entire internet, Mr Malpense. To be honest I feel . . . dirty.'

Otto and Laura didn't stop laughing for a while.

☻☻☻

'Please remain still for retinal identification,' H.I.V.E.mind said.

Nero stood and waited as the bright flash of white light confirmed his identity.

'Identity confirmed, access granted,' H.I.V.E.mind replied and the heavy metal doors in front of Nero slid apart.

Nero walked into the room and surveyed the assorted medical equipment that was arranged around the single bed in the centre of the room. The bed was surrounded by semi-translucent plastic curtains that made it impossible to identify the figure lying on it.

H.I.V.E.'s chief medical officer looked up from the terminal at which he was working and walked over to him.

'His condition has improved slightly, but his injuries are grave,' the doctor reported.

'Can he talk?' Nero asked.

'Yes, but please keep it brief. He's still very weak,' the doctor replied.

'Worse than that, doctor. He's dead,' Nero replied calmly.

'I don't understand,' the doctor said, looking confused, 'his condition is serious but stabilised . . .'

'As far as anyone but you or I is concerned, he's dead, do I make myself clear?' Nero said firmly.

'Yes . . . yes . . . I understand,' the doctor nodded, suddenly realising what Nero was saying.

'And your autopsy report will be on my desk by the morning,' Nero replied.

'Of course.'

'Good,' Nero said, 'and, doctor, if you ever tell anyone about this you will very quickly be joining him in the afterlife. Do I make myself clear?'

'Perfectly,' the doctor replied, swallowing nervously.

'I wish to speak to him alone,' Nero said.

'Very well, I shall be just outside if you need me,' the doctor said, and left the room.

Nero walked over to the bed and pushed the curtains aside. Lying shackled to the bed, hooked up to multiple monitors, his body a mass of shattered bones and internal injuries, was Cypher. At least that was how Nero thought of him now, but once he had known him as Wu Zhang. His head turned slightly as Nero stepped nearer, a twisted, broken laugh wheezing from him.

'Why don't you just let me die?' Cypher said, his voice

little more than a whisper, but filled with hate.

'Because I want answers,' Nero said, 'and unfortunately you're the only one who can give them to me.'

'Why should I tell you anything?' Cypher replied with a sneer.

'Because if you don't I shall just hand you over to Number One and let him get the answers for me, and you know as well as I do that he'll get them. This way will at least spare you that experience.'

'You can't give me to him,' Cypher said, with just a hint of sudden panic in his weak voice.

'Give me one good reason why I shouldn't,' Nero said impatiently.

'Because he's insane,' Cypher replied sharply, 'and so are you.'

'Only one of us is a madman, Cypher, and I think your recent actions make it perfectly clear which of us it is,' Nero snapped back.

'How can you say that, Nero, you of all people, knowing what you know. What you're planning is an act of sheer madness. You have to be stopped,' Cypher said angrily.

'Again you accuse me of something terrible and yet I still have no idea what you're talking about,' Nero replied with clear irritation.

'The Renaissance Initiative. I know all about it,'

Cypher spat. 'That's why I needed the Protocol. With it in my control and the massed offspring of G.L.O.V.E. held to ransom I could have stopped you, but now it's too late. Just deliver the Protocol to Number One and be done with it. Let the world burn.'

'I still have no idea what you're talking about. I've never heard of any Renaissance Initiative.' Nero was starting to think that this was pointless. The man was clearly delirious, or insane.

Cypher looked at Nero carefully, staring him straight in the eye for long seconds before speaking again. The angry, contemptuous look on his face faded, slowly replaced by one of confusion mixed with disbelief.

'You really don't know, do you?' Cypher said, an edge of amazement to his voice.

'Know what?' Nero demanded, the volume of his voice rising in tandem with his impatience.

'If I tell you, you must promise me one thing,' Cypher said, his voice weakening again.

'You know I'm not going to promise you anything. Frankly I'm not even sure why I'm keeping you alive any more,' Nero replied coldly.

'You have to promise to protect Wing,' Cypher said.

'Every pupil of this school is under my protection,' Nero replied. 'You are the only one who's put him in danger.'

'I was trying to protect him,' Cypher said, sudden anger

in his wheezing voice. 'He was never supposed to come here in the first place. He's all I have left of her.'

'Xiu Mei,' Nero said softly.

'Yes. Both of us survived the Overlord incident, but it quickly became clear that all traces of the project were being erased, including the people who had survived.'

'I was told that no one lived,' Nero said. 'I believed I was the only survivor.'

'And Number One was going to great lengths to ensure that was the case. As more and more of the survivors disappeared we soon realised that it was only a matter of time before we met a similar fate, and realising we had no one we could trust but each other, we fled China together. We created new identities for ourselves in Japan as Mr and Mrs Fanchu, husband and wife. We fell in love only after we were married, ironically, and before long we had a child.'

'Wing,' Nero said. 'But then what happened? If you had truly managed to disappear – and the fact that you were allowed to live suggested that you did – then why did you resurface?'

'Xiu Mei discovered something terrible. She was working as a professor of computing science at the university and she was approached by people who were recruiting for something called the Renaissance Initiative. At first she was intrigued, it was high-level research, work that she found fascinating, but then she found out what the true nature of the Initiative was.'

'What happened?'

'She was given some new sample code to work with,' Cypher continued. 'She was told that it was the latest development by another team and that the Initiative wanted someone else to take a look at it. It didn't take her long to assess the code, after all she had written it herself some years previously. It was part of Overlord's core code; she recognised it immediately. At first she did not tell me. She just kept digging and before long she uncovered who was really behind the initiative . . . G.L.O.V.E. But somebody had noticed that she was getting too close to the truth. They killed her, Max.'

Nero's eyes widened.

'Oh, it was made to look like an accident, a burglary that went bad, but she had told me everything she had discovered a few days before, so I knew what had really happened. The only shred of comfort in the whole tragic affair was that they obviously did not realise who she really was and so they let me and Wing live. We were no one to them, just another grieving father and son, collateral damage. I swore I would avenge her, but I also knew that the only way I would ever find out who was truly responsible was from the inside. So Mao Fanchu became a mid-level technician for G.L.O.V.E. and at the same time

Cypher was born. I knew that I had to keep my identity a secret from Number One so I wore the mask. I went to great lengths to ensure that no one could ever find out my true identity, not to protect myself, but for Wing's sake.'

'Did you know that she still had the Overlord Protocol?' Nero asked, stunned by the implications of what Cypher was telling him.

'Only recently did I discover that,' Cypher sighed. 'I knew that while she was alive she never took that amulet off, but it was only when I was digging through encrypted files on her old computer that I realised its true significance. She had encrypted the code of the Protocol on to two separate embedded memory cores, one in each half of the amulet. Wing had one half, as you now know, but I had no idea where the other half was. I assumed her killer had taken it. One half is quite useless without the other, though. Only together can the Protocol be decrypted from the memory cores.'

'Why not just destroy the half that Wing had?' Nero asked. 'Surely that would have rendered the Protocol useless.'

'By the time I knew what the amulet was it was too late. Wing had already been taken to H.I.V.E. and that made retrieving his half of the amulet impossible.'

'His records indicated that you requested he be brought here,' Nero said, looking puzzled. 'Why would you do that if you believed I was involved with all of this?'

'I didn't send him here,' Cypher explained. 'It was someone else, I have no idea who. I assumed that it was someone who knew my secret, that he was a hostage here and that whoever had done it was sending me a message. To be honest, I had begun to suspect that it was you.'

'I knew nothing of this,' Nero said sincerely. 'I had thought it odd that the son of a mid-ranking technician should have been put forward as a potential Alpha stream student, but once I saw what he was capable of I just assumed that someone had taken note of his abilities and approved the admission at high level. It is not H.I.V.E.'s policy to enquire too deeply into such things. Our students' parents often value discretion.'

'And so I was forced to fake my own death. It was simple enough to stage an explosion in my laboratory. After all, such incidents are hardly unheard of at G.L.O.V.E. facilities. Mao Fanchu was too low level an operative to warrant much close investigation of the incident but I had learnt that it was H.I.V.E.'s policy to temporarily release its students for funerals and I knew that would be my only chance to retrieve him. I knew I would have to fake his death as well to ensure that no one would come looking for him, but my hope was that in time I could explain all of this to him and that he would understand why I had to do what I had to do.'

'So why risk the assault on H.I.V.E.?' Nero asked. 'Why not just ride off into the sunset with your son?'

'Two reasons. Firstly, I wanted you dead. Not only did I believe you were a key part of the Renaissance Initiative but I had also recently reviewed the footage of the incident with Darkdoom's son and the plant creature. When I did I saw you lying injured, your shirt torn open, and what do you think I saw?'

'The amulet,' Nero said, things finally beginning to slot into place.

'The amulet, which I believed whoever had killed Xiu Mei had taken, and that made you the prime suspect in her murder. So tell me, Max, how did you come to have it? I can do nothing to you now. Did you kill her?' There was an edge of rage, madness even, in Cypher's eyes as he stared at Nero.

'I swear to you that I knew absolutely nothing of this. If I had known the truth I too would have wanted to find her killers, believe me,' Nero replied, looking Cypher straight in the eye. 'Xiu Mei sent me the amulet, along with instructions to keep it safe at all costs. It seems that she trusted me a great deal more than you did.'

'So it would seem,' Cypher sighed, the look of rage in his eyes fading to be replaced with one of weary resignation. 'The second reason that I wanted control of H.I.V.E. was that it was the perfect place to launch a coup against

Number One. Heavily defended, hard to access and with so many G.L.O.V.E. members' children here, there was no way that the ruling council would allow a full-scale assault. With the Protocol and so many hostages I would have been untouchable.'

Nero finally understood.

'As you know, the Protocol was designed to be the means by which Overlord would interface with the world's computer networks, but it was so much more than that. It's the ultimate hack, a work of pure genius, and something that only Xiu Mei ever understood completely and hence not recreatable without her. It would have given Overlord unrestricted access to every network on earth, including the keys to every military arsenal on earth, drone bombers, submarines, nuclear launch codes, everything. Which was why Xiu Mei had the good sense to not integrate it into Overlord's code until she was sure he could be trusted, which of course it turned out he couldn't be.'

Nero flashed back to the still troubling memories of the incident high in the Chinese mountains all those years ago.

'I understand what you're telling me, but why try to depose Number One?' Nero asked, still waiting for the final pieces to fall into place.

'Why do you think?' Cypher said, staring at Nero.

'Number One *is* the Renaissance Initiative. God only knows why but he's trying to bring Overlord back.'

Nero stared back at Cypher, looking for any trace of deceit in his eyes, but there was none.

'You and I are probably the last two people on earth who know how insane that is,' Cypher continued. 'He has to be stopped.'

Nero's mind raced. Suddenly the very foundations upon which his whole life was built had been shaken. If what Cypher was telling him was true, and he knew he would have to prove that to himself, Number One had to be deposed before he could unleash Overlord on the world.

'I don't understand,' Nero said finally. 'Number One shut Overlord down the first time. He knows what that thing was capable of. Why on earth would he try to bring it back?'

'I have no idea,' Cypher said, suddenly looking tired. 'Just promise that whatever you do you'll keep Wing safe. That's all that matters to me now.'

'I would do that whether you asked me to or not,' Nero said quietly. 'You have to believe that.'

'I didn't believe it, but now I'm beginning to,' Cypher said sadly. 'Can I see him?'

'Out of the question,' Nero responded, his expression hardening. 'He believes you're dead. He has already mourned you twice, I see no reason to add to his torment.

Even if I believe everything you've just told me, I cannot forgive what you have done. No matter how important you thought this was, too many people have died needlessly. You've turned my own people against me and as Cypher you stood for everything that I oppose. Your career has been one of needless brutality and horror. As far as the world is concerned, you're dead, and I intend to make sure that it stays that way.'

'How very noble of you,' Cypher snorted, 'but if Number One gets his way and the streets of the world run red with blood I wonder how well your principles will fare then?' The edge of madness had returned to Cypher's voice, the obsession that had fuelled the fire within him for all these years all too plain to see.

Nero gave him no answer, simply turned and walked out of the room

⊛ ⊛ ⊛

'I am glad that the situation has been resolved,' Number One said, his silhouetted form impossible to identify as usual. 'Cypher was a capable operative once, but this insanity was unforgivable. It is a shame that he is dead. I would have liked to question him about his motives.'

'As would we all,' Nero replied, 'but whatever his reasons for attacking H.I.V.E. he took them with him to the grave.'

'Indeed,' Number One replied. 'And the Contessa?'

'She is being transferred to a G.L.O.V.E. detention facility as we speak. I have instructed everyone who may come into contact with her of the precautions they should take. Colonel Francisco is currently undergoing intensive hypnotic deprogramming to ensure that there is no trace of her manipulation left. He is a proud man, as you know, and I believe it will take him some time to forgive himself for what he did, even if nobody here blames him. I blame myself for not realising what Maria was doing. Her *gift* is a potent weapon when it is turned against you.'

'You need to set your house in order, Maximilian,' Number One said coldly. 'There is much that disturbs me about these events. Not least of which is the ease with which Cypher circumvented your defences, both physical and metaphorical.'

'Yes, sir,' Nero replied, praying that none of the conflicting emotions he was feeling at the moment were visible to the man silhouetted on the screen in front of him. 'We are instituting a full review of all security procedures.'

'See that you do. I shall be keeping a very close eye on H.I.V.E. for the foreseeable future. Rather too many things have gone wrong there recently.'

'Of course,' Nero replied, hiding the clawing anxiety that the thought of increased surveillance by Number

One induced in him.

'I expect your full report by the end of the week. Do unto others.'

'Do unto others,' Nero said, the G.L.O.V.E. motto suddenly having much more sinister undertones.

The screen went black and Nero felt the tension drain from his body. He prayed silently that Number One had not sensed that he was lying about Cypher. He supposed he would find out soon enough if he had.

The entry chime sounded and Nero pressed the button to open his office door. He smiled as Wing Fanchu strode into the room.

'You asked to see me, sir,' Wing said formally.

'Yes, Mr Fanchu. I believe this is yours,' Nero said, handing the white half of the yin-yang amulet to Wing. 'Despite everything that your father did, I am sorry for your loss. If there is anything you need please let me know.'

'Thank you, sir, I appreciate your concern,' Wing replied. 'There is one thing that I need.'

'And what might that be, Mr Fanchu?' Nero asked.

'I need to know something,' Wing said evenly, looking Nero straight in the eye. Nero was suddenly struck by how much the intensity of this young man reminded him of both his parents.

'Yes?' Nero asked, prompting Wing to continue.

'Did you murder my mother?' Wing said, an edge of steel to the tone of the question.

'No, Mr Fanchu, I did not. Your mother and I were once great friends. She sent me the other half of the amulet just before she was killed because she trusted me. But you don't have to take my word for it.'

Nero pulled open a drawer in his desk and handed Wing the letter that had been enclosed with the amulet when he received it. He waited as Wing read the letter and then handed it back to him.

'Thank you, sir,' Wing said softly, 'I hope you can forgive my impertinence. To be honest, it is a relief.'

'And why is that, Mr Fanchu?'

'Because now I will not have to kill you,' Wing replied with a dead straight face.

'Many have tried, Mr Fanchu. Dismissed.'

Wing did not see the broad grin that spread across Nero's face as he turned and left the room.

⊛ ⊛ ⊛

'And I am punching Colonel Francisco's lights out,' Franz said as Nigel just slowly shook his head, a slight smile on his face.

'No doubt about it, Brand. We've got a couple of bona fide heroes here,' Shelby said with mock awe as Laura suppressed a giggle.

'What about Laura "Sea Wolf" Brand here,' Otto said, flopping on to the sofa next to them.

'Och, I dunno, you sink one stealth battleship and people just never let you forget it,' Laura replied with a grin. 'Besides which, who says that you get to have all the fun.' She poked Otto playfully in the ribs.

'I didn't do anything,' Otto replied with a grin. 'I just always seem to be around when things start exploding. It's not my fault.'

'I believe that returning from the dead trumps all, though,' Wing said with a smile.

'I don't think you ever actually did, though,' Shelby said. 'I think you're still dead, zombie boy.'

She got up and shuffled across the open atrium of the accommodation block, arms outstretched in front of her.

'Heelllooo, my name is Wiiing, I want to eat your brains,' she said, doing her best zombie impression.

This even got a slight smile from Wing, something that Otto was very glad to see.

'Come on, Shel,' Laura said grinning. 'It's water polo night, let's leave this lot in peace.'

'We will be coming with you,' Franz said. 'Nigel is promising to show me what is being so good about the library.'

'I keep explaining to him that it's just books,' Nigel smiled, 'but he's convinced that there's something I'm not telling him.'

Otto and Wing watched as the four walked away across the atrium, chatting and laughing.

'I do not want to leave any more,' Wing said, still watching the others leave. 'There is too much I would miss.'

'Well, I suppose that means I'll have to stay as well,' Otto said with a sigh. 'I mean, without me to keep you out of trouble who knows what might happen.'

Wing started laughing and as usual it set Otto off too. As he sat there chuckling away Otto realised something with a slight sense of shock.

It was good to be home.

# chapter twenty

The Contessa struggled uselessly against the bindings that shackled her to the chair.

'Hello, Maria.'

Her blood froze as she recognised the voice that crackled over the speaker mounted above the mirror on the wall.

'I suppose it is pointless to beg for mercy,' the Contessa said.

'Oh yes, quite pointless,' Number One replied.

'Then *release me*,' she said, the familiar sinister whispers of command twining through her voice.

'Oh, come now, Maria, surely you know better by now than to try your voodoo on me,' Number One replied calmly.

'Let's just get this over with, shall we?' the Contessa spat defiantly. 'Kill me and be done with it.'

'Oh, Maria,' Number One replied. 'I'm not going to kill you. You're going to be much too useful for that.'

## Which Stream are you?

- ● ALPHA
- ● HENCHMAN
- ● TECHNICAL
- ● POLITICAL / FINANCIAL

*Turn over to begin the test . . .*

## Answer the following questions to find out which stream you belong in.

**1.** If you were an animal, which of the following would you be?

**A.** Panther
**B.** Rhino
**C.** Spider
**D.** Snake

**2.** How might you make one of your enemies sorry?

**A.** With a hypnotic trigger phrase – so that every time someone says 'Pass the salt', they cluck like a chicken
**B.** Break every bone in their body – even the ones they didn't know existed
**C.** Rewire their alarm clock so that it always goes off at 4 a.m.
**D.** Discover their most embarrassing secret, and publicly expose it – after blackmailing them for a brief, yet lucrative, period

**3.** If you could choose any instrument to aid you in your villainous cause, what would it be?

**A.** Nothing – your cunning is all you will ever need
**B.** A bazooka
**C.** A computer
**D.** Money – after all, it is the root of all evil

**4.** You decide to take over your school. How would you achieve this?

**A.** Simply inform the headmaster that you are indisputably the most qualified person for the job – you had read every book in the library by the time you were four years old, and have a better understanding of the subjects than the teachers do

**B.** Threaten to show the headmaster what his/her spleen looks like if control of the school is not relinquished immediately

**C.** Hack into the computer system and rewrite all of the school's files to show that you are, in fact, already the headmaster

**D.** Infiltrate the local council and appoint yourself as Head of Education — why settle for just your school?

## If your answers are mostly As . . .
Alpha: The Alpha stream specialises in leadership and strategy training. You exhibit certain unique abilities which mark you out as one of the leaders of tomorrow.

## If your answers are mostly Bs
Henchman: Your aggression knows no bounds, and you are happiest when you're doing damage to something, or more likely, someone. Your uncluttered, uncomplicated mind makes you the perfect trusted subordinate.

## If your answers are mostly Cs
Technical: There's not a computer that you cannot hack, or a bomb you cannot defuse (or build, for that matter). You put the 'EEK!' in computer geek.

## If your answers are mostly Ds
Political/Financial: You have a brilliant head for figures (as well as ways to fudge them), and also happen to be excessively charming and a natural born liar — the perfect combination for a successfully sinister career in politics or finance.

# Join the world's most talented villains for more incredible adventures at H.I.V.E. It would be criminal not to . . .

Thirteen-year-old master criminal Otto Malpense has been chosen to attend H.I.V.E., the top-secret school of Villainy. But there's one small catch – he cannot leave until his training is complete. He's left with one option. Escape. He just needs to figure out how.

A new power is rising to challenge Number One, the most formidable villain alive. But who is it? And why do they want to assassinate Otto Malpense, star pupil of H.I.V.E., and his best friend, Wing Fanchu?

H.I.V.E. is in grave danger. Dr Nero, its leader, has been captured by the world's most ruthless security force. It's up to Otto to save him, but first he must escape from Nero's sinister replacement.

One of the world's most powerful villains is threatening global Armageddon, and Otto, Wing and his most trusted villain-friends find themselves in the sights of the most dangerous man alive, with nowhere to run to.

Otto Malpense, star pupil at the top-secret school for Villainy, has gone rogue. In a deadly race against time, Raven and Wing must find Otto before the order to eliminate him can be carried out.

The evil A.I. Overlord is about to put his terrible plans into action. Then no one will be able to stand in his way. It is time to activate Zero Hour, a plan designed to eliminate any villain on the brink of global domination.

Otto and the rest of the elite Alpha stream have been sent on their most dangerous exercise yet: the Hunt. But when Otto and the Alphas arrive in the icy wastes of Siberia, it becomes clear that something is wrong. There's a traitor in their midst, and time is running out to discover who it is.